An Affair in Winter

(SEASONS BOOK 1)

By

USA Today Bestseller
Jess Michaels

AN AFFAIR IN WINTER
Seasons Book 1

For more information, contact Jess Michaels
www.AuthorJessMichaels.com
PO Box 814, Cortaro, AZ 85652-0814

To contact the author:
Email: Jess@AuthorJessMichaels.com
Twitter www.twitter.com/JessMichaelsbks
Facebook: www.facebook.com/JessMichaelsBks

Jess Michaels raffles a FREE Kindle or Amazon gift certificate EVERY month to members of her newsletter, so sign up on her website: http://www.authorjessmichaels.com/

DEDICATION

There are so many people to thank for this book making it to publication that it could make a book itself. But here we go:

Thank you to Audrey Sharpe and Vicki Lewis Thompson who helped me wiggle through some plot holes when Gray and Rosalinde's story was just a scene in my head.

Thank you to the amazing Jenn LeBlanc. Doing the custom cover shoot for this book was not only so fun that it shouldn't be legal, but it helped me hone my entire process. An extra shout out to Ellen, Shelly and Kim for their hard work on the day. Also to Tricia Schmitt for tuning those images into a gorgeous cover.

To the cover models, Ashley and Dean: having you two in my head while finishing the book made these characters even more real. Thank you for smoldering and being good sports.

Next, a huge thank you to my "team". Mackenzie Walton, the editor *everyone* should hire because she's great. Millie Bullock, my mama and copyeditor.

And, of course, Michael. For putting up with my quirks and questions and loving me through it all. Like Rosalinde, I tend to live my life with my arms wide open, and knowing you are there makes that so much more amazing.

CHAPTER ONE

October 31, 1810

Rosalinde Wilde pulled the edges of her worn pelisse tighter around her body, and yet she still shivered. The thin fur lining did almost nothing to block out the bitter wind that seemed to swirl in the carriage. Her poor maid, Gertrude, huddled closer, the two women seeking body heat to save them from the chill.

"Great God," Rosalinde muttered as she fought to keep her teeth from chattering. "Grandfather meant to punish me by making me take the oldest carriage in his fleet to Stenfax's estate, but this is beyond the pale."

Gertrude shrugged. "H-how could anyone guess that a snowstorm would hit in October?"

Rosalinde kept her counsel on that question. She feared that even if her grandfather had known a chance storm would overtake them on the road, he might have still forced her to follow him and her beloved sister Celia to the country now instead of allowing her to accompany them when they had made their own trek ten days before. After all, he claimed Rosalinde was a bad influence on Celia. And he seemed to like hurting them both.

A blast of loud wind hit the vehicle, rocking it back and forth violently. Rosalinde squeezed her eyes shut. Without the inclement weather, their carriage would normally be rushing along at a brisk clip. Now they hardly moved as the snow swirled and the wind howled. She pitied their poor groom Thomas and the driver, Gertrude's husband Lincoln, who were forced to ride out in the elements.

"We'll never make it to Caraway Court tonight, Mrs. Wilde," Gertrude all but wailed.

Caraway Court. It was the estate of Celia's intended, the Earl of Stenfax, where Celia would be wed in a fortnight. The name made it sound very grand, indeed, but Celia had written that parts of it were somewhat in shambles, proof of Stenfax's need for a bride with a dowry. Of course, Celia needed to wed a man with a title, so the match was perfect.

Rosalinde sighed, determined to push away troubling thoughts. She squeezed Gertrude's gloved hand and focused instead on comforting her frightened maid. Rosalinde was strong. She'd always had to be.

"Oh, Gertie," she said softly. "We'll be fine!"

She smiled in the hopes Gertrude would not see her own hesitations and fears about the idea of being stranded in the freezing cold. But no sooner had she managed an expression she hoped didn't resemble a grimace than the carriage came to a stop.

Rosalinde pulled back the curtain covering the drafty window. Outside the storm swirled on and the late afternoon sun was fading far faster than it should have been. Fear gripped her despite her best efforts to keep it at bay.

The carriage rocked again, and suddenly her groom appeared at the window. Thomas smiled shakily and opened the door. Although he tried to block it, wind and snow blew in around him.

"I'm sorry, Mrs. Wilde," he said, "but I don't think we can go much farther. There isn't much snow itself, but the wind is blowing it around so much that it's near impossible to see."

Rosalinde nodded. "I can see it's getting treacherous, indeed. But what are we to do, Thomas? We may freeze if we remain out in the elements overnight."

Thomas shot the frightened Gertrude a look. "Lincoln has

an idea," he began.

Gertrude leaned forward, smiling at last, as she always did when she heard her new husband's name. "Does he?"

Thomas pressed his lips together in worry before he said, "Aye. He says there is an inn a few miles east of the main road. If we can make it there, we'll be safe for the night."

"Mr. Fitzgilbert will be furious if we don't make it to the estate as planned," Gertrude whispered.

Rosalinde swallowed hard. That had been her own notion, and she couldn't deny the anxiety in her chest when she thought of the potential for his wrath. Even an act of God like the snow wouldn't appease her grandfather, she was certain.

She looked at her groom, his face bright red from exposure to the wind and cold. She could imagine Lincoln was just as miserable, not to mention the poor horses. There was no way she would deny them all shelter and perhaps sentence them to death.

"Grandfather can hang if he thinks I'll get us all killed for the sake of his foolish timeline," she said. "Thomas, tell Lincoln to try for the inn."

Relief flashed over Thomas's face, making clear how dire the circumstances were. He nodded. "I will, ma'am. But be warned, it will likely take close to an hour to get there on these roads."

Rosalinde flinched at the prospect but forced a smile. "Just do your best."

He closed the door and Gertrude reached out to readjust the curtains on all the windows to hold in as much heat as possible. As the maid turned her head, Rosalinde could see the increased worry on her face. The fear.

She reached out to touch Gertrude's arm. "Gertie, Mr. Fitzgilbert won't hold you responsible," Rosalinde said softly. "I will ensure that he blames *me* for our delay."

Gertrude didn't look fully convinced, but nodded nonetheless.

Rosalinde settled back against her seat and shoved her

hands into her pelisse pockets. "Celia will worry, though," she mused out loud.

"Yes, but she must be very caught up in arrangements for the wedding. That will distract your sister."

Rosalinde pursed her lips. She wasn't so certain of that fact. Celia was the most disinterested bride she had ever known. Neither she nor Stenfax seemed to have allowed emotion to come into the equation of their nuptials at all. After her own bitter experience with marriage, Rosalinde supposed she should be relieved that Celia wasn't letting her heart lead.

And yet she was uncomfortable with the fact that her younger sister was only being practical. Would she be unhappy with that decision in the future? Would she regret being forced to make the choice Rosalinde had not?

Rosalinde glanced over to find Gertrude watching her closely. Apparently she was awaiting some kind of answer to her earlier statement about Celia's impending wedding.

Rosalinde shrugged. "Well, worried or no, we'll get there tomorrow and it will have to be enough. All we can hope now is that we arrive safely at this inn of Lincoln's and that tonight is more uneventful than today has been."

"How could *anything* be as eventful as today?" Gertrude asked with a laugh.

Rosalinde joined her in the laugh, for she knew in her heart that her maid was right. The inn couldn't be anywhere as shocking as the road had been. Not at all.

Gray sat in the corner table at the Raven's Wing Tavern, nursing his ale and watching the crowd fall in from the storm that raged outside. Normally he would curse the weather, which currently kept him from his business, but since he wasn't actually looking forward to the duty before him, he toasted it instead.

"One more night won't change a thing," he muttered to himself.

He sipped the ale and grimaced. If the snow hadn't forced him off the road an hour before, this was not the kind of establishment he would normally patronize. It was worn out, ill kept, and the ale was terrible. But beggars, it seemed, could not be choosers. A proverb that had always chafed Gray, as he was not accustomed to *begging* anyone for anything.

Even a drink. And it didn't seem he had to, for the round innkeeper's wife who had greeted him and shown him to his small but serviceable room when he arrived now stepped up beside him with another tankard in her hand.

He smiled his thanks. "You are getting busy," he said, nodding toward the door where another group of travelers had just staggered in, brushing snow from their clothing as they were welcomed by the portly innkeeper.

The woman's eyes gleamed with greedy pleasure. "Aye. When you travelers lose, it seems we win. We have only a room or two left for the night."

Gray tilted his head. "And what happens when they are full? Being stuck in this storm could be deadly."

"My husband says we'll stack them out in the great hall here like firewood," she said, rubbing her hands together with glee, "and charge them half of what we'd have them pay for a bed and a fire of their own. We're already doubling up the servants in the back."

Gray pursed his lips. He was glad he'd gotten his room when he had, for the idea of sleeping out here in this sea of wet and sniffling humanity was unpleasant, indeed.

The door opened yet again and a swirl of snow entered before the new arrival. As the door was shut and the flakes fell away, Gray straightened. It was two women who had entered this time. They were obviously lady and servant by their posture. The lady wore a red coat, its hood up around her face. When she pushed it back, Gray caught his breath.

She was stunningly beautiful. Her dark hair was almost jet

black, but her eyes were icy blue, piercing the room even from the distance between them. She was the kind of woman who men turned to stare at if she passed them on the street. Now the main hall of the inn grew silent as those within did just that. The lady shifted as a grumble rustled through the crowd of mostly men.

"Ah, here's another!" the innkeeper's wife cackled. "And I bet she'll pay a pretty penny not to have to sleep out in the main room with the riffraff."

She hustled off toward the lady without another word for Gray. He was just as glad for it. Right now his body was doing things he had not allowed it to do for months, hell, years. He'd been a veritable monk during that time, focusing on his investments, his fortune, his family.

Now he wasn't feeling particularly monk-like as the lady newcomer smiled at the innkeeper's wife and began to speak to her softly.

She looked nervous, though Gray could hardly blame her for that after her entrance. Every man in the room was still casting side glances at her like she was a sweet and all of them were starving. Gray included, it seemed.

She looked sophisticated, as well. Every movement of her body spoke of quiet elegance. She must have had money, for the innkeeper had now joined his wife in their discussions and both of them were practically drooling all over the newcomer.

The newcomer who was still unaccompanied except by her maid. There was no man who had yet marched through that door to wrap his arm around her and stake his claim before the masses.

The innkeeper's wife smiled and motioned for the lady and her maid to follow her, guiding them through the crowded hall and up the stairs where the bedrooms awaited.

Once the mysterious lady had gone, the room drew breath again and the men around him began to make various lewd conversation about the beauty who had just been in their midst. Gray gripped his tankard a bit harder as he heard just snippets of the conversation of those close to him.

"Beautiful eyes—"

"...those breasts..."

"I'd like to—"

It seemed everyone in the room had the same lascivious thoughts about the lady. Gray certainly hoped she would be wary when it came to the men in the hall. Most would likely do no more than talk about her behind her back. But a few...Gray looked around. A few did not look savory.

The innkeeper now circulated into the crowd, taking over his wife's job of pouring fresh whiskey and checking on the men in his company. As he passed by Gray's table, he paused.

"And may I get you another tankard, sir?"

Gray stared at his still full glass. "Not right now, thank you. But I wonder if you might have more information about the lady who just arrived."

The innkeeper's eyes lit up with mirth even as he feigned shock. "Ah, I see, sir. You're not the only one who has an eye on the lady."

Gray pursed his lips, hating the teasing tone of the man beside him. "I thought I recognized her," he lied.

"You and every bloke in the hall," the man laughed.

Gray scowled before he reached into his pocket and drew out a coin. He pressed it into the man's palm. "As I said, I think I know the lady. Perhaps you could verify that for me."

The greedy innkeeper pocketed the gold piece swiftly. "Mrs. Wilde, she told my missus," he said, his tongue now freed by heavier pockets. "I came in late to their conversation, but it seems she's from a very important family to the west. She was trapped on her way to their great country estate, I think."

Mrs. Wilde. Gray smiled at the name. The lady at the door hadn't seemed particularly wild, but then, looks could be deceiving.

"And her husband is seeing to the horses?" he pressed.

The other man laughed again. "She don't have one," he

said. "A widow, I think."

Beneath the table, Gray gripped his fists on his thighs and tried to ignored the aching of his cock.

"Hmm, well, I thank you for the information," he said.

The innkeeper took the dismissal as it was intended and bowed away to the next table, leaving Gray to ponder his situation.

He scowled as he thought about the foolish thing he'd just done. Asking after a lady he had no intention of pursuing? Paying for the damned information? A foolish waste of money. Yes, she was striking, and yes, his body was reacting in ways he'd made himself forget, but he hadn't allowed himself to be distracted by a woman for a very long time.

He certainly didn't intend to start now.

CHAPTER TWO

Rosalinde sat in a lumpy chair before a roaring fire, her eyes shut as Gertrude refashioned her hair. The wind had spun it up wildly, probably leading to all the stares in the hall below when she'd entered the Raven's Wing Tavern an hour before.

"It isn't much of a room," her maid mumbled, pulling a pin from between her lips and sliding it through Rosalinde's mass of curls and coils.

Rosalinde opened her eyes and looked around. Gertrude was correct in her assessment. The room was very small, with just a double bed a few feet from the fire and a tiny table beside the rickety window. The wind rattled the pane, and through the frosty glass, Rosalinde could see the outline of a swinging tree.

"It's warm," she said, leaning in toward the fire and yet still feeling her earlier chill down in her bones. "And it will do. Especially since we have little other choice in the matter."

Gertrude sighed as she slid the final pin in place. "Are you certain you don't want me to stay here with you?"

Rosalinde pushed to her feet and turned to face her maid. "Gertie, I'm sure you'd rather stay with Lincoln. You told me the innkeeper gave you a room together."

Gertrude blush was swift and bright. "Er, yes. When I told her that Lincoln and I had only been married a short time, she declared we'd have a room away from the others. It's tiny as a mouse's house, but it *is* private."

"Tiny might be a good thing when it comes to a marital

room," Rosalinde teased, laughing as Gertrude's red face got even redder.

"I-I suppose," her maid stammered.

"Honestly, I will be fine on my own," Rosalinde said, squeezing Gertrude's hand. "You go and see that Lincoln and Thomas have gotten warm in the servant's quarters. They had a much worse ride than we did. I'll have some supper and you'll come see to me later to help me ready for bed. It will be morning before we know it and then we'll be on our way."

Gertrude sighed. "Very well. But if you're going to eat in that main hall, do be careful, Mrs. Wilde. I didn't like some of the looks the men were giving you."

Rosalinde blinked. "Looks?" she repeated. "You must be mistaken."

Gertrude drew back, lips pursed. "You underestimate yourself. Every man in that room noticed you when we came in. And some of them weren't too genteel, neither."

Rosalinde shook her head slowly. It was hard for her to imagine her appearance would cause the kind of notice Gertrude implied. She just never pictured herself as an object of men's desire. Her late husband Martin had made sure she knew just how *undesirable* she truly was.

"I'll be careful," she reassured her maid. "Now go on. Lincoln is waiting, I'm sure, and you'll want to fill your own bellies too."

Gertrude gave her one last uncertain look, but then she bobbed out a nod and said her goodbyes before she slipped from the room and left Rosalinde alone. Once she was gone, Rosalinde sagged against the chair once more.

In truth, sending Gertrude away had been for her own sake as much as the maid's. In the past eighteen months, everything in Rosalinde's life had shifted significantly. A night alone before she had to face the chaos that would surely surround Celia's Society-approved wedding was something she actually looked forward to.

With a sigh, she straightened and walked to the window.

The curtains were flimsy and did little to block out the chill that pierced the glass. She wrapped her arms around herself and watched the storm outside. Since her arrival, darkness had almost entirely taken over outside. Still the snow was swirling, the wind slamming against the inn and banging through the trees until they swung in time to the rhythm of the storm.

It was a devilish night, but Thomas and Lincoln had both assured her they believed the worst would be over soon and that tomorrow they would be able to continue their way to Caraway Court, even though they might not reach the place until late the next night.

Her stomach rumbled and she dropped a hand to cover it. "I suppose I should go down and find some sustenance," she said to herself. "I do hope the food is decent."

She walked from the room, securing the door behind her, and down the hallway to the stairs. Already she could hear the buzz of the crowd below, mostly men's voices echoing in laughter and talk. She smelled the mixing scents of food and ale wafting up the stairs as she made her way toward the hall.

But as she stepped from the last stair, she stopped. The hall, which had been about half full at her arrival, was now packed. Every table was in use, with men gathered together, shoving food into their mouths and drinks down their throats. A few looked up as she made her way into the light.

She thought of Gertrude's implication that she might not be safe in such company, that the men would look at her with wanting eyes. Her body thrilled just a little at the thought, though she couldn't exactly picture herself falling into the arms of any of the men she saw. They were all coarse and unkempt and…

Her thoughts trailed away as her gaze shifted toward a table in the corner of the room. There was room there only for two, but the man who sat at it was alone. There was something different about him. Unlike the others, he was seated ramrod straight, his shoulders even and broad. He was clean-shaven, with a harsh jawline and a full-lipped mouth. She couldn't see the color of his eyes from this distance, but they were very dark.

They were also focused on her. Not in a leer like some of the others in the room exhibited, but merely in an even, intense stare that seemed to draw her in. She actually nearly took a step toward him and was only saved from such a foolish act by the appearance of the innkeeper's wife. The frazzled woman stopped beside her, a tray brimming with drinks balanced precariously on her hip.

"Good evening Mrs. Wilde," she said, blowing a stray lock of hair away from her forehead with a gust of breath. "Have a seat, luv."

Rosalinde looked around the room, this time purposefully avoiding the corner where the intense stranger sat. "Er, where?" she asked. "I see no open places."

"Aye, it's busy with all the guests," the innkeeper's wife conceded. "I'm afraid you'll have to share a table with some of the others. Excuse me now."

The woman took off before Rosalinde could ask a question or lodge a protest. She took a long breath and looked again at her options in the room. There was a spot at a long table, but it was currently inhabited by a large group of rough men, some of whom leered openly at her.

There *was* a table with a few women, the only others in the tavern, but it was full already. Rosalinde sighed. She could return to her room and ask for food to be sent up, but with the way the innkeeper and his wife were bustling around, she would wager her order would not be filled for hours, if ever. Once again her stomach rumbled, as if to mock her plight.

"Break bread with me," came a low, rough voice.

She spun to find the very handsome man from the corner table now standing at her elbow. He was almost touching her, and a spicy scent, perhaps cinnamon or cloves, seemed to exude from his pores and warm her body. Up close, she could see his eyes were chocolate brown, dark and intense when focused. And they were *very* focused now on her face as he awaited her answer to his request.

"I—" she began, then cut herself off. She didn't really know what to say. What he was suggesting wasn't proper. It was entirely forward at best, dangerous at worst.

"Trust me, Mrs. Wilde, I am your best bet." His mouth turned up in the slightest hint of a smile. He motioned his head toward the crowd in the hall. "If this lot sees you with me, they won't trouble you."

Rosalinde arched a brow. "And how am I to know that *you* won't trouble me?"

That smile grew to a grin, and Rosalinde caught her breath. God's teeth, but he was handsome. She didn't think she'd ever seen such a well-favored man. He had a hard face, yes, but his features were each uniquely beautiful. Together they made up a picture of someone not to be trifled with, someone who got what he wanted, when he wanted it.

"You ask a good question," he said. "What if I vow on my honor?"

She tilted her head, her breath now coming short for some reason. "I don't know the value of your honor, sir. Some men have very little."

What was she doing? Verbally sparring with the man? And rather flirtatiously at that? This was not her normal way of behaving. And yet she couldn't seem to stop herself.

"Another good point scored by fair lady," he conceded, and lifted a long, lean finger to his lips. The action drew her attention there yet again and she noted how full those lips were. Full lips meant for kissing.

She shook the thought away.

"And—and what is your rejoinder, sir?" she gasped.

"I am a gentleman," he began, "though I may not be practiced at it as of late. I vow to you now that I have no ill intent toward you. But I do admit that I saw you enter the inn earlier and your beauty caught my attention. I cannot deny that I ask to share supper with you for my pleasure as much as in a noble attempt to save you from unsavory attentions."

She blinked. How long had it been since she heard such compliments? She could hardly recall, but she liked the way he looked at her when he said those words. And though it was foolish to be seduced by such praises, she found she couldn't deny their power.

"Your honesty does you credit," she said softly. "And lends some credence to your claim of honor. And since you are correct that my other options here are...*suspect*, I-I will dine with you. With my thanks for the invitation."

He held out an arm and she stared at it. A very muscled arm, she could tell that even beneath his jacket. With just a small hesitation, she reached out and closed her fingers around his muscles, shivering as they rippled slightly beneath her hand. He guided her back to his table and helped her into her seat.

She took a deep breath before she settled in. There was nothing to fear. It was just supper.

And yet her heart stuttered just the same.

Gray internally cursed himself with all the worst vocabulary in his vast library of profanities. What had happened to not pursuing the delectable Mrs. Wilde? That had been the plan and yet instead he'd leapt to his feet and asked her to join him in his supper. A rational explanation would have been a gentlemanly urge to protect her from any unwanted advances she might find at another table. But that excuse was not correct. His thoughts were nothing gentlemanly as he stared across the table at her. In truth, he had been driven by far more wicked impulses.

Ones best left ignored, even if it took a lion's strength to do so.

He smiled at her and she returned the expression with some awkwardness. Of course it would be awkward. Since they'd taken their seats ten minutes before, they had been in a silence that felt like it cut the air.

Luckily they were spared any further discomfort when the innkeeper arrived with two heaping plates of food. He practically threw them down before darting off to pour more wine for those at an adjacent table.

Gray looked at the food before them. The plate consisted of a roast Cornish game hen with root vegetables set around it. He leaned in and took a long sniff before he let his gaze return to Mrs. Wilde's face.

"It smells safe enough."

She laughed. "It smells divine. Come, I will try it first and we'll see if we have something to fear."

He watched as she carefully cut a slice of meat and lifted it to her ruby red lips. She licked them slightly before she took her bite, and his groin throbbed. Goddamn it, why did he have such strong sexual urges toward this blasted woman? Was it just the length of time between conquests? Was it the odd circumstances? Was it only because she was uncommonly beautiful?

"Oh my," she murmured as she swallowed. "That is *good*."

He lifted his eyebrows at her sentiment, briefly distracted from his lusty thoughts by disbelief at her claim. "Could it be?"

She motioned at him with her fork and he took a bite of his own. To his surprise, the meat burst with flavor and wasn't the slightest bit dry or undercooked. The vegetables were tender and the light sauce that covered the dish was fresh and delicious.

"Well, that *is* unexpected," he admitted as he swallowed. "After trying the ale, I thought I was in for the worst meal of my life."

She nodded. "I have not tried the ale, but the quality of the establishment is obviously questionable. Still, this must be one of the best meals I've ever had the pleasure to consume." She cut another slice of meat and gave him a long look before she ate it. "You know, I just realized we never introduced ourselves."

He watched her eat a moment before he shrugged. "That is because *you* were busy trying to talk yourself out of sitting with me. And *I* already know your name, Mrs. Wilde."

She blinked and her cheeks filled with pink heat as she broke their gaze. Once again, she wetted her lips and he all but growled with the action. Damn his body. He would have to use all his tricks to stifle this ridiculous desire.

And he feared no matter what he thought of, nothing would help.

"How *did* you know my name?" she asked, her voice so soft it barely carried even at such close proximity.

"I told you, I noticed you when you entered. I asked." He left the answer short in the hopes it wouldn't inspire follow-up. Given his lack of ability to control himself tonight, he might just say something he regretted if given the chance.

"And what is *your* name?" she asked, daring to look at his face once more.

"Gray," he said simply.

"Mr. Gray," she said. "A pleasure."

He stiffened slightly. She was not correct in her address. His first name was Gray, not his last. But perhaps it was better not to say anything after all. This was beginning to feel like a strange night stolen out of time. Anonymity might be best.

"How did you come to be stranded on this night?" she asked. "Was your carriage stuck in the drifting?"

He shook his head. "I was riding a horse, not in a vehicle. And though I could have perhaps made it farther, it didn't seem prudent for the animal's health to try to do so."

Her expression softened slightly at that admission. So she was an animal lover.

"The innkeeper tells me you are a widow," he said, pressing into a more intimate topic.

He watched her face for pain in her reaction or regret, but there was none. She nodded slowly. "Yes. For about eighteen months."

"I'm sorry for your loss," he said, though in that moment he was anything but sorry. A husband would have made this stolen moment impossible. Well, more impossible than it already was.

"Thank you." She sighed. "It was a fever."

Gray pressed his lips together. He shouldn't ask more, but he couldn't seem to stop himself. He wanted to ask more. He wanted to know more, despite the circumstances. And he surrendered to the urges, hoping they would prevent darker ones from pushing to the forefront.

"But you are back in Society now, back in color," he said at last.

She looked down at herself for a moment, almost as if she'd forgotten what she was wearing. He followed her look and couldn't help but notice the elegant curve of her throat, the fine swell of her breasts. She was truly lovely.

"Yes," she said. "To both your questions."

"You must be busy dealing with suitors."

She shook her head. "Certainly not. Why would you think that?"

He arched a brow, uncertain if she was being coy or just totally unaware of herself. He thought perhaps the latter, which was utterly charming. "Please, Mrs. Wilde, you must see yourself in the mirror each morning. You are well aware that you are exceptionally beautiful."

Her cheeks filled with color and she turned her attention to her food for a few bites, to avoid responding, he supposed. Finally, she took a gulp of wine, and when she lifted her eyes she swept her gaze across his face, focusing for just a beat too long on his lips. He almost snarled in triumph. So he wasn't alone in this attraction.

"And what of you, sir?" she asked, her tone shaky. "Is there a Mrs. Gray?"

"No," he said simply. "I am a confirmed bachelor. I leave the marrying to my siblings."

Her brow wrinkled, and for a moment he thought she might press him on the topic. Then she shook her head. "We are straying into intimate topics, Mr. Gray. Perhaps it would be wise to steer away from them."

He held her stare a moment. She was right, of course. It was dangerous to speak of familiar things with a stranger, especially a stranger who he wanted so desperately to touch. But there was something about the circumstances, the oddity of being trapped together like this, that gave their meeting a sense of magic. Of freedom. Like there could be no consequences if he did and said exactly as he desired.

And he *knew* now that the strange connection wasn't one sided. Even now he felt the hum of desire, like a wire between them that connected them in a way neither would have guessed was possible. Her hands trembled slightly on the table, her gaze continued to flit to his mouth and she licked her lips every time it did. The attraction between them was most definitely mutual.

And dangerous. He'd avoided such things for a long time. There was part of him that told him to continue to avoid them. And another that told him to reach over and touch her bare hand, to trace her skin and see if her pupils would dilate with want.

He cleared his throat and straightened. "You are correct, of course, Mrs. Wilde. I didn't mean to cause you any discomfort. Why don't we talk of something less intimate? Are you a reader?"

Her face lit up. "I am, indeed."

He smiled at her pleasure, for it was impossible not to do so. "Then tell me, what are you currently reading?"

She leaned in, the subtle scent of lemons wafting to him from her silky hair, and began to speak passionately about her current reads, a few of which he had also enjoyed. And yet, as they ate and talked, he felt less than satisfied by the discussion. Because the longing he'd stifled was coming back, and he doubted any veneer of politeness would make it go away.

Not on this night.

CHAPTER THREE

As the clock on the mantel began to chime, Rosalinde gasped. Was it truly midnight? That meant she had been sitting in the hall with Mr. Gray for hours now, without noticing the passage of time in the least. The last time she'd made any note of the time was at ten when Gertrude had come looking for her to help her with her nightly rituals. She'd sent the maid away, reluctant to end her conversation with the man who sat across from her.

She'd been hesitant to join him when the night began, for he was an intimidating person, with his handsome yet hard face and his intense stares. Something about him made her nervous. And it still did.

But now…well, now she couldn't deny that her body reacted to every movement of his. She knew full well what those reactions were about. She'd been married. She'd even liked the marital bed for a time.

What she was feeling was *desire* for this man. Much as she would like to deny it, it seemed she was just as her grandfather had long accused her of being: a wanton. She should have felt ashamed of that fact and yet she didn't. The tingling need that pulsed through her body felt natural, not wrong.

"You look very serious now," Mr. Gray drawled, leaning in to examine her face. It felt like he saw into her mind, her soul, and she was not afraid to bare both to him, no matter how foolish a notion that was. "What thoughts are in that pretty head of yours?"

She swallowed hard. There was no way she was about to tell him she had been pondering what it would be like to kiss him, to do *more* than merely kiss him. So she shrugged as she looked around the room.

"I was thinking about how late it was," she said.

He joined her in examining the room and seemed as surprised as she was by what she found. During the stolen hours when they'd talked, many of the patrons of the inn had slipped away to their rooms. Those left were drunkenly sprawled out here and there, including the innkeeper and his wife, who leaned against each other in the corner crooning a bawdy song as they passed a bottle between them.

"Time has flown, it seems," he agreed.

"We should go to bed," Rosalinde said, then jerked her face to his as her words rang in her ears. "I mean, I should go to my room. You should—well, you are obviously capable of doing whatever you like. You're a man, a grown man, a-a man able to make his own decisions."

Her cheeks grew hot at the stammering she suddenly couldn't control and Mr. Gray laughed softly. It wasn't a mocking laugh, but warm as the fire behind them.

"I am very glad we have determined that I am a man. It takes a great deal off my mind," he teased. "But you are right when you say that it is time for both of us to retire. After all, tomorrow will likely be a long one, for the storm may pass but the remnants will not make travel pleasant."

He rose to his feet and she caught her breath. She'd forgotten how tall he was. And now his big hand reached out to her, an offering of assistance. A temptation.

"I will take you," he said.

She shivered despite herself. Of course he meant take her upstairs, but her errant, wicked mind conjured up other kinds of *taking* before she could stop herself. It must have reflected on her face, for his smile fell, and for a moment his gaze took on a heated quality that made her stomach flip and her legs squeeze together.

She rushed to her feet.

"Yes, yes, thank you," she said, her words running together rather embarrassingly. "I would appreciate it."

She hesitated a fraction of a moment before she took his offered arm. She'd touched him earlier in the night, in this exact manner. That moment had been burned into her body and now she knew him even better. Now she could recognize that she wanted him even though it was foolish and ridiculous and dangerous to feel thusly. Touching him now was going to affect her even more.

But she did it. She folded her fingers around his bicep with a shiver and forced herself to stare straight ahead as he guided her to the staircase. As they climbed up together, their bodies touching far too intimately thanks to the narrowness of the passageway, she desperately sought a topic of conversation to fill the heavy silence that had come down between them.

"I'm certain you're looking forward to getting wherever you were going when you were waylaid," she said, knowing she was chattering mindlessly but unable to stop it. "I was expected today and I'm sure they'll be worried. This is my door."

She motioned to the door they were approaching and he came to a stop before it. "*This* is your room?"

"Yes." She looked at him, for his tone was hard to read. He was staring at the barrier without releasing her. "Why?"

"Mine is the next," he said, pointing just a few steps down the hall.

Her body clenched against her will and she began to throb between her legs. Cursing her body, she took a long breath. "My. Isn't that…funny?"

"Yes, funny," he said, his voice suddenly rough.

She slid her hand from his arm and took a step away. She was trembling, he had to have felt it. And judging from the way his dark stare met hers, he knew exactly why. It seemed she was incapable of hiding her desire.

Chance was a funny thing. Here she was, trapped in this place, thrown into a stolen night with a devastatingly handsome man and now he was going to be separated from her by just a thin wall. She would not sleep well knowing that fact, that was clear.

"Well, good night," she managed to choke out, turning away from him at last.

"Yes, good night," he said, but didn't move to leave. Apparently he was going to see that she got into her chamber safely. Which was gentlemanly of him, even if it felt the opposite as he stood behind her, watching her fumble with the door.

At last she got it open, but she was greeted with an unpleasant surprise. Instead of the warmth of a fire to welcome her, a blast of cold air burst from the dark room.

She recoiled from it with a gasp and he rushed to her side, touching her elbow.

"What is it?" he asked, even as he peered into the room.

The fire was cold and all the lamps in the room save one had died out. But by the faint light, the problem Rosalinde had encountered was clear. The rickety window where she had stood what seemed a lifetime ago had been broken when a branch from the tree outside cracked and fell into it. Glass and wood were spread halfway into her room, along with piles of snow on the soggy, worn carpet.

"Oh no!" she gasped, and stepped inside the chamber.

"Careful now," he said as he followed her in. "There's glass everywhere."

"I watched that tree swinging around in the wind earlier," she said with a shake of her head. "I actually thought it was pretty when it swung to the music of the storm."

"Well, you're lucky it wasn't deadly," he said, lifting the remaining lamp and holding it toward the bed. A heavy clump of the branch now rested in the middle of it and glass was strewn all over it.

She shuddered. "Yes, I suppose I was very lucky, indeed.

But what can I do now?"

"It isn't salvageable," Mr. Gray said as he picked up a shard of glass, examined it and then tossed it aside. "Even if you could clean it up and block the hole, which you couldn't, the bedclothes are soaked by the melting snow and you'd likely freeze."

Panic lifted in her chest as she spun to face him. He was no longer looking at the damaged room, but at her. His gaze was penetrating but unreadable.

"Then what do I do?" she repeated. "Should I see if there's another room at the inn?"

He shook his head slowly. "You heard the innkeeper tonight. He came by crowing about being at full capacity more than once. He only had a few rooms left before you arrived and a dozen or more came after you."

She broke their gaze and stared at the floor as reality began to become clear. "You're right. That was why so many were piling up in the great hall. They have taken over every available cushion and carpet. Damn."

Tears swelled and she blinked so she wouldn't let him see. But he did. Even in the dim light, his face tightened as he explored her face.

"Could you join your maid?" he asked. "It isn't the most comfortable solution, but it would be far better than what you see here."

She sighed. "My maid and my driver were married just a month ago. Despite her mercenary tendencies, it seems the innkeeper's wife is also a romantic. She was kind enough to allow them to share what Gertrude described as a tiny little private room. And when she stopped by our table a couple of hours ago, she told me the rest of the servant quarters are unbearably full. There is not an inch of bed or floor to be shared there."

"I see." There was a long hesitation before he spoke again. "Then there is only one alternative, Mrs. Wilde."

She swallowed hard, trying to focus over the pounding of

her heart. "And what is that?"

He took a step toward her, his body filling up the space between them, warming her in the chilly room. "Come to *my* room. Stay with me tonight."

The words had been said. Gray couldn't take them back. He didn't want to take them back, though he knew he should. Mrs. Wilde's cheeks filled with high color, her breath grew short, and in the dim light of the remaining lantern, her pupils dilated.

It was undeniable that his request was welcomed. Damn. It would be easier if she would set him down with a solid slap that he so richly deserved. Perhaps it would snap him out of this fog of need that clouded every judgment.

"I—" she began, then swallowed a few times, searching for breath. "I—but—I…what?"

"You must see there is little choice. You cannot stay here and there is nowhere else for either of us to go in this situation." He drew in a long breath. "I would depart the room before dawn, before your maid came. You could tell her I surrendered the room to you. No one would be the wiser."

She lifted her stare to his and he was lost in cerulean blue, the color of faraway oceans and unreal fantasy. He wanted so badly to kiss her in that moment, to drag her against him and make some part of her his, even though he knew it wouldn't last.

"We don't know each other," she whispered. "Not even our first names."

He shrugged. "In this case, perhaps that is best." He edged closer again. The distance between them was almost gone now, and yet she didn't step away. She just shivered and he knew from her expression that it had nothing to do with the cold. "If it helps, I would not touch you. Unless you wanted me to do so."

Her eyes widened and that dratted pink tongue darted out again to wet those full lips. She was testing him. Trying to make him a liar.

"Come."

He held out a hand and she lifted her own, almost in a daze, to take it. She had taken his arm twice tonight and each time had sent a thrill through him. But this was the first time that bare skin met bare skin. Electricity seemed to flow between them as their fingers tangled.

He drew her from the room and shut the door, then took her to the next in the hallway. He opened it wide and ushered her in, leaning against the barrier once he'd closed it to allow her to explore his chamber.

He knew what she saw. It was small, just as her room had been small. In fact, the bedrooms were almost identical, with just a bare table near the window and a bed wide enough for two. There was nowhere else to go or hide here. If she stayed, there would be intimacy to it, even if he never so much as grazed her cheek with his fingers.

She turned slowly and met his stare. Her hands were shaking, as was her voice when she said, "It seems I have no choice, Mr. Gray. Thank you for your kind offer to let me stay here. I'll—I'll take it." She shifted a moment and then clasped her hands before her stomach. "What did you mean when you said you wouldn't touch me unless I wanted it?"

He squeezed his eyes shut. And there it was. Temptation embodied and unavoidable, forcing his hand. He would give in to it now. He knew he wasn't strong enough to do otherwise, not when she was standing in the middle of his chamber, her expression telling him exactly what she wanted. What she *needed*, even though she was afraid and uncertain.

And it was the same need that coursed through his veins.

"We have spent several hours together," he said. "And I know you're clever. You must have sensed how attracted to you I am."

25

Her eyes widened and her voice cracked when she asked, "Yes?"

He folded his arms, mostly to keep himself from reaching for her. "Don't pretend you are naïve. It doesn't suit you. I felt your attraction to me, as well."

She blushed. "You are immodest."

"No. I am honest. In this case, I think I must be, for we only have tonight. Do you deny what I've said?"

She bent her head and he could see her struggling. She was a lady and expressing her desire wouldn't come naturally to her. She'd been taught to deny it, she'd probably been shamed for feeling it. She would have been told to avoid it at all costs unless it was in her marital bed, and perhaps not even there. He waited, although he wouldn't say patiently, for her to decide how to answer.

"I suppose I cannot deny what you already know is true," she finally whispered, and her shoulders were trembling.

He took a step toward her at last, and she leaned in before she caught herself and straightened.

"Let me be clear," he said. "I am in no way suggesting anything more than a night to explore that attraction between us. After all, it seems the stars have aligned to bring us together."

"The stars?"

"Fate," he clarified. "There was a storm that never should have been which stranded us both at a tavern in the middle of nowhere. We were forced to break bread together by the crowded hall. And now your damaged room has brought us here. *Fate* seems to want us to be together."

"I wouldn't think a man like you would put much stock in fate," she said softly.

He smiled slightly. "In this case, how can I deny it when it is offering me such a delectable prize? This is one night where we can give in to fate without consequences. Without censure or judgment. What do you say?"

CHAPTER FOUR

Everything wicked in Rosalinde screamed at her to do exactly as Mr. Gray suggested. No one would ever know, no one would see, with the right precautions, no one could possibly be hurt. Afterward, she would never even see him again.

But could she do something so daring? So foolhardy? So wanton? She could all but hear her grandfather's angry voice as the reply to those questions, calling her a whore like her mother.

"You're uncertain," Mr. Gray said, his low voice hypnotic. He moved toward her once more, and then he was practically pressed against her. He was all heat and heaven and want and *man*. "Let me try to persuade you."

He leaned in and Rosalinde caught her breath just as his lips brushed hers. It was a soft kiss at first, just a gentle exploration, but as the seconds ticked by it grew harder, more purposeful and infinitely more passionate. She lifted onto the balls of her feet, letting her hands rest on his forearms, then his shoulders. His arms came around her, tucking her in closer, his mouth grinding against hers and his tongue gently tracing the crease of her lips.

She opened to him—how could she not? After all, he was worshipping her with his mouth and it had been such a long time since anyone kissed her. He made a low, hungry sound in his throat as his tongue breached her, dueling with hers in long, languid strokes.

Her body jolted to life as she clung to him. She was hot and yet shivered at the same time as pleasure poured from their clinging mouths, cascading down her body, making every nerve hum and tingle. She felt the pulse of growing need in her hardening nipples and between her legs, and she let out a broken sigh against his lips as she gave in to all that heady desire he so easily inspired.

He pulled away, his dark stare exploring her face. "Is that a yes?"

There were dozens of reasons to refuse this man. Dozens of reasons to turn away and be the lady she'd been raised to be. But she couldn't remember them anymore, or at least she chose not to.

"Yes," she murmured, her voice breaking as she said it. "Please."

He smiled slightly and cupped her chin, tilting it before he kissed her again. She melted into the caress, giving herself over entirely, shutting off her uncertain mind and letting her heated, wanting body lead.

Letting *him* lead. And he did. He guided her farther into the room, back toward the bed. But when they reached it, he stopped and drew away, squeezing her hand before he walked to the fire.

"Wh-what are you doing?" she asked, barely able to form coherent words.

He tossed two logs onto the low flames and the fire sprang to life, immediately bringing more light and heat to the chamber.

"I want to see you," he explained as he turned back. "I want you to see me."

She swallowed hard. Although she had experience with such things, thanks to her previous marriage, Martin hadn't put much stock in what he saw. He'd started out trying to give her pleasure, but as their relationship deteriorated, he'd gone to just flipping her nightgown up, grunting over her a few times and then returning to his chamber without even a gentle word for her.

Now this man stalked back toward her and she knew by instinct that what was about to happen wasn't going to be that. And she reveled in it.

"May I remove your dress?" he asked.

She started at his politeness. "I assumed you were the kind of man who would just tear it off me. Or flip it up without preamble."

"In another circumstance, I might just tear it off you," he said. "But you must wear it again tomorrow and I wouldn't want to cause you embarrassment. As for simply flipping it up and having you..." He made a tsking sound. "That would be a waste of a perfectly good stolen evening, wouldn't it?"

She turned so the buttons that ran down her spine faced him. "Please remove it."

She held her breath as his big hands caressed her shoulders first. But that same breath gasped out when he leaned in and touched his lips to the side of her throat.

"This isn't going to be quick, Mrs. Wilde," he assured her between kisses that tasted her skin. "It isn't going to be perfunctory."

She shuddered and leaned back against his chest. "What will it be then?"

He lifted his fingers to the top button of her gown and unfastened it, letting his fingers slide into the gap he'd created.

"A night to remember," he vowed. "For both of us."

She squeezed her eyes shut. The idea of a night to remember, a night just for her, a wicked thing she could recall at her darkest and loneliest hours...

Oh, she would take that.

He parted three more buttons, and now there was a significant opening in her dress. She blushed as she realized just how worn out her chemise beneath was. Her grandfather refused to allow her to buy new things anymore. Her punishment for her "bad decisions", along with a great many other punishments.

But Mr. Gray said nothing about it, just leaned down to sweep the tip of his tongue on the flesh just above the torn lace of the undergarment.

"You taste as sweet as you smell," he whispered. "I wonder if that is true everywhere?"

She wasn't quite certain what he meant, but the low, seductive tone of his voice was undeniable. When he unhooked her last button, she let out a long sigh and he chuckled.

"You sound as though you've been waiting for that for a long time."

She stared straight ahead, pondering her response. If he was correct that this was a stolen night out of time, that it was an alignment of wicked stars which had forced them to this moment, wasn't it her duty to be honest?

"I have been waiting for that since the moment you approached me in the hall downstairs," she admitted, feeling blood heat her cheeks. "Since the first moment my body betrayed me by making me ache for you, by letting me know how much I wanted you."

He said nothing, but placed his hands on her shoulders and slowly turned her to face him. He searched her gaze for what felt like an eternity, and then said, "I wanted you from the first moment you stepped into the inn. Desire is something I have tried to stifle for a long time. But now we'll both have what we need at last."

She nodded, though she wondered what he meant by his statement that he had stifled his needs for a long time. The question left her mind when he tugged on her dress and it fell forward around her waist.

Heat flooded her cheeks as he shimmied the fabric away until it pooled at her feet. Then he stared. Just *stared* at her.

"You are truly lovely," he murmured, almost more to himself than to her.

He reached up and threaded his fingers into her hair, plucking away the pins Gertrude had so meticulously placed there hours before. Her locks fell around her shoulders, covering her partially, and he smiled as he glided them back to look at her again.

"Much better," he drawled.

"And what about you?" Rosalinde asked, her hands shaking as she lifted them. "Wouldn't you like to be more comfortable as well?"

He chuckled, but didn't argue as she slid her hands beneath his jacket. She hissed out pleasure at the body heat she found trapped there and the muscles that were present beneath his shirt. If she was going to be wicked and take a lover, she had certainly been gifted with a remarkable specimen of a man. Whatever fairy godmother had placed her on this path, Rosalinde intended to write her a long note of gratitude the moment she had time.

With a shiver, she shoved his jacket away, letting it fall to the floor in a pile with her discarded dress. She met his eyes as she began to unbutton his shirt and his gaze lit with unadulterated desire. He wanted her. Truly. It was a thrilling prospect to inspire such a feeling in a man such as this.

And she intended to savor every moment.

She parted his shirt and took in a harsh breath. "Oh my God," she murmured as she dragged her fingers across his chest.

Martin had been soft, a gentleman who never went outside unless required by some kind of royal edict. This man, though, *this* man was made of stone. Beautifully carved stone that only masqueraded as warm, living flesh.

It made her wonder, briefly, just who he was outside of these walls. Was her Mr. Gray a highly educated laborer? A handsome farmer? A man so far removed from her sphere that her grandfather would ban her from his house for life if he found out she'd stooped so low? Again.

She pushed the unpleasant thoughts from her head and

focused instead on the man in front of her. She stroked his chest, shivering as his muscles rippled beneath her fingers.

Slowly, he lifted his hands and removed his shirt on his own. She glanced up to find his gaze focused on her face. She blushed.

"I-I'm sorry. I was…you are…I've never—"

He kissed her to cut her off and she sank against him, her body going soft as her chemise-clad breasts flattened against the warm, hard expanse of his chest and his strong arms encircled her.

His tongue massaged hers and she whimpered as electric desire coursed through her, pulsing and teasing and demanding she find release in some way, any way, *every* way she could. One of his big hands found its way into the small of her back and drew her closer, while the other dragged the strap of her chemise halfway down her arm.

His lips broke from hers, dragging down the column of her neck and down her bare shoulder, tracing the path his finger had just taken. She fisted her hands against his chest and arched into his body, swept away now by need, propriety torn to shreds at last.

He tugged the chemise lower and her breasts came free. He made a low sound once again, possessive and hot, and his mouth dragged over her collarbone, down the swell until he latched onto her already hard nipple.

She cried out. She couldn't have stopped herself from doing so, even if she were in complete control of her faculties, which she was not. The gentle scrape of his teeth over the sensitive nipple, the rough laving of his tongue, the way he sucked her and then swirled his mouth over her…her vision blurred and pleasure pooled between her legs with frightening speed. There was nothing left to do now but hold on, and she did, clinging to him as he pulled the rest of her chemise away and left her naked to his touch.

He pressed her across the room as he continued to suckle first one nipple, then the other, torturing her until she was trembling. She felt the bed at her backside, felt him lift her to sit on the edge as he continued his erotic assault, but she could do nothing, say nothing. She was too lost now.

He nudged her legs open with his hips and stepped inside the space there. She gasped as she felt the hard ridge of his erection, still hidden beneath his trousers, pressed against her sex. She lifted against it with a moan, seeking out the friction that action created.

"God, woman," he gasped, breaking his mouth from her flesh at last.

Her eyes went wide at his reaction. She hadn't thought her movement would bring anyone pleasure but herself. Seeing his glazed expression now, she ground against him again and he dipped his head back with another long moan.

"All right, enough of that," he grunted, pushing her fully onto the bed and taking a place beside her. "I have more to do before *that*."

She shook her head, not understanding what he meant, but before she could ask, he dropped his head down to her belly, dragging his tongue across her flesh. Then lower to her hip. Lower to her thigh. And suddenly he was sprawled at her sex.

She stiffened as he parted her clenched thighs and her most private of areas was now on display for him. She stared at him as he looked at her, a smile on his face that made even more liquid rush to her sex.

He slid his hand beneath her backside, dragging her closer and tilting her hips toward him. Then, to her shock and utter pleasure, he kissed her quim. And it was no chaste peck, either. He slid his tongue across her exquisitely sensitive flesh, swiping away the evidence of her arousal as he swirled his tongue around and around.

Her cry echoed in the room around them as she fisted the bedclothes. This was amazing. Incredible. And he wasn't finished. He licked her up and down, tasting and teasing, flicking his tongue over the nub of her clitoris and then diving into her sex to slide in and out in the rhythm with which he would eventually take her.

She began to lift her hips to meet him, mewling out pleasure as he relentlessly feasted on her body. Eventually, he moved his focus to just one part of her quivering flesh. He flicked her clitoris with the tip of his tongue, then alternated with gentle sucks of that tingling nub. She gasped, arching and thrusting as her pleasure grew, crested, and finally it exploded. She thrashed her head on the pillow as wave after wave of release rolled over her. He drew her through them all until at last she shivered one last time and lay still.

"Very sweet," he growled as he moved up the length of her body with his tongue and finally kissed her.

She tasted herself on his lips and glided her fingers into his hair to angle his head differently. They warred that way for a while before he finally drew away and stepped back.

"Oh no, don't go," she whispered, heedless of the desperation in her tone.

"I would not go if the inn caught on fire," he assured her as he unfastened his trousers and stripped the last barrier between them away.

She sat up partially, staring at his hard, ready cock. He was thicker than Martin had been, longer too. She was going to have that inside of her and she couldn't wait. It had been too long, far too long, since she'd had that pleasure.

He crawled back over her and settled between her legs, but he didn't claim her. He kissed her again, slow and languid, and she sank into it, letting go of any remaining fears and questions about right or wrong or proper.

And just when she was almost boneless with surrender, he caught her hips and rolled, dragged her on top of him.

She straddled his hips immediately, her tingling body driving her for more, for everything. Now she was too far gone to deny herself, or to deny him, the ultimate end to this wicked night. He gripped her hips, helping her position herself, and she reached between them to grasp his cock.

He sucked in a breath through his teeth and she smiled as

she stroked him once, twice, then slid him to her entrance. They both stopped breathing, their eyes locked, as she finally glided down over him. Inch by inch, she took him, reveling in the stretch of his body inside of hers. Oh yes, he was bigger than Martin, certainly bigger than her own fingers, which had been the last thing to breach her. When he was finally fully seated, she felt full and womanly and her body screamed at her to move.

She did not deny herself. Placing hands on his shoulders for balance, she began to grind down on him in small circles. He squeezed his eyes shut, meeting her movements, their short breaths matching as she worked them both toward yet another release. This one would be more powerful, she could already tell from the rapidly growing tension and pleasure in her loins.

He caught his breath. "Jesus," he grunted, and surprised her by sitting up. His arms came around her, his mouth sought hers, and as she continued to thrust over him, he lifted to meet her.

It was too much, and at last she lost control, whimpering into his mouth as pleasure mobbed her once more. It was only when her body went limp in his arms that he shifted her, flipping her on her back, her head at the end of the bed, her legs locked around his waist. Then he began to take her harder.

She lifted to meet him, watching his face in fascination as he finally sought out the pleasure he had thus far denied himself. His neck strained, sweat formed on his brow and after a few long thrusts his face twisted. He withdrew from her clenching sex and came between them with a long, deep moan that seemed to shake the very room.

Then he collapsed on top of her, his mouth seeking hers, his arms dragging her closer. She could feel his pounding heartbeat through his chest, its rhythm matching her own erratic one, and she held him close, pretending, just for a moment, that this was real. That this would last.

Even though she knew it wouldn't. After all, it was only a dream. A stolen night. When morning came, it would be over.

CHAPTER FIVE

It didn't seem fair that dawn came with a burst of bright sunlight. As Gray let the curtain fall, he sighed. Today should be cloudy and gloomy, as he was. He turned to find Rosalinde in his bed, her eyes open and watching him. She said nothing, she asked for nothing. She just watched. He couldn't find a smile to give her, so it was with a frown that he snatched his discarded trousers from their pile of abandoned clothing and shoved his legs into them one by one.

"The roads will melt off before noon with the sun up as it is," he said. "Your carriage will be able to make its destination by tonight, I would wager, even with the inevitable mud."

She didn't respond. Her bright blue gaze tracked him in silence for a moment, and then she sighed. "I suppose I should be happy for that."

He frowned even more deeply. Why couldn't the weather trap them another night? What would he give to stay in this room, pretending all that existed was the two of them?

But that was longing talking, not sense. Longing for more passion, but also longing for something else. Something he would not name, but felt as though he'd lost as he prepared to leave this woman's side.

He buttoned his shirt swiftly and then turned to her again. She'd sat up, the sheets tucked around her bare breasts, her dark hair tangled around her face. It took everything in him not to fall back into her arms, consequences be damned.

How that was possible, he didn't know. After all, he'd

made love to her, how many times the previous night? Four, five? He'd lost count of the pleasures they'd shared. But it wasn't enough. Somehow it wasn't enough.

"I must go before the others wake," he said, hating the words as they echoed in the room.

"I know you must. But will you come here before you leave?"

She motioned to a spot on the bed beside her. He joined her, perching on the edge, looking down into that upturned face that had inspired such foolhardy actions.

She smiled, and his world froze.

"Thank you," she whispered, reaching up to trace his lips with her fingertips gently. "Last night was incredible. I never knew, Mr. Gray."

He nodded, for he knew what she meant. "Nor did I."

She curled her fingers around the line of his jaw, drawing him down, and their lips met. In that moment, Gray knew this was the last time he would ever kiss her. Ever see her. Ever touch her. And it shattered some part of him that he'd never even known existed. He slid his fingers into her hair and kissed her more deeply, hoping to brand her in some way. To brand himself. To make a permanent mark that wouldn't fade.

But it had to end. At last, he pulled away and stood. "If I don't go now, I never will," he choked out. "Goodbye."

She blinked furiously, as if she were fighting tears, but she merely whispered, "Goodbye."

He took his jacket from the floor and strode out, forcing himself not to look back. Forcing himself not to stay. And when he was in the hallway, the door shut behind him, he tried to lie and say their night had been nothing but a bit of fun in the midst of a storm.

But it felt like so much more. And it felt like he'd lost everything as he walked away from her door, from her and back to reality.

Gertrude pulled back the curtain and let a bright blast of sunlight into the carriage. It was all Rosalinde could do not to hiss at the light as she lifted her hand to shade her eyes.

How dare the day be so beautiful when her heart hurt?

"Funny how we can have such an unexpected storm one day and the next it's gorgeous," Gertrude laughed, completely oblivious to the pain in her mistress.

"Funny," Rosalinde repeated.

"When we stopped a while back, Lincoln said we'd make it to Caraway Court by midnight," her maid said, watching her face carefully. "That ought to cheer you up."

Rosalinde pressed her lips together and nodded. "Good," she said, though she was barely attending anymore.

Her thoughts had turned, yet again, to last night. She did not regret those hours with the mysterious Mr. Gray. She only wished she could have stayed longer. That the stolen night could have been a stolen week. Or a stolen month. Or a stolen lifetime.

She blinked. Foolish thoughts, those. Mr. Gray hadn't even looked back when he walked away from her. He certainly felt none of the connection to her she had toward him.

"It was good luck that the gentleman next door to you as willing to give up his chamber after that awful tree came through the window," Gertrude continued, digging out some sewing from her bag and beginning to fuss with it. "Was it the man who shared supper with you?"

Rosalinde stifled a sigh. She had given her maid just a few details about how she'd ended up in Mr. Gray's room. She'd rather hoped Gertie would leave it at that, though she had not believed it. In truth, she was surprised the inquisition had been stayed for so long.

"Yes," she said past a thick tongue and a dry throat. "The very gentleman. He kindly slept on the floor downstairs with the others to save me trouble."

"Hmmm," Gertrude hummed, and Rosalinde shot her a look.

Gertrude was still sewing, but there was something about her maid's pursed lips, her slight glances in Rosalinde's direction. Did Gertrude not believe her?

In the end, it likely didn't matter. Gertrude had been her maid for many years and had proven herself to be a loyal companion. She didn't have loose lips, she never had. In fact, Rosalinde might have even confessed the truth to Gertrude, but for one fact about her passionate night.

It was hers. Hers alone. It was too precious and private to share with anyone but the man she would never see again.

She turned to the side, leaning her head against the carriage wall as she fought the tears that stung her eyes. It was foolish to let them fall for a person she didn't know. One who'd she'd known from the start was not meant for her. She'd lost *nothing*.

"With all the excitement last night, I hardly slept," she admitted. "I think I'll close my eyes for a while."

"You do look exhausted," Gertrude said with a smile. "You sleep now. I'll wake you if you're needed."

Rosalinde let her eyes close and the rocking carriage began to lull her to sleep. But she feared, as she drifted away, that there would be no rest to come. Just dreams of Mr. Gray. Dreams of what would never be.

"Mrs. Wilde?"

Rosalinde shifted, but did not open her eyes. She didn't want to wake. She didn't want Mr. Gray to leave again.

"Mrs. Wilde? We've arrived at Caraway Court."

Rosalinde opened one eye and realized she was not back at the inn. She was in her carriage and it had stopped. Gertrude was already outside—Rosalinde could hear her talking to Lincoln. It was the groom, Thomas, who now stood in the carriage door, his face uncomfortable as he tried to rouse her.

"What time is it, Thomas?" she asked as she sat up slowly.

"Nearly midnight, ma'am," he said. "A few of Lord Stenfax's men are helping with our things, but the rest of the household is already abed. I've heard Miss Celia is still awake, waiting for your arrival."

Rosalinde let out a sigh. "Well, at least I shall not have to deal with Grandfather tonight."

Thomas said nothing, but took a step back and held out a hand to help her from the carriage. She stretched her back as she stepped down. She was achy all over, both from the long, cramped ride and from the passionate night she'd shared with Mr. Gray. She knew that stiffness, that well-used ache between her legs would fade soon, and she hated it. It would make that night nothing more than a distant memory.

"Come, Mrs. Wilde," Gertrude said as she approached. "Lincoln and Thomas will help the others put away the carriage and horses. I'll take you to the room you'll share with Miss Celia."

Those words cleared Rosalinde's mind. This was the last time she and her sister would share a room. The last time she'd be with Celia before her sister became Countess of Stenfax.

She couldn't let memories of one wicked night keep her from fully concentrating on matters at hand. She followed Gertrude into the house and gave over her coat and gloves to Stenfax's butler. He gave Gertrude directions to Celia and Rosalinde's chamber and the two women trailed up.

"We're here so late, I'll just help you into one of Miss Celia's nightgowns," Gertrude said. "And you'll have your things tomorrow morning when you rise."

"Good idea," Rosalinde said. "Celia has nicer clothes than I do anyway."

She laughed, but Gertrude didn't. In fact, her maid pursed her lips in annoyance at the statement that was pure truth.

While their grandfather punished Rosalinde for her "bad choices," he still thought Celia had a use. Her sister received the benefit, even if she didn't want it.

As they reached a door down the hallway, it flew open, and there stood Celia. She wore a wrap tied tight around her waist and her dark hair, so like Rosalinde's, was braided and fell around her shoulder. Her younger sister let out a little gasp, then dragged Rosalinde into a tight hug.

"You're here," Celia breathed. "I'm so glad. Hello, Gertie."

The maid smiled. "I'm just here to help Mrs. Wilde into a night rail and—"

"Oh, I'll help her," Celia said. "You should go to bed. You must be exhausted."

Gertrude gave Rosalinde a questioning glance, which Rosalinde returned with a smile. "Celia can help. I'll see you in the morning."

Gertrude nodded. "Very well, good night to you both."

The moment she turned to go, Celia dragged Rosalinde inside. Once she'd shut the door, Celia hugged her once more. "I was worried sick."

Rosalinde heard the true anxiety in her sister's tone and squeezed her a little harder. "I'm so sorry. That dratted storm came up from nowhere and stranded us at this little inn."

She said no more, not sharing the secrets of her stolen night with her sister any more than she'd shared them with her maid. Celia would no more breathe a word than Gertie would, but Rosalinde still wished to hold her memories close to her heart.

"That must have been awful," Celia said, hurrying her toward the roaring fire to warm up. "Was it a very terrible night?"

Rosalinde bit her lip as she held her hands up to be warmed by the flames. "No. Not at all."

She looked around the room to keep her mind from wandering. It was a fine chamber, well suited for the future

Countess of Stenfax. No expense had been spared in the furnishings or silky bedclothes.

"Let me help you undress, you must be exhausted," Celia said, moving behind her to unfasten her gown.

For a brief moment, Rosalinde had a clear picture of Mr. Gray doing exactly the same thing, his rough fingers brushing her skin. She jolted and tried to shake the memory off.

"Are you all right?" her sister asked. "That was a great shiver."

"It was not a pleasant ride," Rosalinde gasped. "That carriage is drafty."

"Well, now you're here. No more unpleasantness to be found," Celia said as she unbuttoned the dress.

Rosalinde shrugged out of it as her sister moved to the wardrobe across the room and drew out a nightgown for her to wear. As Celia approached, Rosalinde looked at her evenly.

"I'm not certain I believe you. Was Grandfather angry when I did not arrive last night as planned?"

Celia didn't have to answer for Rosalinde to know what she'd say. Her sister blanched and her gaze darted away before she let out a long sigh. "Yes. He blustered fiercely, even when Stenfax tried to explain the weather was to blame. Even his own brother couldn't make it until earlier today and *he* was on horseback."

"His brother?" Rosalinde said, sliding her shift aside and taking the nightgown from her sister.

"Rosalinde!" Celia cried. "What are those bruises?"

Rosalinde froze and let her gaze slowly slide down her body. There were bruises on her hips. Finger-sized bruises that told her a tale of a strong man holding her while she rode him. Her cheeks flamed and she shoved her nightgown on to cover herself.

"I-I don't know. The ride was very bumpy," she said. "I must have rattled around."

"I'm sorry," Celia said. "How awful for you. I tried so hard to convince Grandfather to let you come with us when we came here almost two weeks ago, but you know him."

"Yes," Rosalinde said softly. "He made it clear he was punishing me by leaving me behind."

Celia folded her arms, frustration clear on her face. "If he had done as I asked, you never would have had to endure last night."

Rosalinde turned her face. Celia would never know that Rosalinde wouldn't give up last night for anything.

"It is no use blustering over what has already happened. But what is this about Stenfax's brother? I didn't even know he had one," Rosalinde hurried to say, hoping the change of subject would distract her sister from other dangerous topics.

The color slowly drained from Celia's face and she let out a shuddering sigh. "Well, he does. And the man doesn't like me."

Rosalinde drew back in surprise. "Why? He hasn't ever met you before, has he? I'm certain I would recall meeting him, or you would have told me if you met him without me in attendance."

Celia's frown grew longer. "No, I've never met the man until this afternoon when he arrived. He has business in the North, Stenfax says. That's why we never crossed paths until today. I thought I'd told you about him, but I guess I never thought it very important for the few times Stenfax spoke of him. But he was smiling when he entered the room…until he heard *my* name. I could tell he didn't like me at once."

"How?"

Celia shivered. "He grew very cold."

Rosalinde shook her head. She couldn't believe someone wouldn't like Celia. Her younger sister was a sweet, lovely woman with a kind heart and an intelligent mind. There had to be another explanation.

"Some men are just like that, Celia," she said, reaching out to grasp her sister's hand. She could tell Celia was truly troubled by this development and wanted to ease her pain. "Especially ones who come from such families. Coldness is sometimes bred into them."

"But it's more than his distant reaction," Celia said, her stare moving to her feet. "At supper I caught him...*glaring* at me."

Rosalinde tilted her head, anger beginning to burn in her chest. "If he doesn't like you, it's proof the man is an idiot. Who couldn't like *you*, Celia?"

"At least his attitude doesn't seem to trouble Stenfax," Celia said with a sigh. "At least, not yet."

"And how are things with the earl?"

There was a brief flicker across Celia's face. An emotion Rosalinde couldn't place, but it troubled her. Then her sister shrugged. "Fine."

Rosalinde pursed her lips at the curt response. "Fine?" she repeated.

Celia paced away to tug the covers back from the bed. "Yes. Fine. He is polite and kind and does everything an upstanding fiancé should do."

Rosalinde watched her sister fuss with the bedclothes and folded her arms. "That isn't exactly a glowing review, Celia."

"Why *should* it be glowing?" Celia said, giving Rosalinde a look over her shoulder. "This is no love match. He needs Grandfather's money, I need his title."

Rosalinde swallowed hard at the frank description of their situation. "It is desperately unfair that you must make the sacrifice."

Slowly Celia turned, and there was a brief longing to her face. "But there is no other way. Marry a title and Grandfather tells us the truth about our father."

Rosalinde flinched. She and Celia had been raised by their grandfather after their mother's death, and had long believed their father had also died. They had even grown up with their grandfather's last name, Fitzgilbert, rather than their father's, and all questions regarding the man who had sired them had been rebuffed by their guardian.

But once Rosalinde had married so far beneath their

grandfather's expectation, he had cruelly revealed to Celia that their father actually lived. The price for giving his name was that Celia must marry a title to further their grandfather's ambition.

Rosalinde had never regretted her marriage more than the day she'd received her sister's shaky letter, revealing the truth and the bargain their guardian had forced her to make.

"Do you think what he tells us will even be the truth in the end?" Rosalinde asked, suddenly weary in the face of it all.

Celia faced her again. "You mean, is Grandfather only saying this to manipulate me into doing what he wants? I've thought of it, of course. But we won't truly know until this deed is done."

"I suppose not," Rosalinde whispered.

"And I could do worse," her sister said, lightening her tone. "Stenfax is well-landed and handsome, a catch, or so my jealous friends say."

"Still, I had hoped he wouldn't be entirely uninterested," Rosalinde said with a long sigh.

"Oh no. He is attentive in his own way."

Celia shrugged as if none of it mattered, but Rosalinde knew better. She had experienced a man who grew to think little of her. She had recently experienced one who wanted her. She knew which was better.

"Celia—"

Her sister lifted a hand. "It is the way of our world, Rosalinde. Marriage for love is nothing more than a fairytale."

Rosalinde nodded slowly. She had learned that lesson the hard way.

"You must be exhausted after the past few days," Celia said, motioning to the bed. "Come, let's go to sleep and we will talk more about all of it tomorrow when everything will be far less bleak."

Rosalinde sighed and all but fell into the comfortable bed. She smiled as her younger sister flitted about the room, blowing out candles and lamps before she snuggled in next to

Rosalinde.

Rosalinde closed her eyes, but though she was tired, sleep didn't come right away. She was troubled with thoughts not just about what her sister had revealed to her, but about Mr. Gray. Had he reached his own destination safely after the storm? Did he think of her at all or had she been a faceless conquest after a long string of the same?

She shook her head. It was foolish to allow such things to trouble her when Celia needed her. Tomorrow she would meet this brother of Stenfax's, and perhaps she would find a way to soften him in his ill-informed opinions of her sister. That was the best she could do for Celia now.

The best she could do for them all.

CHAPTER SIX

Rosalinde linked arms with Celia as they stepped off the last step together and headed for the breakfast room down the hall. It was amazing what a good night's sleep in a comfortable bed could do for a person. Rosalinde felt rested and ready to come to her sister's aid in whatever way Celia needed her. No more thoughts of her mysterious lover or regrets about a past she couldn't change.

They approached the room and heard voices drifting into the hall from inside. Both she and Celia stiffened at once when their grandfather's voice rose above the others. He was blustering about eggs.

"Doesn't sound like he's in a good mood," Rosalinde mused.

Celia laughed, but it was a brittle, unhappy sound. "Does it ever?"

"I suppose not. Into the lion's den we go."

They walked through the door arm in arm and found their grandfather, the dowager countess, and Stenfax's sister Felicity all gathered in the room. There was a long table on one side of the chamber and a sideboard heavy with delicious-smelling breakfast treats on the other.

"Ah, Mrs. Wilde," the dowager said, moving across the room to greet her. "You have arrived at last, we were all so worried."

Rosalinde smiled. She had met the dowager a handful of times since Stenfax had begun his courtship of Celia. The woman was warm and welcoming…and flighty as a gnat. It was funny, for she had produced very intelligent children. Her daughter Felicity, the Viscountess Barbridge, who was just a year younger than Rosalinde, was obviously clever.

The viscountess joined her mother as she greeted Rosalinde. "What a harrowing time you've had," Lady Barbridge said, squeezing Rosalinde's hand with a friendly smile first for her, then for Celia.

"I—" Rosalinde began, but before she could say anything her grandfather turned from where he had been standing at the sideboard and glared at her.

"A *harrowing* time? More likely you were dancing and laughing in your sleeve as you spent my money on a ridiculous night at an inn," he snapped.

Rosalinde blushed at the set-down, delivered so cruelly in front of their hostesses. She drew a breath and tried to keep her own demeanor calm to combat his. His round face was red, which made his white hair even more shocking. And his blue eyes, the ones she and Celia had both inherited, were cold as ice when he stared at her.

"I assure you, Grandfather, had I not paid for an inn, *you* would have been paying for four coffins," she said softly.

He did not say anything more, but spun away, muttering something about value that stabbed her directly in the heart. She forced a smile for Lady Barbridge and the dowager, who both looked uncomfortable with what they'd witnessed. And why not? Mr. Fitzgilbert usually maintained a false joviality around the Stenfax family and a pretended affection for Celia.

This was likely the first time they'd ever seen the truth of him.

"Your home, or what I've seen of it, is lovely," Rosalinde forced out as she willed tears not to fall.

The dowager's face lit up, the unpleasantness of the previous moment clearly forgotten. "Oh, thank you. I did most of the decorating myself, you know, when I came here as a young countess years ago. I would love to show you around after breakfast."

Lady Barbridge nodded swiftly. "An excellent idea. It may even warm up enough today to be able to look at some of the grounds."

"I would like that," Rosalinde said, and meant it.

"Ah, you have made it at last."

Rosalinde turned to watch as the Earl of Stenfax entered the room. He was well over six feet tall and exuded a wiry strength that women in the *ton* had been cooing about for years. And yet he didn't have much arrogance about that fact. He hardly seemed to notice it at all. Now he had a warm smile on his face for Rosalinde. She shot Celia a look to see her sister's reaction. There was none. Though her handsome fiancé had just entered the room, her sister was caught up talking to Lady Barbridge rather than noticing her intended's entrance.

"I have," Rosalinde said, moving toward him. "I do apologize for the inconvenience of my delay."

"Not at all," the earl assured her. "Why, my brother was waylaid by the same storm, weren't you, Gray?"

He stepped aside, allowing a man behind him to enter the chamber. Rosalinde looked at him—and her world stopped. Time didn't move, her heart didn't beat, she didn't draw breath. All she could do was stare, the blood draining away from her face and making her lightheaded.

She knew this man. She knew him all too well. He was the man from the inn.

And he was staring right back at her, the recognition just as plain on his face as it was on hers.

"Mr. Grayson Danford, may I present Mrs. Rosalinde Wilde, Celia's sister," Stenfax said, motioning to her.

Mr. Gray…no, that wasn't right. He wasn't Mr. Gray and he never had been. That had been a lie. Mr. *Danford* ducked his head toward her rather dismissively. "Mrs. Wilde, is it?" he drawled.

Her body clenched as it remembered all the ways he'd said her name just two nights before. All the ways he'd touched her and pleased her and made her feel alive.

Now he looked at her like she was nothing.

"Yes," she managed to squeak out. "A pleasure to meet you."

She couldn't bear to hold out her hand to him, nor did he offer his own. He merely nodded toward her a second time, then moved off to the sideboard to look at the food there.

Stenfax moved past her to where Lady Barbridge, Celia and his mother were speaking, leaving Rosalinde frozen in her spot, shaking in her slippers and wishing she could wake up from the nightmare she was currently in.

Gray looked down the table toward Mrs. Wilde—*Rosalinde*—and pursed his lips. She was not eating, just as she had not eaten from the moment they all sat down together. She was simply staring at her plate, not engaged with those around her. Certainly she never looked at him.

What the hell was going on?

He'd left this woman in his bed at the inn the previous morning, his mind filled with longing and faint desires for something he knew he could never have. To see her here, to know she was the sister of a woman he was bound to break from his brother...

It set him on his head.

As did she. Had she known his true identity all along? Was her behavior toward him, her surrender, all a way to divert him from his path?

And why did she have to be so beautiful? More beautiful than he'd remembered, if that was even possible. He'd been dreaming of her since, obsessed with each second they'd shared.

Stenfax cleared his throat gently. "You are quiet, Gray."

Gray blinked, focusing on Lucien as best he could. "You

never told me the last name of Celia's sister," he bit out softly.

Lucien wrinkled his brow and looked down the table at the subject of their conversation. Rosalinde was picking at her food with her fork now, but still hadn't taken a bite.

"I didn't find it all that important," Lucien said, leaning in to give their conversation more privacy. "And it wasn't as if you were around to meet her until now. Why do you inquire about her at all?"

"No reason," Gray said, fisting his hands against his thighs under the table.

Lucien's mouth tightened with obvious irritation and he glared at Gray. "You and I are going to have to have a talk about your coldness toward my fiancée and her family."

Gray almost laughed. Coldness. Well, that might apply to the grasping Miss Fitzgilbert and her grandfather, but he had been anything but cold toward Rosalinde. The absolute opposite had been true in that tiny chamber on a stolen night.

He could already imagine Lucien's horror if his brother ever found out about *that*.

"I would very much like to discuss it," Gray said.

"Stenfax," their mother said, drawing Lucien's attention away from Gray for the moment.

Gray took a long breath and stared at Rosalinde once more. At last she let her gaze dart to him, and when she found him staring she immediately blushed and refocused on her plate. Her hands were shaking, so she shoved them beneath the table's edge. Celia was sitting next to her and leaned in, whispering something to her. Rosalinde shook her head and murmured words in return, but her gaze didn't return to him.

Anger bubbled up in him, joining the confusion he'd felt since first seeing her here in his brother's house. He hated to think Rosalinde might be part of her sister's game, but he had to consider it. He didn't trust Celia, she was a title hunter if ever he'd met one, and his brother had already suffered from one of those in his life. He'd nearly…well, Gray wasn't going to consider what Lucien had nearly done after being tricked by a woman with greed in her heart. Gray was determined never to have it happen again.

Rosalinde licked her lips, and slowly her gaze sought his. For the first time since he walked into the room, she held her eyes on his and he was lost, albeit briefly, in the bright blue. He had touched this woman, tasted her, felt her writhe above and beneath him. Worse yet, he still ached to touch her, even now when he questioned her motives.

He ached to feel her body wrap around his.

"Grayson, you have hardly touched your food," his mother said, leaning forward to talk to him around Lucien.

Gray forced a smile for her. "I find I'm not very hungry, Mama, that is all."

"You and Mrs. Wilde have the same affliction, then," Lady Stenfax laughed. "She has also hardly eaten a bite."

Rosalinde jerked her gaze up at the mention of her name. "I apologize, my lady. I suppose the travel has turned my schedule around."

Lady Stenfax nodded. "It will do that to the digestion, I know. Perhaps a walk will help. You wanted to see the house, yes? I know Celia and her grandfather have some issues to discuss with Stenfax. And Gray, you could join us, just to get a little exercise."

Gray looked at Rosalinde. She was tomato-red now, staring straight ahead, clearly trying to find some way out of this situation. Obviously hoping he would refuse his mother's suggestion.

But they had much to discuss. And sooner rather than later. But not in front of the others.

"Why don't you let *me* show Mrs. Wilde around, Mama?" he suggested, watching as Rosalinde's eyes widened and her delectable lips parted in shock. "I know you like to keep to your schedule and write your letters after breakfast. And Felicity, didn't you say something about your seamstress coming?"

His sister and mother exchanged a look before Lady

Stenfax said, "Well…"

Rosalinde pushed to her feet, drawing all attention to her. "I—no one need go to any extra trouble for me," she said, her tone breathless.

"Nonsense," Gray said, arching a brow in her direction. "It would be *my pleasure*, Mrs. Wilde."

Her eyes fluttered shut on his emphasis, as well as the hardness he couldn't keep out of his tone. She bent her head and he saw the defeat in her demeanor.

"If you insist," she whispered.

"I do," he said, rising as the others did to start their various days. "Come, Mrs. Wilde."

She turned toward him, her shoulders back. She looked like she was about to face a firing squad as she moved toward him.

"Thank you," she said, not meeting his eyes. "It is very kind of you."

"Not at all," he drawled as he motioned her from the breakfast room. And it wasn't kind. Not in the slightest.

Rosalinde had begun the day determined. When she'd seen Gray, she'd been terrified. And now she had progressed to being angry, with a hearty dash of confusion, hurt and abject humiliation.

Gray had not spoken to her since they left the breakfast room almost ten minutes before. He had merely marched down the long hallways of Caraway Court, turning and twisting, barely allowing her to keep up with him. Obviously he had some destination in mind. Someplace far from the others, who had disbanded to their duties throughout the house.

At last he paused at a door and faced her. "And here, Mrs. Wilde, is the music room," he said, calm and cool, like he was truly intent on giving her a tour of the household.

Suddenly he darted a hand out and gripped her upper arm, pushing the door open and dragging her through. He released her and quickly shut the door behind them.

She backed away from him out of instinct, moving toward the fire and the window beside it, as if the light could save her from the dark man before her.

"Did you know?" they burst out in unison.

She drew farther away from him in shock and anger. "How could *I* know? I'm not the one who gave a false name, *Mr. Gray*."

He shook his head, his mouth a thin, grim line. "Gray *is* my name. You were the one who assumed it was my last. I simply didn't correct you."

"A fine way to explain away a lie," she said, folding her arms. His gaze shifted to her breasts and she gasped, shoving her arms to her sides again. "At any rate, *I* gave my real name how could *you* not know my identity?"

He shrugged. "I knew *Miss Fitzgilbert* had a sister, but Lucien never referred to you by name in his letters, when he mentioned you at all. I had no idea that you were a widow and your last name was different from Miss Fitzgilbert's. You never gave me your first."

"At *your* insistence!" she cried out, now unable to keep the frustration from her voice.

"I believe that is something we agreed on," Gray said, his tone low. "That we would keep some level of anonymity in our encounter."

"Why would I wish to do that if I were somehow fully aware of your identity?" Rosalinde asked. "Certainly you cannot believe that I would purposefully have a scandalous affair with the brother of my sister's intended."

He was the one who folded his arms now. His dark gaze, which two nights ago had been hooded and filled with passion, was now cold and emotionless. He was almost not the same man.

Except he was.

"Why wouldn't you, if you thought it would help Celia's case?" he asked, his tone as frosty as his expression.

She shook her head. "Her *case*? What case?"

"Come, don't tell me that you haven't heard about my objections to the match between Stenfax and Miss Fitzgilbert."

She thought of Celia's upset the night before, the anxiety this man had caused her beloved younger sister. She glared at him. "Until I arrived last night and saw my sister, I had no idea of your existence, let alone that you wished to interfere in their arrangement."

He snorted out a sound of derision that cut her to very core. "Please."

"Don't insinuate that I'm a liar," Rosalinde said softly, proud that she didn't shout when that was exactly what she wished to do. "You don't know me."

His eyes lit up at that statement, and for a moment the same passion that had flared between them two nights past returned to his expression. Only now it was angry passion. He took a long step toward her and her errant mind bombarded her at once with a dozen images from that night. Of his mouth lowering to hers, of his arms around her, of the pleasures of his tongue, of his taut expression as she rode him.

She saw those same things reflected in his eyes along with his mistrust, his anger, his cruelty. She was a fool, for even now, facing him for what he truly was, she wanted him.

She had to remember how hateful he was. Devastatingly handsome. But utterly hateful.

"Don't I?" he whispered, his low tone trembling down her spine, making body clench against her will.

"N-No," she stammered. "You don't."

For a moment, his gaze flitted over her face and his expression softened a fraction. But then he spun away with a cruel laugh.

"Perhaps I *don't* fully grasp all your schemes, Mrs. Wilde. In fact, that is perfectly clear now. But *you* don't know how far I am willing to go to stop my brother from making the biggest mistake of his life. I *will* bring this wedding to a halt. And not even your considerable wiles will stand in my way."

He didn't say anything else and he didn't wait for her response. He merely strode out the door and left her standing in the music room, heated by both her anger toward him and the desire she didn't want, didn't need and apparently couldn't control.

CHAPTER SEVEN

Gray threw the reins of his horse to the groom who rushed to greet him and stormed into the house. A long ride in the cold morning air had done nothing to restrain his out of control emotions. He was still just as angry as he had been when he walked away from Rosalinde in the music room.

Worse, he still wanted her just as much as he had then when her denials had sunk into his skin and made him want to believe their meeting was coincidence, the fate he had once whispered to her it was. He could have kissed her in that moment, he could have drawn her against him.

And had he done so, he would have been a fool all over again.

The best thing he could do was get rid of her. Her and her scheming sister and grandfather. So he rushed down the hallway until he reached Lucien's office and threw the door open without even bothering to knock.

His brother sat at his desk, papers strewn around him. He lifted his gaze slowly as Gray entered without leave and slammed the door behind him. Although Lucien pressed his lips together in a deep frown, otherwise he seemed unfazed by Gray's obvious temper.

"What is wrong with you?" Lucien asked. "And where have you been? You were meant to show Mrs. Wilde around the house, but it was obvious she got a truncated version of the home, judging from how swiftly she returned to the parlor. Felicity had to take up the duty after her seamstress departed."

Gray waved his hand to dismiss his brother's question. "That doesn't matter. Mrs. Wilde does not matter." Those words sounded false, but he continued regardless. "I want to reiterate my strenuous objections to this marriage."

Now Lucien set his quill aside with a long, tired sigh and pushed to his feet. "This again?" he asked as he moved to the sideboard and poured himself a drink, despite the early hour.

"Yes." Gray pursed his lips. "This again. It is important, Lucien."

"So you say," Stenfax replied with a glance in his direction.

"It *is*." Gray threw up his hands. "Great God, doesn't it bother you that Celia Fitzgilbert and her grandfather are title grabbers?"

Lucien's brow wrinkled. "Unlike two-thirds of the *ton*, you mean?" he asked, sarcasm dripping from every word.

"Like Elise," Gray bit out.

The color drained from Lucien's face and he slammed his drink down before he returned to his desk. As he settled back in to his work, he said, "Do not mention that name to me."

Gray flinched at the coldness in Lucien's tone. It didn't match the hot emotion he knew his brother felt about the woman he'd once loved. The one who'd thrown him over when she had been offered the chance to marry a rich duke over an almost penniless earl.

Gray had watched his brother suffer massively from that broken engagement. He'd watched him step out on the edge of a terrace wall in a drunken stupor and nearly throw himself to his death. Gray's stomach turned at the memory that sometimes rushed back to haunt him in both his dreams and in waking moments that were like a nightmare.

"I don't want to see you hurt," Gray said, this time softly.

Lucien didn't look up from his paperwork, but his jaw clenched and unclenched. "I won't be," he vowed. "I was hurt before because Eli—because *that woman* made me believe she cared for me. Celia and I have no such illusions between us.

Our marriage will be one of mutual convenience, nothing more. Her dowry is large and allows me to refill our family coffers. My title will elevate her and her grandfather as they wish."

"My investments are paying off," Gray said. "I have money. Let *me* refill the family coffers."

Lucien's cheeks flamed, and he finally looked at Gray. "Take your charity? No thank you. You have found your way, Grayson. Allow me to find my own."

"But there are plenty of rich women who *aren't* only interested in a title," Gray suggested. "You are a popular man."

"I don't want ridiculous romantic entanglements," Lucien insisted with another heavy sigh. He finally looked at Gray. "You are the younger brother, Gray, not the eldest. You needn't play nursemaid to me. I am perfectly capable of making my own decisions. This subject is closed."

Gray opened his mouth to argue, but his brother shook his head. "It is *closed*, Grayson. I mean it. Now go find something else to do and allow me to finish my business."

Gray let out his breath in a frustrated sigh as he turned on his heel and left him alone. He had no choice at the moment but to do as Lucien asked, for his brother was not in any mood to hear the truth. But whatever Lucien said, the subject was not closed to Gray.

Rosalinde paced the parlor, frustration growing in her every time she turned and took another lap around the room. That she could still be so angry almost two hours after her encounter with Grayson only proved what a hateful man he was. He and his accusations and his full lips could hang for all she cared.

She fisted her hands at her sides with an angry growl just before she made the next turn in her endless pacing. And as she did so, she found her grandfather standing in the doorway to the chamber, watching her through a narrowed gaze.

She stopped, forcing her hands to unfist, trying to calm her expression and her racing heart. "Gr-grandfather," she said. "I didn't see you there."

He stepped into the room. "Clearly, as you were hurtling yourself around the room like an angry harridan."

Rosalinde took a long breath and readied herself for yet another unpleasant encounter with the man who had raised her. He had aged a great deal in that time, but his attitude remained the same. He was still cold, he was still unyielding, he still held grudges for crimes committed years ago. Hell, he still despised Rosalinde and Celia's mother, his own daughter, and she had been in the grave for over two decades.

"I am restless, that is all," Rosalinde lied. "I suppose it comes from being trapped in a carriage for two days."

"Lying, are you, Rosalinde? I shouldn't be surprised. You are like your mother. Agatha was a liar, too."

Rosalinde shut her eyes briefly, swallowing back the defense of the mother she didn't even remember.

"I'm not lying," she said softly.

He shook his head. "So you say. But I saw the way you reacted this morning at breakfast. You made a spectacle of yourself by not eating, by acting so strangely in front of Stenfax and his family. Have a care, Rosalinde. You will not like the consequences if you ruin this engagement."

"I assume I would not," Rosalinde replied. "I have already suffered your wrath in the past, Grandfather. I have not forgotten its sting. I am in no way trying to hurt Celia or her chances with Stenfax."

In fact, she was trying to *help* her sister, but she wasn't going to tell Mr. Fitzgilbert that. If he knew the engagement was being threatened by anyone, his temperament would only become less and less pleasant. He might ruin things, himself, by flying into a temper, though he would blame Rosalinde and Celia quickly enough.

"You'd best not be," he grunted with a quick nod. "You know I hold all the cards. If you two want to know your father's identity, Celia must get her title first."

"Yes," Rosalinde said, setting her jaw in anger and disgust. "We are both well-aware of the terms of your devil's bargain. You needn't repeat them."

"A devil's bargain?" her grandfather repeated. "Only if the devil you refer to is my daughter."

"My mother has nothing to do with you taking us from our father and making us believe he died," Rosalinde said through clenched teeth. "She has *nothing* to do with your blackmailing Celia into marrying a title to satisfy you in exchange for the information you've kept from us all these years. She has nothing to do with your cruelty."

Fitzgilbert waved his hand to dismiss her claim. "If your mother hadn't seen fit to spread her legs for someone so beneath her and if *you* hadn't done the same just to thwart me, none of us would be in this position."

Rosalinde turned away tears stinging her eyes. Leave it to Mr. Fitzgilbert to be so cruel as to throw her desperately unhappy marriage in her face.

"Why do you hate us so much?" she whispered.

"Because you represent such a failure. A failure to produce sons and proper heirs. A failure to produce good women who wouldn't destroy my name."

"You could have loved us," she said without looking at him. "We would have loved you in return if you had tried even a little to care."

"*Love?*" he repeated on a laugh. "My dear, *love* is weakness and it does nothing to carry on a name or a legacy. And if you feel you have been wronged by my attitude toward you, recall that it is only by *my* good graces that you have a place here at all. You would do well to be grateful."

He said nothing else, but turned on his heel and left her alone in the chamber. Rosalinde moved to the settee, where she sank down, covering her face with her hands. Her entire life she had been trapped by her grandfather's hate. She'd had Celia to love, of course, to share her pains and triumphs with.

But she'd failed Celia and put her in her current situation. And once Celia was gone? Well, she had no idea if Fitzgilbert would put her on the street. Or even if he would share the information he claimed to have.

"That sounded heated."

Rosalinde sucked in a gasp and jumped to her feet to face Gray as he came into the room. "Are you in the habit of listening in on private conversations, Mr. Danford?"

He shrugged, and her heart stuttered. God, what had he heard exactly? Certainly he would turn much of that conversation against her if he could. He would use it to condemn Celia and damage her in front of Stenfax.

"I am not," he said. "But your grandfather's angry tone was hard to disguise, even if his words were unclear."

Rosalinde sagged in relief. So he hadn't heard the specifics of the exchange. The anger he'd been privy to was humiliating, of course, but Gray couldn't hurt Celia with it.

He moved closer, tilting his head as he examined her face. "There are tears in your eyes," he murmured. "What is it, Rosalinde?"

She gasped. That was the first time he'd ever addressed her by her given name, and the way it rolled off his tongue, the way it reverberated in his voice, touched her deep inside. Added to the tenderness in his tone, it was very confusing, indeed.

She shook her head. "You have already accused me of being a liar," she whispered, reminding herself as much as reproaching him. "And insinuated I would trade my body for the purposes of…God, I don't even know what you think I tried to gain from our night together. Is it blackmail of some kind? So please don't pretend to care about my wellbeing now."

He moved on her so suddenly that she didn't have time to recoil. One moment he was three feet away, the next he was right in front of her and his hand was reaching out, his fingers stroking over her cheek so gently.

"I'm not pretending," he murmured.

She stared up into his face, trying desperately to keep herself from doing something foolish like lift her lips to his. Like beg him to hold her. He was her enemy. He'd made that clear just two hours before. She couldn't forget all that just because he touched her.

That would mean surrender in this war they were secretly fighting.

"Rosalinde," he groaned, and lowered his lips toward her.

Her rational mind briefly screamed at her to back away, but it was overridden at once by her desire to taste this man once more. Just once more. Then never again.

His mouth covered hers and she let out a low moan of pleasure and relief. She lifted her arms to wrap them around his neck, she opened her mouth and he drove inside with his tongue, claiming her and tasting her and teasing her just as he had done two nights before. She sank into the swirling, heated sensations, setting aside all her tangled emotions when it came to this man and their opposing goals.

She was just a woman in that moment, he was just a man, and this was just pleasure that gently pulsed through her body, awakening every nerve and settling between her legs. He grunted out a needful sound and his arms came tighter around her, molding her fully against him, letting her feel how much he wanted her. Her body responded to the hardness that now pressed against her belly. She felt soft and wet and womanly and ready for him.

But she couldn't have him. Rationality returned with that thought. She couldn't have him because he could use that surrender against her. Because this desire he inspired was now a tool for him, to be wielded against her.

She pulled back and he released her immediately. He only watched her as she staggered away. She kept her back to him for a moment, touching her hot lips, trying to regain some control over herself. But she couldn't find that. Only confusion and aching need were to be found inside of her. She wasn't strong enough for anything else.

And so she staggered away from him and the desire he inspired. But in the hallway, away from his touch, from his overwhelming presence, she felt no more grounded. Only more confused and driven to touch him, to have him, to surrender to him, even though she knew that could only bring her pain.

Gray wanted to follow Rosalinde into the hallway. To press her against the wall and kiss her again until surrender was all that was left in her. Until their bodies merged as one and he could truly claim she was his.

He'd never felt that strong a need for a specific woman before. And the past few years, he hadn't indulged in desire at all. But now Rosalinde was here, in his home, so close he could pluck her and taste her and claim her all he wanted.

And that attraction was not one-sided. Even though she was as wary of his intentions as he was of hers, when he touched her she melted. Her longing was clear in her bated breath, her responsive body, the kiss that she returned with as much fervor as he gave.

"Bloody hell," he muttered, walking to the sideboard to pour a drink. He slugged it back and the liquor burned down his throat, but did nothing to ease the coiled tension of his hungry body.

This was out of control. This was unstoppable.

He flopped down in the chair before the fire and propped his feet up on the ottoman, tapping his fingers along the glass in his hand. Right now this unexpected desire for Rosalinde felt at odds with his plans to break up the engagement between Lucien and Celia. If his attention was on Rosalinde, how could he fully commit to any plans? How could he see through

Celia's beautiful but disinterested exterior into her secrets?

Unless…

He straightened. Rosalinde and her sister were thick as thieves. If Celia had secrets, surely Rosalinde knew them. If Gray gave in to the desire between them, if he convinced Rosalinde to let down her guard in his arms, in his bed, she might let something slip that would condemn Celia.

He could be with her *and* get what he wanted.

Now that realization should have made him feel triumphant, it should have made him happy. And yet the core of this potential deception of Rosalinde didn't do either of those things. Instead he felt guilty.

He lifted his gaze and found himself staring at a family portrait, painted years ago, before their father had died. His parents stood on either side of their three children. Somehow Gray had ended up in the middle, though he wasn't the heir. Probably because his father had wanted to stand next to his favorite son. Gray had never been anything but an afterthought. A standby.

Gray swallowed the bitterness of that thought and instead examined both his brother's and his sister's faces. These had been more innocent times. They both looked untroubled, unbroken.

Now when he looked at them, he saw lingering pain in their faces, bitter emptiness in their eyes. That pain had been caused by bad matches and poor decisions in love. He'd seen them both shatter, he'd helped pick up the pieces. He would not do that again. Even if it meant sacrificing some of his own morality, he had to at least consider any plan that would save Lucien from heartache.

So he set his drink aside, steepled his fingers and continued to ponder his newly minted plan. To seduce or not to seduce. That was the question. Now he just had to find an answer he could live with.

CHAPTER EIGHT

Rosalinde sat on the edge of the bed, watching Celia's maid, Ruth, fix her sister's hair. Gertrude was still fussing with Rosalinde's gown, tugging at the fabric and primping her ceaselessly.

But Rosalinde was only half-aware of all of it. She was thinking of Gray. It had been three days since he kissed her in the parlor after her run-in with her grandfather. Three days, and since then he had scarcely been around. Oh, she sometimes saw him at supper or passing through the hallways, but he never spoke to her.

"Did you see him?" Celia asked, the question piercing through Rosalinde's distracted fog.

"See him?" she repeated in blank confusion.

Celia turned to look at her. "Grayson Danford. Great Lord, Rosalinde, have you been listening to me at all?"

Rosalinde blinked. She had not, of course, and it seemed she had missed out on information about her very obsession.

"I'm sorry, I must have been woolgathering," she admitted.

Celia rolled her eyes. "I was saying that *he* was staring down the table last night, watching me. We were sitting right next to each other, Rosalinde. I was wondering if you'd noticed."

Gertrude let out a snort. "Perhaps he weren't looking at you, Miss Celia. Perhaps he was looking at Mrs. Wilde. After all, he—"

Rosalinde jumped to her feet. "Gertie," she said sharply, cutting her maid off before she could reveal her secret about that night at the inn. "That's enough."

Gertrude shot her an odd look. "I'm sorry, Mrs. Wilde," she said.

Celia stared at the two. "What is it? Is there some reason Mr. Danford would have an interest in you, Rosalinde?"

Rosalinde pushed to her feet and forced a smile on her face. "Lord, no," she lied. "Ruth, are you finished with Miss Celia?"

Ruth looked her charge over once and nodded. "She's as pretty as a picture."

Rosalinde smiled broadly, despite her nervousness about Celia's current choice of conversational topic. "Indeed, she is. Why don't you and Gertrude leave us, then?"

The two maids both bobbed their heads and made for the door. Rosalinde followed. Ruth stepped out first and as Gertrude made her way past, Rosalinde caught her arm.

"Gertie, please don't mention to *anyone* the fact that Mr. Danford and I met before," she whispered.

Gertrude shook her head. "Of course, ma'am, but do you mind if I ask why?"

Rosalinde worried her lip as she pondered a response. How in the world could she explain herself to her maid? To anyone? If the fact that she and Gray had spent a night in each other's arms ever came to light, the consequences would be swift and terrible.

"Mr. Danford is not kind to my sister," she explained at last. "And the fact that he represented himself as a gentleman to me that night, deceived me, would likely only upset her. I would like to avoid that, as Celia is already nervous about her marriage and fitting in with Stenfax's family. So please, do not say a word."

Gertrude nodded. "All right, Mrs. Wilde. I won't say anything."

"Thank you," Rosalinde breathed. "I'll see you later."

As her maid turned, Rosalinde shut the door with a sigh. At least that issue had been subverted. For now.

"Why are you being so short with Gertie?" Celia asked, rising and turning to face Rosalinde.

She couldn't help it—Rosalinde caught her breath. Celia did look beautiful in a pale green gown with a darker green overlay that was spun with flowers. She looked like a future countess should. Even Gray couldn't deny that.

"Rosalinde?" Celia said, her brow wrinkling.

Rosalinde moved toward her, catching her hands. "I'm sorry, I was just taken aback by how utterly lovely you look, Celia. Truly, you have never been more beautiful. Stenfax will be set on his heels."

Her sister, who had at first smiled at the compliment, now frowned. "I doubt that. Stenfax isn't moved by such things. I'm certain he'll be pleased that I am presentable and appropriate, but otherwise..." Celia waved her hand as if to dismiss any other connection.

Rosalinde frowned. "But Celia—"

"Oh, Rosalinde, I don't want to discuss Stenfax," Celia said. "I want to know why Gertrude thought Mr. Danford might have been staring at you rather than at me last night."

"Gertrude probably just heard he showed me around the house a few days ago," Rosalinde suggested weakly. "And she reads all those silly romantic stories—they put wild notions in her head."

Celia pursed her lips and actually looked disappointed. "Oh, is that all? Damn, I hoped there might be something more to it."

Rosalinde drew back. "What in the world do you mean? You couldn't be suggesting that Grayson Danford and I..."

"Of course not," Celia said, and paced away. "You have better taste than a man who always looks as if he ate something sour. But I do admit that I selfishly hoped if he *did* like you, perhaps that could help *me*. At least it might be a distraction to him."

Her sister let out a long sigh and it shuddered, like she was just keeping tears at bay. Rosalinde rushed to her side, sliding an arm around her for a comforting squeeze.

"Oh, darling," she said. "I'm sorry his attitude toward you is so upsetting."

Celia shook her head. "He's just so cold. He hardly speaks to me, and when he does, his tone is always dismissive. And those glares of his. They're so pointed. I just wish he would stop."

"And he will," Rosalinde reassured her. "You'll marry Stenfax in less than ten days and then nothing Gray... Mr. Danford...does will matter. He will have to accept you at some point."

"Unless he does something to stop the wedding," Celia all but wailed. "I have been trying to keep myself from believing it, but I..."

When Celia trailed off, Rosalinde tightened her embrace. "Tell me."

"I-I fear he is working behind the scenes to ruin our engagement." Celia's voice broke. "And if he succeeds, I know Grandfather will *never* tell us the truth about our father. It will be my fault!"

Rosalinde's lips pursed. Gray had all but said he was doing just that after their encounter in the music room the morning he'd taken her for their "tour" of the house. Now she looked at her sister, saw Celia's deep fear and pain, and anger swelled in her.

"It *wouldn't* be your fault if that happened. And I have no idea why Mr. Danford would interfere, but if that is his intent, I'll stop him, Celia. I swear to you that I will," Rosalinde said, though the words sounded more certain than she felt.

"How could you possibly do that?" Celia asked, swiping at the tears that now glistened in her eyes.

Rosalinde paused to consider the question. Celia had hit on an interesting theory earlier, that if Gray liked Rosalinde, perhaps he would be kinder to Celia. He'd even suggested himself that Rosalinde had gone to bed with him in order to help her sister's "case".

Now, perhaps he didn't *like* her, Rosalinde couldn't be certain of that. But he did want her. Their unexpected kiss in the parlor, so heated, so passionate, had proven it.

And she wanted him, God help her.

But could she sink so low as to trade on their attraction just as he'd suggested? She'd been offended by the accusation when he made it, but now it seemed to be a viable path to helping Celia.

If she pursued the attraction it would certainly kill two birds with one stone. She could keep an eye on Gray, even distract him from whatever nefarious plans he was hatching, but also be with him.

She shivered at the thought of his hands on her skin, his mouth on her, his body inside of her. Those were overwhelming images, ones she felt were burned into her.

But she didn't have to start there. A flirtation with the man might help as much as an affair would. It was an easier place to begin, at least.

"Celia," she said, taking her sister's hand. "I will find a way to help you whatever it takes. To help *us*. I promise."

Rosalinde had been to many a ball in the three years she'd been in Society before her marriage to Martin Wilde. She'd even accompanied Celia to a few in the last year. But none had ever been so fine as this one.

Stenfax's ballroom seemed to be modeled after a Grecian temple with pillars and marble and statues all around. The servants were finely liveried, the drinks were plentiful and not as watered down as some at other fetes. Truly no one would know the man's financial situation if this party were the sole way to judge.

There were over a hundred in the ballroom and the dowager countess had claimed this to be a "small" gathering.

Rosalinde drew a long breath. "Intimate friends, my left foot," she muttered.

Her gaze slid to Celia on the dance floor. She was spinning in Stenfax's arms, but they didn't appear to be speaking. Rosalinde frowned. Although they seemed to like each other as people well enough, there was never even a hint of deeper connection between the pair. She supposed it was foolishly romantic to hope for more, but she didn't want her sister to end up in a loveless, empty marriage.

She knew too well the consequences of such a thing. But what choice did they have? None, thanks to the machinations of their grandfather, who stood off to the side of the dance floor, puffed as a peacock as he chatted up the titled attendees.

Her gaze shifted again and she found herself looking at Gray. It wasn't the first time she'd found him in the crowd. In fact, her eyes seemed naturally drawn to him. He was dressed impeccably, not a dark hair out of place as he stood on the other side of the room with the dowager and Lady Barbridge.

It had been just two hours since she'd made her vow to Celia to help her with the infuriating man. Two hours since she'd committed herself to flirting with him. But now she wasn't sure how to do that. How did one approach one's greatest enemy and deepest temptation? How did one flirt with the most confusing and appealing man in the room?

He turned his gaze into the crowd, and suddenly his eyes focused on her. His expression all but smoldered as he held her stare evenly, not allowing her any route for escape. He leaned over to his family and said a few words, then moved in Rosalinde's direction.

She caught her breath as he approached her, thinking as she always did when she saw him, of that night at the inn when he had stalked her way, passionate intention in his dark eyes. He had almost the very same expression on his face now and her entire body reacted against her will, readying for him as if

71

he would take her right here, right now.

"Mrs. Wilde," he said as he reached her at last. "Would you like to dance the next with me?"

He held out a hand. It was gloved, as was her own, but she had no doubt those thin layers of satin would do nothing to reduce the impact of his touch. She knew what his skin felt like, what it tasted like. She wasn't likely to forget just because a few fragile layers of propriety now separated them.

But there was no choice in the matter. She had promised Celia that she would help. The only way she could do that was to use their mutual attraction against this man.

"Yes," she said, hating how breathless she sounded. Hating that he obviously heard her desperation, if his smirk was any indication.

She took his offered hand, ignoring the jolt of awareness that came along with touching him, and let him lead her to the dance floor. As they took their places, the orchestra began a waltz. Rosalinde just barely held back a curse. Of course it would be a waltz. There would be no respite from his embrace with a country jig or quadrille. Just her in his arms, almost scandalously close, until they were released by the music.

He glided her into motion with an effortless grace, and for the first few bars of the dance, they were both silent. His hand rested on her hip, his fingers splayed almost too intimately. Her other hand was in his, their fingers entangled. From this viewpoint, looking up at him, she could see every angle of his face. And she remembered all too clearly what those features had looked like when rapt with passion and release.

"We don't have to be enemies," he said, his deep voice breaking the spell between them at last.

She swallowed hard. Now was the time to focus. For her own sake, as much as Celia's. "I agree," she said.

He seemed surprised by her response. "You do?"

She nodded. "Of course. I liked you at the inn, Gray... Mr. Danford."

His fingers tightened on her hip. "Gray," he said softly.

That was inappropriate, and she knew it. And there was no way she could ever call him by his given name in front of anyone else. But when they were alone…if it served a purpose…

"Gray," she whispered. "And I thought you liked me in return."

His smile was brief, but oh, so wicked. "You *know* I liked you. There was no denying that I *liked* you."

His statement, so inappropriate because of what it referenced, made her blush hot. But she also found herself smiling at his gentle teasing, his pointed reminder of the deep connection they had shared that stolen night.

If this was flirtation, it didn't seem as hard now that they were together.

"I can't deny that seeing you here again gave me a charge, Rosalinde," he continued. "Can you?"

She hesitated. Ladies should not talk of such things, she knew that. And yet his tone was almost hypnotic. It made her want to say and do such inappropriate things.

"I can't deny it," she gasped out.

His pupils dilated as his expression grew more focused. "I will also admit that seeing you makes me want…*more*."

"Yes," she said. "You kissed me a few days ago. I think that proves what you say."

He nodded. "And *you* kissed me back."

"I-I did," she admitted.

He smiled, and that expression softened his normally hard face. "Then it seems I'm not alone in this…this wildly inappropriate attraction between us."

"No," she said before she thought. The moment the admission was out, she ducked her head, missing the next two steps as embarrassment filled her. Helping Celia was one thing. Labeling herself a wanton to a man whose intentions were unclear…well, that was another.

"You are honest," he said softly, his voice free of the censure she had feared would be there.

She lifted her gaze to his and held as evenly as she could. "I thought you believed I had no honesty in me."

"*Did* you know who I was that night at the inn, Rosalinde?" he asked with a frown.

She huffed out her breath. "You asked me that already."

"And this is the last time I will do so. Did you know?"

"No," she said, not blinking, not breaking her gaze, all but willing him to see the truth. His face relaxed, as if he was relieved to believe her. "Did *you*?"

"No," he said, with just as much certainty and honesty as she had. He leaned a little closer as they danced. "But I will tell you, Rosalinde, even if I had known your identity, I might have done the same thing. Because I wanted you. And God help me, I still do."

CHAPTER NINE

Gray had tried to talk himself out of this wild plan of seduction. He'd tried to find some other way to deal not only with his brother, but also with the rapidly escalating desire he felt for Rosalinde. But nothing had changed in the past few days, no matter what he did.

He avoided Rosalinde, and he still dreamed of her. He tried to distract himself and she was still in the corners of his mind. And now he was here and there was no going back.

She blinked as she stared up at him. His expression was one of surprise at his admission, but not disregard or disappointment. The woman was off kilter if the way she stumbled in her steps was any indication.

And that's what he wanted. To keep her off her game so that he could obtain both what he desired and needed.

She licked her lips and his groin clenched. Goddamn, but she was beautiful.

"Do you still want me, Rosalinde?" he asked, softer, more seductive.

She opened and shut her mouth, then turned her face. "This is—we shouldn't talk about this here," she gasped out.

"Then where?" he asked, sliding his fingers across the swell of her hip in what he knew was an entirely inappropriate way. But she shivered at the intimacy, known only to her. "Your bedroom?"

Her breath caught, but she didn't respond.

"Oh, that's right," he continued. "You share a bedroom

with Celia. Then mine."

Her lashes kept fluttering wildly against her cheeks, like she was searching for purchase. "I—Gray…"

He could hardly contain himself when she said his name. Especially in that breathless tone that sounded so much like she'd sounded in his bed less than a week before.

"Tell me you don't want that, Rosalinde," he pressed, ignoring all semblance of propriety and any boundaries that should have stopped him. "That you haven't dreamed of our night together since we parted."

"I—" Her voice broke, almost on a sob. "I can't tell you that."

The admission was like a gunshot, cutting through all other sound, breaking off any attention he might have been paying to those around them. He reveled in the fact that she wanted him. In that moment, nothing else on heaven or earth mattered.

"The song has ended," she whispered.

He froze and realized she was correct. The other dancers were beginning to bow to each other and make their way from the floor. He released her from the embrace of the waltz and instead slid her hand into the crook of his arm. He had to take her back to her grandfather now. It was twenty paces there, give or take.

He was running out of time.

"What if we could do it again?"

Her body stiffened. "Again?"

"Oh yes," he groaned, wishing he couldn't picture that exchange so perfectly. "Would you do something so *wild*, Mrs. Wilde?"

Her grandfather was now ten paces before them. He had a scowl on his face that he seemed to reserve especially for Rosalinde. Gray could feel her grow even more tense as they approached him.

"Gray—"

"Don't answer now," he interrupted. "Just think about it."

He said the last words just as they reached Mr. Fitzgilbert. Gray was reluctant to release her, but he somehow found the ability. He gave her a bow.

"Good evening, Mrs. Wilde. Mr. Fitzgilbert."

She nodded in acknowledgment of his farewell, but it was a jerky action. Her voice was small as she squeaked out, "Good evening, Mr. Danford."

He strode away, content with the knowledge that he'd laid the groundwork for moving forward with her. But the energy that coursed through his body, making him smile, had nothing to do with furthering his quest to break Celia and Lucien's engagement.

It had everything to do with the idea that he could steal yet another moment with Rosalinde Wilde.

Rosalinde tightened her robe around herself and stepped into the quiet of the library. The candle in her hand trembled as she moved to the long line of shelves and began to peruse their contents. She needed something tedious to help her in her quest for sleep. She needed something engaging enough to make her forget why slumber eluded her.

She pressed her forehead to the line of books before her with a long, shaky sigh. For the past few hours, she had been tormented by memories of her dance with Gray. Her mind and her rebelling body had relived every seductive word that left his lips.

He wanted her. He wanted to have her again.

And the thought both aroused her beyond measure and terrified her to the point of sleeplessness. The storm and the magical, fated quality of that unforgettable night in the inn had made surrendering to a stranger seem somehow acceptable.

But what Gray suggested now was something far different. Far more dangerous. They knew each other. They were in a house full of watchful eyes. And perhaps worst of all, they were enemies. Any man who would work to hurt her sister *had* to be Rosalinde's enemy.

And yet she wanted his wicked hands on her, his hot tongue on hers, his big body stretching her as she trembled beneath him.

There was a soft click behind her, and Rosalinde spun around to find Gray standing at the now-closed door. He had removed his formal jacket and cravat, leaving him in a crisp shirt, the sleeves rolled up past his elbows and unbuttoned to the collarbone. He held her gaze evenly, but said nothing as her candle began to shake in her hand.

And then he moved on her. He reached her in three long strides, slipping the candle from her fingers, setting it aside on a nearby table. He lowered his mouth to hers and she melted against him, arguments gone, reason departed, nothing left in her but pulsing need for this man.

His tongue probed her mouth, tasting her like she was something to savor, and she arched against him with a mewling cry that sounded so loud in the quiet room.

His arms tightened around her waist, lifting her against him, letting her feel the hard ridge of his erection through his trousers. She rubbed it with her hips, out of control as emotion took her, making her forget everything but him.

She felt his hands dragging down her back and gasped as he cupped her backside, kneading the sensitive flesh there as he rhythmically ground against her. She could hardly breathe as sensation gripped her, overcame her, and she cried out in his mouth.

He yanked his lips from hers, his dark eyes wild as he pushed her toward a settee near the fire. They collapsed backward on it, his heavy body pinning hers to the cushions.

She lifted her pelvis to his, moaning softly as she grabbed for his shirt. She unhooked the buttons with shaky hands and pushed at the fabric, nearly tearing it as she parted it and revealed his chiseled chest.

He shrugged out of the garment and then went back to kissing her. Heated, claiming kisses that began on her lips, but then he dragged his mouth to her throat, to the edge of her robe. His hand found the knot and he made swift work to open it. He licked lower, all the way to the scooped neckline of the nightgown beneath.

She felt like she was on fire and he was the one making her burn. But she also knew he was the only one who could grant her relief. And she needed that. Now.

He nudged a knee between her legs and she opened without argument, sighing as he shoved her nightgown up past her hips and then settled in the cradle of her thighs.

He was still dressed, but the hardness of his cock bumped her entrance as he tugged the neck of her night rail down and revealed one breast. He sucked her hard nipple between his lips and swirled his tongue around and around the peak until she was writhing beneath him.

She managed to wedge a hand between them and found the flap of his trousers. With so little room, unfastening it was a challenge, but she managed, and he hissed out a sound of pleasure as she tugged the fabric away and wrapped her hand around his erection.

He pulled from kissing her and stared down at her. Their gazes locked and suddenly there was nothing else in the world. She could hardly breathe as she guided him to her entrance.

"Rosalinde," he whispered.

She ignored him and lifted her hips, pressing him inside of her one glorious inch. He took over after that, sliding all the way inside in one long, heavy stroke.

They moaned together as he fully seated himself. Though it had only been a matter of days, Rosalinde felt she had been deprived of his touch for weeks, months. She was shaking as he began to move, rotating his hips as he took her one short stroke at a time.

She braced against him on every thrust, digging her fingers into his bare back as pleasure swirled between her legs, rising and lifting until she jolted with an orgasm. He grunted at the feel of her body flexing around him. His thrusts increased as her pleasure crested, and he slammed against her just a few more times before he withdrew and spent between their sweaty bodies.

He collapsed on top of her, his lips against her neck, his arms around her back, his sharp, panting breaths slowing to meet her own as they lay together in the afterglow of intense passion.

Finally she opened her eyes and stared up at the crisscrossed pattern of the exposed wood beams on the ceiling high above. The reality of what she'd done hit her and she buried her face into his shoulder with a shuddering sigh of both pleasure and self-recrimination.

"We shouldn't have done that," she whispered against his flesh. "It was wrong."

He pushed away from her, getting to his feet to tuck himself back into his trousers and search on the floor for his shirt. She also sat up, drawing her tangled nightgown over herself and retying her robe.

"It didn't feel wrong to me," he said as he buttoned his shirt. His eyes never left her. "It felt as good as being with you the first time did."

She bit back a sigh at those words. At his steamy look. This was not a man who regretted anything. Since arriving here, she'd heard enough about him from his family to know that was true. He had that luxury, given the family he came from and the money he'd made with his various ventures. She had more to consider when it came to the potential of a scandal.

And yet she shut her eyes and nodded. "Yes, it did," she admitted softly.

She felt his fingertip on her chin, tilting her face up, and opened her eyes. He was leaning over her, his face dangerously close to hers.

"Then why stop?" he asked, every word seeming to take

an eternity.

She pondered the question. She had so many reasons to stop. That he had so much more control than she did was one reason. That she didn't trust him. That this was too wild, too dangerous. That she feared what would happen when he tired of her at last. That she feared what would happen if she never tired of him.

But those things, as powerful as they were, did not rise too loudly to the forefront of her mind. Instead, she thought of Celia and the promise she'd made to her sister. And in truth, Rosalinde thought of her own pleasure. Being with Gray would bring her more of it. So much more.

"I don't want to stop," she croaked out. "I may be a fool of the greatest kind, I may be a wicked wanton with no sense of right, but when I look at you, all I want is for you to put your hands on me like you did tonight."

His eyes widened like he was surprised at the candor of her response. She supposed she was surprised by it, too.

"I'm glad of it, Rosalinde. During our dance tonight, I was afraid you would refuse me, calling on honor and propriety to shield you. That you want me as much, that you are willing to trust me with your body, means a great deal to me."

She shrugged. "I know I shouldn't trust you," she whispered. "But all I could think about after you left me with my grandfather tonight was what would happen if I said yes to your offer. And what would happen if I turned away. I couldn't sleep with such thoughts pounding in my head. It's how I ended up here, searching for something to quiet my mind and let me rest."

"You found me instead," he drawled, sliding his thumb along her jawline until her body felt hot and shaky.

"Technically, you found me," she whispered. "And without a word, you made me see exactly what my decision had to be. No question, no doubt, I had to be with you. I'm certain you judge me for that."

He shook his head. "I don't. I felt the same way. There

was something about you, from the moment I met you, that made me forget everything I had ever promised and vowed. It made me a slave to animal hungers I once foolishly told myself that I could control. With you, I cannot."

"Is that true?" she asked in wonder. "Could you really want me so much?"

"How could you not be certain after what we just shared?" he said with a short laugh. "Certainly you have been wanted before."

She turned her face, thinking of her husband and his attentions. Yes, he'd been gentle at first, but once he realized his fortunes wouldn't be increased by their marriage as he had hoped…well, her pleasure had gone by the wayside. He hadn't wanted her, not really. He'd only wanted what she could provide. When that was gone, everything had been broken.

"Never like this," she whispered, just barely keeping her voice from cracking in pain.

He hesitated, searching her face like he was seeking some kind of truth. She bent her head so he wouldn't see it. Trust him with her body? Oh yes, she would do that. Trust him further? It would take a fool to not see how utterly dangerous that would be.

She rose to her feet, dodging his touch and his glance as best she could. "So what will we do now?"

He stepped away from her, and his voice was gruff as he said, "Steal time, just as we did at the inn. It will be more challenging here, but I think it will be worthwhile."

She nodded. "Yes, so do I."

He moved toward her, and her heart leapt as he slid his fingers into her hair, tilting her face so that he could kiss her deeply, passionately. Her toes curled, her body heated, she melted like ice in an inferno. But he didn't continue the encounter. Instead, he let her go.

"Your sister will wonder where you are," he said as he turned her toward the door and pressed her toward it. "You'd best go as to not rouse her suspicions."

Rosalinde walked away as he was encouraging her to do. He was right, after all. They had taken a risk to make love in a public room like this one. She'd have to be more careful in the future.

But as she reached the door, she stopped and turned toward him. He was rumpled now, his hair tangled by her fingers, his shirt wrinkled from being torn away and tossed aside. He didn't look like a gentleman anymore. She doubted she looked like a lady.

"Goodnight, Gray," she whispered, smiling at him one last time before she slipped away toward her bed.

And though nothing had truly been resolved between them, she felt lighter than she had since her arrival. Everything had changed. And she would never again be the same.

CHAPTER TEN

Gray took a long breath of cold morning air before he urged his horse forward and dashed past Lucien. He heard his brother's laugh, so rare now, and then Stenfax thundered past him in return. They did this back and forth a few times, playfully racing each other. Of course, Gray knew the competition would get more serious as they neared the lake ahead. That was their traditional finish line.

As predicted, with the lake visible in the distance, both men urged their horses faster, faster. Gray pulled ahead, his heart racing with triumph, as the last hundred yards became the battleground. He would have whooped in victory, but seemingly out of nowhere another horse appeared. It was Felicity, who had been riding behind them, above all their games. Even riding sidesaddle she flew by and reached the water's edge before her brothers.

Gray patted his horse's side and muttered, "Next time, boy."

All three got off their mounts, laughing and panting as they let the horses roam off to drink and rest and graze.

"Do I win something?" Felicity asked as she adjusted her hat over the blonde hair she'd inherited from their mother, rather than the dark tresses her brothers shared. "Or is it just boyish bragging rights, as usual?"

"I could give you a farthing," Lucien suggested with a bark of laughter. "But it's all I have. You and Gray have far more money in your coffers between you."

Gray's smile fell even though his brother was teasing. It was no secret that the Stenfax reserves had been dwindling for some time. Their brother had inherited gambling debts and the poor management of three generations before him. Lucien was working to recover what the prior earls had so foolishly squandered and he still refused to take help from Gray, who had built his own small inheritance back into a fortune, or Felicity, who had inherited quite a sum herself when her viscount had mercifully breathed his last.

Of course, their brother's stubborn desire to fix things on his own was exactly why Lucien was poised on the edge of a dangerous precipice with Miss Celia Fitzgilbert. Gray scowled.

"Lucien—" he began.

"Oh Lord, he's about to start," Lucien said to Felicity. "Look at his face."

Felicity smiled softly as she turned to look at Gray. "He does have a certain expression that says he's going to start acting like the older brother instead of the middle child. That's our Grayson, trying to save the world."

Gray scowled at the playful words of his siblings. "This is nothing to jest about. You talk easily about the financial situation of the title, but I know it weighs on you. Without the troubles, you might not have ever chosen such a title hunter as Celia."

Felicity moved on him, her smile gone. "For heaven's sake, Gray, enough! Not only is Lucien well capable of making his own decisions, but you judge Celia Fitzgilbert too harshly. I've spent time with her in London as well as here, and she is a lovely girl."

"Her ambition doesn't trouble you?" Gray asked, tapping his boot.

"Not when it is made so plain," Felicity snapped back. "She is not pretending."

"Unlike Elise, you mean," Gray said, ignoring how his brother recoiled at that hated name. "Yes, I agree, Celia is open as can be about her desires when it comes to Lucien. She could hardly be less interested in him and shows no romantic inclination whatsoever. I have seen him hurt before. I've seen you *both* hurt before by the decisions you made in spouses."

Both his siblings flinched and Felicity spun away with a soft sound in the back of her throat. Gray hated to make them relive their worst moments, but if the reminder of past suffering would help him save Lucien from a desperate and irrevocable mistake, it was worth it.

Lucien stepped toward him, hands fisted at his sides and face red with more than just the cold air. "Damn it, Gray! Did it ever occur to you to ask *why* I chose Celia?"

"The money," Gray said flatly.

Lucien shook his head. "No, you ass, it's *not* just the money."

"Then what?" Gray threw up his hands in frustration.

"I don't want any of the damned romantic entanglements you say Celia doesn't show. She and I are clear on what we both want. On what we expect from each other."

Gray huffed out his breath. It seemed Lucien had an answer for everything. "But doesn't it make you question her character that she is so driven to marry a title and title only? And if there is a crack in her integrity in that arena, what others could exist?"

"You think Celia is walking around with a passel of secrets tucked in her reticule, waiting to pop out and hurt Lucien's reputation?" Felicity faced him again, her eyes wide and bright with unshed tears.

Gray rocked back at the sight of them and clenched his hands together behind his back. What his brother and sister didn't know, at least not yet, is that was *exactly* what he feared. He'd even launched an investigation back in London to address that very concern. He'd hoped to have some answers before he departed for Caraway Court, but when that hadn't panned out, he'd arranged to have a friend who was attending the wedding pick up his investigator's report before he made his way to the country estate.

Of course, if he told them that, they would both tear into him about his actions and motivations. So it was best to wait until he had something concrete to share.

"You mock me," Gray finally said, glaring at her. "But in truth, we know little about her past or her family. Her grandfather has a good pedigree, but you cannot say that he is a solid person. I walked in on him arguing with Rosa—with Mrs. Wilde just a few days ago. It was heated enough that I was forced to stop and check on the lady."

He cut himself off before he said more. After all, what was he going to confess? That he'd kissed Rosalinde in the parlor as some kind of comfort? That he'd done so much more last night in the library?

He doubted that revelation would help him in this argument with his siblings.

An argument that seemed to have found a mark, at last. Lucien's defensive posture softened a little and he exchanged a brief look with Felicity.

"I will grant you that Mr. Fitzgilbert's behavior is sometimes not gentlemanly," he said softly. "And that he has a great many demands about what Celia's dowry will 'buy' as far as access and influence."

Felicity reached out to Lucien, touching his arm. "But can you blame his behavior on Celia or Rosalinde?" She squeezed before she glared at Gray. "And why do you care so much, Gray? Rosalinde and her grandfather could hate each other to the core and that would have nothing to do with us. It is Celia who will join our family, not Fitzgilbert or Rosalinde."

No, Rosalinde would not be part of their clan once this was done. She would be just an in-law who they saw from time to time.

"Do stop scowling, Gray," Felicity said, crossing over to him to slide an arm around his waist. "We both know you mean well, but sometimes you go too far."

Gray pressed his lips together. He could see from Lucien's tight expression that he'd done just that today. The last thing he wanted to do was alienate his brother. So he sighed.

"I'm sorry if I'm too forward. I hope you know it comes from a good place." Lucien nodded wordlessly, and Gray continued, "I only want you to at least say you'll take my concerns into account. Consider *all* the outcomes in your association with this woman."

Lucien rolled his eyes. "I'll think about what you've said, Gray. But don't expect things to change. This wedding is happening in less than ten days. I don't see anything stopping it now."

In the three days since her last encounter in the library with Gray, Rosalinde could have written a book about how difficult it was to carry on an affair in a household filled with nosy people. Thanks to dress fittings and outings, gatherings and plans, she'd shared little more with Gray than a few meaningful looks and a lightly flirtatious banter. By the time each day came to a close, she felt unbearably tight, but there was no chance for release with her sister sleeping beside her.

"How do you take your tea, Mrs. Wilde?" the dowager countess said as she poured for her.

"Just milk," Rosalinde replied, pulling herself from her inappropriate thoughts with great difficulty.

She sat in the midst of the parlor surrounded by both bridal families, including Gray, who sat in a corner watching her. The intensity of his stare was so distracting that when Lady Stenfax held out her tea, Rosalinde didn't notice right away.

"Take the cup, girl," her grandfather snapped.

It felt like everyone in the room jumped at his harsh tone. Lady Stenfax even sloshed the cup so tea fell onto the floor between them.

Rosalinde grabbed the cup. "Oh, I'm sorry!" she burst out

as blood rushed to her cheeks.

"It's all right," Lady Stenfax said, smiling at Rosalinde even as her gaze slid to Mr. Fitzgilbert. "No harm done."

"Let me fetch you a napkin for your hand," Rosalinde said, setting her cup aside and rushing to the sideboard to get the cloth. As she reached it, a servant trailed behind.

"I've got it, ma'am," the maid said, taking the napkin and returning to her mistress.

Rosalinde stayed at the sideboard, trying to calm her breath. She felt Gray watching her, wondered if he would come to her, but before he could Lady Barbridge got to her feet and slid over with a warm smile.

"Don't worry," she said, touching Rosalinde's shaking hand lightly. "It was an accident, it could happen to anyone."

Rosalinde smiled at the other woman's kindness and her gentle tone. "Thank you, Lady Barbridge."

She flinched ever so slightly. "Oh, please, I know it is proper to call me by my title, but I do prefer Felicity. Especially from my friends."

Rosalinde lifted her gaze to Felicity's face. There was no censure there, no judgment. Was it possible she truly wanted to be Rosalinde's friend? Oh, she'd been kind before, the few times Rosalinde had encountered her in London, but now that she knew Gray's drive to break Celia's engagement, she wondered if the rest of his family felt so strongly.

"Thank you," she said with caution. "Felicity."

The pair watched the others for a while. Celia was speaking to Lady Stenfax while the earl seemed to be locked in intense conversation with Mr. Fitzgilbert. Only Gray sat outside it all, observing everyone, including Rosalinde. Whenever his dark gaze speared her, her body reacted almost against her will.

"I hope Gray isn't being too hard on you," Felicity said, drawing Rosalinde from her thoughts with sudden and violent force.

"I—he—we—" Heat flooded Rosalinde's cheeks and she

cleared her throat as she tried to find some level of calm. "Whatever do you mean?"

"Well, he is very protective of our brother." Felicity's voice grew softer and smaller. "And of me. Sometimes to a fault."

Rosalinde shifted. It didn't feel right to talk about such private things, and yet what choice did she have? Gray had made his war against Celia so clear, Rosalinde had to fight him just as hard if she were going to shield her sister from his plans.

"He *does* seem protective," she admitted. "Do you mind if I ask you why?"

Felicity shifted slightly, and a great pain came into her eyes. "Lucien and I have both been…*unlucky* in love before."

"I see," Rosalinde said softly. "How so?" Felicity glanced at her and Rosalinde rushed to continue. "I'm sorry. That was forward. If you don't want to—"

"No," Felicity interrupted. "It is a painful subject, yes, but not exactly a secret. I'm sure you know that Lucien was engaged once before and it…well, it ended badly. He was brokenhearted. As for me…" She cocked her head. "Well, I think you and I are not so different, Rosalinde."

"How do you mean?"

"I think we married men who we believed were one thing and turned out to be violently different." As Rosalinde's eyes widened, Felicity nodded. "Women in our situation recognize each other, yes?"

Rosalinde swallowed hard. "I'm sorry to hear your marriage was so unhappy."

"It happens," Felicity said, her words dismissive but her eyes telling a tale of pain that wasn't quite gone. "But it's over now. How did you lose your husband?"

"A fever," she admitted.

She pursed her lips as she remembered him drawing a last breath, his glaring eyes on her. "I wish it were you" had been his last words, and sometimes they hung in her ears.

"And you?" she asked, turning her face as she tried to

wipe clean the pain of that memory.

Felicity's face drained of some color momentarily before she said, "An—an accident." She took a few breaths before she motioned to Gray and brought Rosalinde away from her past and straight into her current predicament. "That is why Grayson is our defender, though. He simply wants to see us happy. And he is arrogant enough to believe he knows the only path to that outcome."

Rosalinde let out a long breath as she tried to keep her annoyance and frustration from her voice. She had enough enemies in this family—she didn't need to make more by alienating Felicity.

"And he is convinced Celia won't make Stenfax happy," she said through clenched teeth.

Felicity's shrug was answer enough. "Just so you know, I like Celia very much. Gray will get there. Eventually. He is stubborn, not unreasonable."

But there was something in Felicity's tone that made Rosalinde stare at her more closely. Made her doubt that the viscountess believed her own words.

"You don't seem certain," Rosalinde pressed. "Has he—has he said anything?"

Felicity shifted slightly, and Rosalinde's irritation turned to full anger. Gray *had* been talking about Celia to his siblings, that was clear, despite how Felicity immediately began to shake her head.

"Not anything of merit," she said weakly.

Rosalinde folded her arms. "Does he not think that I wish to protect *my* sister, as well?"

Felicity laughed at that question. "You two are so alike. You should be friends."

Rosalinde blanched at that off-hand comment. Felicity clearly didn't know anything about the relationship she and Gray had. She didn't know about the passion between them, which was always tinged by being on opposite sides of a battle neither felt they could afford to lose.

"I-I don't think your brother and I will ever call each other friends," Rosalinde whispered.

Felicity looked at her for a long moment. "Never say never," she said, then squeezed Rosalinde's hand and returned to Celia and Lady Stenfax.

Rosalinde watched her go and then let her gaze shift once more to Gray. He held her stare evenly, his gaze smoldering into hers. Her body wanted so desperately to melt at that look, but then she thought of Felicity's words. Her anger arced and she turned her back on him, shutting out his gaze, though she still felt it focused on her back.

Desire and connection was one thing, yes, and she could use those against him if she could gain some small control over her own reactions. But the fact that he was speaking about her sister to his family could not stand. And as soon as she could get him alone, she was going to have it out with him once and for all.

CHAPTER ELEVEN

The sun was just cresting over the horizon, signaling a new day, as Gray strode down the long, winding path to the stables below the house. A groom rushed to greet him, but he waved the man off.

"I'll take care of it, Stevens, thank you. Go about your business," Gray said.

"Yes, sir!" Stevens called out as he rushed off to make preparations with the house staff regarding the guests who would begin to arrive tomorrow.

Gray pursed his lips as he entered the silent and empty stables and moved to prepare his horse for riding. Thoughts of Lucien's nuptials had been more and more intrusive in the past few days. And yet he made no headway getting his brother to listen to reason.

It was frustrating and part of why Gray was up so early now. He needed a ride to clear his head. He'd just gotten the saddle on when the stable door slid shut in the distance.

He turned to see who had entered, expecting it to be Stevens, but when he saw the intruder, he caught his breath.

Rosalinde stood in the corridor, her arms folded, her lips trembling and her eyes flashing fire. She was dressed in a plain morning gown in a deep blue, but the somber clothing did nothing to reduce her vibrant beauty. It made him all too aware that it had been four long days since he last touched her. Another frustration that kept him up nights.

"Rosalinde," he said, moving toward her. "What are you

doing here? Are you following me?"

She lifted up a hand as if to ward him off, and he stopped. She was not teasing—she truly wished him to stay back.

"Of course I'm following you," she hissed. "I have not had a moment to speak to you privately since our...since we...since that night in the library."

He smiled at her stammer, her blush, and took another step in her direction. "And now you want to *talk* to me? Like we did that night?"

He looked toward the stable doors. Stevens would likely be up in the house for an hour for orders and food. More than enough time to enjoy a few pleasures with Rosalinde.

"You disparaged my sister to your siblings," she said, her voice shaking.

Gray wrinkled his brow as the true nature of her reasons for following him became clear. "You came here to talk to me about Celia?"

She nodded. "Of course. After all, she has no one on her side but me, it seems. Not when you are fighting hard to turn everyone else against her."

Gray stopped advancing on her and folded his arms. "Rosalinde, I made my stance on your sister's marriage to Lucien clear more than once. It can't surprise you that I would speak both to him and to Felicity about my concerns."

"You make it sound like you're addressing a business issue," Rosalinde said, and her voice cracked. The painful sound hit him in the gut. "Celia is a *person*. She is the person I love more than any other on this earth. And you're trying to hurt her."

He caught his breath. "I'm not trying to hurt anyone. I'm trying to make sure my brother *isn't* hurt."

"How many times must it be said that Celia has no intention of harming Stenfax? The two of them have made their agreements, *both* will benefit from them. Not only will Stenfax receive my sister's generous dowry, but she will make a good countess for him."

She said the words, but he could see a flicker of hesitation on her face. Was she aware of some betrayal on Celia's mind, or was it just that the two of them had no connection and it troubled passionate Rosalinde?

Either way, her words didn't sway him as she likely hoped. He leaned in closer, getting a whiff of the lemon scent of her hair on the cold breeze.

"Are you trying to convince me or yourself?"

Her jaw stiffened and lifted in outrage. He supposed he should have been put off by that, but he wasn't. He liked her loyalty to her sister. He liked her fire when she was angered. He liked that she faced off with him directly, not simpering or playing or hiding how she felt.

As if to prove that point, she pushed her face closer to his and hissed, "I despise you."

She moved to turn away, but he caught her arm and pivoted her back, dragging her almost into his arms. She made no move to resist and her pupils dilated with the desire she was obviously trying to deny.

"Do you?" he whispered.

She held his gaze, mouth twitching, her cheeks growing pink. Then she looked straight at his mouth and licked her lips.

He was lost. He tugged her firmly into his embrace and crushed his mouth to hers. She was stiff only for a fraction of a second, then she parted her lips and met his tongue. He kissed her as he backed her up until she was flat against the stable wall, tilting his head to taste her, panting as he took what he had been missing these four long days and nights.

And he knew there would be no stopping the tide now. He would have her. Here and now.

She seemed to sense the same thing, for she began to arch against him with a breathless, eager fervor that only stoked the need driving through his body.

He broke from her lips with a gasp and looked down at her upturned face. "Do you want this?"

She nodded. "God help me, yes. Yes, I want this."

He almost sagged in relief at her acquiescence, given despite her anger toward him. He cupped her face and kissed her again, this time more gently. She moaned softly in her throat and her hands came up to grip his jacket lapels as she lifted against him.

He knew they didn't have much time, so as much as he wanted to make love to her slowly and sweetly, until her body was limp and languid from orgasm after orgasm, that wasn't an option. Instead, he crooked her leg up with one arm and used the other to ratchet up her skirts.

She let out a cry as he leaned into her, unfastening his trousers as he ground little circles against her bare sex. His cock came free and they sighed together.

"Hurry," she murmured, her fingers digging into his jacket.

"Your wish is my command," he responded as he adjusted his position and gently thrust, sliding into her as deeply as he could.

They both moaned together and she immediately began to rock, forcing him to thrust in time to her shaking body.

He kissed her as he took her, lost in her softness, her heat, her unrestrained passion. He'd never known anyone like this woman and he'd never know anyone who came close to her again once she had departed his life.

It was why he felt so driven to have her, despite all the very good reasons to stay away. Despite the knowledge that it wouldn't last, just as no connection ever lasted. Right now he had her. Right now he would celebrate that fact by driving hard into her, sliding his hand between her legs where she was slick, stroking her clitoris with his thumb.

She jolted at the caress, her eyes going wide and her cries louder and sweeter in the warmth of the stable. Her body fluttered around him in sweet release, massaging his cock, milking him until the pleasure crested and he was forced to withdraw from her heaven and spend his pleasure with a roaring cry of her name.

"You judge Celia," Rosalinde panted a few breaths later as she smoothed her skirts back down and watched him fasten his trousers. "But you are willing to take advantage of my vulnerability."

He froze at the accusation and slowly lifted his gaze to her face. Sunlight streamed through a window in the loft above and hit her so that she looked almost angelic, but she held herself like a warrior. An interesting dichotomy if he'd ever seen one.

"Is that what you are? Vulnerable?" he asked.

She laughed, and in that sound he heard her rawness, a pain she had never before revealed to him. "We are women under the control of men, Gray," she said. "Of course I am vulnerable."

She said nothing else, but walked out of the stable without so much as a backward glance.

He thought of chasing after her, but didn't. Why? Because the look on her face had been too genuine. If he followed her, this connection to her would no longer be a mere twist of fate, plucked from the ether. No, if he pursued her, if he pushed her, if he really grew to know the weakness and pain and emotion that she hid deep in her soul...

That would make this real. He didn't want real.

And yet he couldn't stop thinking of what she'd said before she walked away. He returned to his horse with her words haunting him.

We are women under the control of men.

She'd meant under his control, she supposed. That Celia was in some ways under his brother's control. That Rosalinde had once been under her husband's control.

But he thought she'd also been referring to someone else—her grandfather. She and Celia were under his control and he held the cards to their future in a way Gray didn't fully understand.

But maybe it was time to change that. Maybe it was time to start finding out more about these sisters and the man who held the key to all they did and said.

Rosalinde sat in the chair by the window, staring out at the rolling hills of the estate far below. In the distance, she saw a rider. Gray. She knew it was him. She was beginning to know the way his body moved far too well.

She sighed. Her plan had not been to make love to him when she went to the stable. She'd wanted to confront him about his interference. To try to convince him that he was wrong about her family. Instead she had ended up consumed by pleasure.

She was a selfish girl, just as her grandfather had always accused her.

The door to the chamber opened and she glanced over to watch Celia come inside. Her sister shut the door and looked at her, concern written on her face.

"There you are," Celia said, moving toward her. "You were gone so early this morning, and when you weren't at breakfast I worried."

Rosalinde smiled sadly. Celia wouldn't be *worried* if she knew the truth. "I-I thought of taking a ride around the grounds but decided against it."

Celia sat down on the chair across from her and examined her carefully. "Do you want to tell me what's wrong?"

"Wrong?"

Celia nodded. "I have eyes in my head, Rosalinde, there is no reason to deny the truth. Since your arrival here you have been *odd*."

Rosalinde tensed. Leave it to her sister to notice even the slightest of changes in her mood. "Odd? How so?"

"You are distracted, for one. I catch you staring off into the heavens so many times each day. And troubled. You are the one of the two of us who smiles and I have barely seen that expression since you came to the country. I can't help but be concerned by this change."

Rosalinde shrugged. "Perhaps I am just lamenting the loss of a dear sister when you wed in—God's teeth—just days now!"

She had meant Celia to laugh at that statement, but she didn't. Celia folded her arms as if irritated.

"Please don't pretend the truth away or try to distract me. I want to know what is in your heart, Rosalinde."

Rosalinde sighed. "I suppose I feel…guilty."

"Guilty?" Celia edged closer. "Why?"

"I ran away to marry a man I knew grandfather would despise," she said. "And that rebellion led to his threats to you, to his devil's bargain that you must marry a title for us to find out the truth about our father. If I had been good, if I had stayed home, if I had—"

Celia lifted a hand. "Stop. There are many things that are regrettable about your marriage, Rosalinde. Watching your heart break when it became clear Martin had only held an interest in money and connection was horrible. But you can't blame yourself for Grandfather's actions. He wanted me to marry a man of rank and he would have wanted that whether you turned away from his path for you or not. Your marriage may have pushed him to the timing of his threats toward me, but I have no doubt he would have made them no matter what."

"Still, it could have been *me* making this sacrifice rather than you," Rosalinde said. "After all, it is clear you don't care for Stenfax."

Celia bent her head. "No," she said slowly. "I have tried, I truly have. After all, he is handsome and intelligent and kind enough. Most women would give their arm to have him. And yet when I look at him, I feel nothing."

Rosalinde shivered. "Oh, dear."

"But one can live in a loveless union, can't one?" Celia asked, but it sounded like she was trying to convince herself. "People do it every day. Stenfax and I will surely find some common ground along the way, develop a friendship and a partnership when it comes to children."

Rosalinde bit her lip. "And what will you do about making those children?"

"You've explained to me already about the marital bed," Celia said, and her face twisted, as if the thought of sex was unpleasant. "I'll bear it."

"You should experience more than just that," Rosalinde declared, her mind turning to Gray and his searing touch, his ability to awaken her body with just an expression or a glancing touch. "Celia, the moments shared between a man and a woman should be passionate and tender. You should feel heights of pleasure and then a connection afterward that is unlike any you've felt before."

Celia's eyes narrowed and she said, "That is a far different story than the perfunctory touches you described to me weeks ago."

Rosalinde gasped. She'd been so caught up in her worry for her sister, she hadn't thought through what her words would reveal. Now Celia stared at her.

"Rosalinde," her sister said slowly. "What has suddenly made you so passionate about the marital bed?"

"Nothing," Rosalinde lied. She moved to get up, but Celia caught her wrist and held her in place.

"You told me that there was little pleasure with Martin," Celia said. "You said that you wished you could have experienced something more like what you've just described. So what changed between then and now? What makes your eyes light up when you describe what a woman should experience with a man?"

Rosalinde sucked in her breath. Celia was too clever to be distracted from this line of questioning now that she had gotten the scent of Rosalinde's lies. The truth *would* come out.

And perhaps it was best that it did at last. Despite being two years younger, Celia had always been the more rational of the sisters. She could help Rosalinde in the tangle she had created for herself. But only if Rosalinde could manage to say the words that now stuck in her throat.

"I didn't know who he was when I met him," she squeaked out.

Celia shook her head. "Who?"

"And he drew me in, made me want…made me want things I had long ago declared would never be mine."

"*Who?*" her sister repeated, this time more strenuously.

"Gray," Rosalinde whispered. "Grayson."

The blood drained from Celia's face as recognition dawned. "*Grayson?*"

Rosalinde nodded slowly. "We were trapped in the same inn the night of the storm, my room was damaged and there was no choice…I stayed with him. Just one night, just a stolen night."

Celia jumped to her feet and stared. "You shared a night with *Grayson Danford*. My fiancé's younger brother, the man driven to find any reason to have me ousted from Stenfax's life?"

"I didn't know it was him," Rosalinde reminded her. "And then I got here. We were both shocked, especially since I knew by then that he had a desire to break you apart from Stenfax."

"And then what?" Celia pressed. "Did you call him out for his seduction? Did you threaten to tell Stenfax of his ungentlemanly behavior unless he stopped his torment?"

Rosalinde blinked. She could have done just that, but she'd never thought of it. Perhaps because she had wanted that night with Gray as much as he had, so she couldn't pretend she had been used when she was an equal party to the passion.

"No, I-I thought if I could get closer to him—"

Celia skittered back, her hand flying up to her face, but not before Rosalinde saw the horror of her expression. It cut her to the bone.

"You're *still* bedding down with him?" Celia asked, her voice muffled by her fingers.

Rosalinde flinched at the stark description of her actions. Stark, but not inaccurate. She pushed to stand and straightened her shoulders.

"I have, yes."

Celia let out a strangled sound and spun away, racing across the room as if getting away from Rosalinde would make this right, make it better.

"I thought you would flirt with him," she gasped. "Not this!"

"But—"

"No! No! You know what he wants to do," Celia all but sobbed. "How he is driven to hurt me and my chances of a future."

"Yes," Rosalinde admitted, and hated herself for the betrayal her beloved sister now felt. "Oh God, Celia, it wasn't my intention to—"

"Your intention?" Celia cried out, spinning on her. "You want to speak to me about *intention* now?"

"Gray sees you as a potential harm to his brother," she explained. "But he is not entirely unreasonable. I thought if I could grow closer to him, I could make him see—"

"That we Fitzgilberts have no morals? No control?" Celia interrupted.

Rosalinde recoiled at the accusation. "I—you don't mean that."

Celia shrugged, her voice calm even though tears were now streaming down her face. "How could I not? Thanks to Grandfather's coldness, you and I have always been more than sisters. You were my best friend. I watched you dance around Martin Wilde and what did I tell you?"

Rosalinde swallowed hard. "I—you—" She dipped her head. "You told me it was a bad idea."

Celia nodded. "I told you Grandfather would retaliate, I told you we might *both* suffer. But you declared you were in love, and so I closed my eyes and prayed I would be wrong."

"You weren't, though. He cut me off," Rosalinde whispered. "And when he did, Martin realized there would be no great sum settled upon me, upon him, as he hoped."

"Yes, we both know how your husband turned against you." Celia stepped toward her. "But do you know what Grandfather did to *me*?"

Rosalinde drew back. "Did to you?"

"I always kept it from you, so you wouldn't feel guiltier than you already did." Celia lifted her chin. "He locked me in my chamber for a *week*. When he brought me out, it was only to read Bible verses which described punishments for disobeying the Lord, disobeying *him*. If I didn't seem impressed enough by his readings, he made up punishments of his own. He let you escape, but he made it clear *I* never would."

Rosalinde reached for her. "Oh, Celia. I didn't know, I didn't—"

"Of course you didn't know. You were busy running off to marry, to thwart Grandfather, and only deal with the easiest of consequences." Celia dodged her hand. "And when he told me that our father hadn't actually died, as we'd always been told, and that if I did as he wanted, he would tell me about him…I was shattered, Rosalinde. And you were *gone*. I was left to deal with it alone."

Rosalinde could hardly breathe as the full weight of her selfishness hit her. She had always only seen her own pain, but now Celia's burned bright and accusatory.

"You suffered because of me. I cannot tell you how sorry I am."

"When Martin died and you were going to be on the street, I had to *beg* to have you return," Celia continued. "Grandfather was horrible, Rosalinde. It was almost unbearable to hear him disparage you, compare you to our mother and make you both sound so terrible."

Rosalinde tried a weak smile for her. "But it worked. He allowed me back, not with open arms, but back nonetheless."

"And it is *me* he rails to about you," Celia said. "When he forced you to remain in London when we came here to begin final wedding preparations, do you know what the topic of conversation was the entire time in the carriage?"

"No," Rosalinde whispered.

"How when you came, I had best control you so you wouldn't ruin this engagement. That and how I better not let any romantic notions of a happy and loving marriage keep me from doing as I'd promised. He holds *me* responsible for both our behavior and now you do *this*. Do you know what he'll do if he finds out?"

"He won't find out."

"Why? Because you fully trust this man who would destroy all my hopes with a wave of his hand if he could?" Celia asked, her tone flat and sarcastic.

Rosalinde flinched. She deserved her sister's censure, but it cut her nonetheless.

"What can I do to earn your forgiveness?"

Celia stared at her, her face filled with disappointment and betrayal, but also love. Her sister still loved her, and Rosalinde clung to that.

"You said this man can be reasonable," Celia whispered. "I've seen no evidence of that."

Rosalinde thought of him. There were times when he could be so tender. Times when she could believe…

Well, she didn't know what to believe.

"I think he could be."

Celia didn't look convinced, but she said, "Then perhaps that can be used to help us. I don't want my future husband's brother to despise me, to poison his family against me. See if you can talk to him, see if you can convince him that I am not so bad as he wants to believe. Perhaps you can even convince him to discuss his problems with me directly."

Rosalinde nodded. "I can try, but…but that might mean I have to trust the man a little more. Give a little more."

Celia stiffened, her aversion to that plan clear on her face. But she finally jerked her head up and down. "All right. If you believe that is best, I'll agree to it."

Rosalinde reached for her again, and this time Celia

allowed her touch. She squeezed her sister's fingers as she said, "I let you down. I know I did. But I vow to you, Celia, I will be sure never to do it again."

Celia held her stare, but it was clear she didn't fully believe Rosalinde. And that hurt the most. Her sister thought she was willing to sacrifice her for her own pleasure.

And Rosalinde was going to have to be certain she never did that again.

CHAPTER TWELVE

Gray entered the parlor, intent on grabbing a few cakes leftover from tea and then heading to his chamber to prepare for the night. But as he moved to the sideboard, someone cleared their throat from the corner of the room.

He turned to find Rosalinde and Celia's grandfather, Mr. Fitzgilbert, sitting in a chair, the paper he'd been reading now draped over his lap.

Gray stiffened. He liked this man even less than he liked Celia. And yet his conversation earlier with Rosalinde in the stable, when she'd said she and her sister were women under the rule of men…well, it rang in his ears.

This was an opportunity to find out more not only about Celia, but also about Rosalinde. To understand what she meant when she whispered those bitter, painful words.

"Good afternoon," he said, bringing his plate to the chair opposite Fitzgilbert. "I seem to have missed tea with the others, but would you mind if I joined you?"

Fitzgilbert shrugged one shoulder as he folded his paper and set it aside. "Of course not. I admit I have been very interested in speaking to you, Mr. Danford."

Gray met the older man's stare evenly. "Have you now?"

"Indeed, I hear so many interesting stories about you from both gossip and your own family. I wonder if they can all be true." Fitzgilbert smiled, but there was little realness to it. He was pandering.

"I am eager to hear what tales are being told," Gray

drawled.

Fitzgilbert crossed his legs. "They say that though you were raised a gentleman, you have become a man of business."

"I have."

He waited for the other man's reaction. There were only two responses most in their sphere displayed when hearing Gray had decided not to sit on his ass and watch his inheritance dwindle to nothing, all while he pretended to still be rich.

Disgust…or interest.

Fitzgilbert was hard to read as he steepled his fingers and examined Gray. "An interesting thing, though I suppose you had little choice what with your family's…*issues*."

Gray stiffened. "Issues?" he repeated.

Fitzgilbert shrugged. "Come, we can be honest, can't we? Discuss things plainly."

"I'm not sure what it is you wish to discuss."

"It's no secret that your brother needs my granddaughter's dowry." Fitzgilbert reached out to grab his teacup from the table beside him. He took a slow sip before he said, "Some of the best marriages start that way."

Gray nodded slowly. His dislike for this man was growing by the moment and yet he didn't pull away. Fitzgilbert had opened a door that led to the answers Gray wanted.

"Some men wouldn't see it that way. It seems to be in vogue at present to encourage love matches."

Fitzgilbert wrinkled his nose in disgust. "What use is it to have children or grandchildren if one cannot increase one's value through them? Encourage a love match? That is pure poppycock."

"How did you further yourself through Rosalinde's first marriage?" Gray prodded, trying to remain nonchalant.

Fitzgilbert's eyes narrowed, his face twisting with cruelty. "That nothing she married? Laughable. Rosalinde has never brought me anything but heartache. She is an out of control, impertinent she-devil who lives to torment me when I was kind enough to take her in. I should have taken her to a foundling hospital. I've told her so a dozen times since I took her in."

Gray flinched at the icy tone of his companion's voice. At the cruelty in his eyes. *This* was what Rosalinde had endured her entire life. It was no wonder she was so protective of her sister.

"I can't imagine you would say something like that to a child," Gray said, now through clenched teeth.

"If it keeps a child in line, why wouldn't I?" Fitzgilbert sputtered. "If I'd done the same with that mother of hers, we never—"

Gray straightened up as the other man cut himself off. He could see from the expression on his face that he'd gone too far, revealed too much.

"Your daughter?" he pushed.

Fitzgilbert sniffed. "Such as she was."

Gray was stunned by the coldness. This man's daughter had died, leaving him with two young children to raise, and he couldn't even bother to look sad at that fact. He was truly a bastard.

But a bastard who had given Gray an insight. Rosalinde had run off with a man of no title or money and it had angered Fitzgilbert. More importantly, it also reminded him of his own daughter.

Gray had looked into the history of Celia's parents in the past. It was vague, at best. Their mother had at some point gone to live with relatives, where she had married a gentleman who no one seemed to be able to identify. When she and her husband died, Fitzgilbert had come to collect his grandchildren. But it had always been curious to Gray that their grandfather had insisted they go by his last name rather than that of their father.

Who had that man been? And why did Rosalinde and Celia's mother inspire such hatred in her own father?

More to the point, could the answers to those questions be Celia's undoing? If the scandal was big enough, it was possible straight-laced Stenfax would shy away from it.

Gray's investigator was already working on the answers to those exact questions, but now more than ever he felt this might be the path. He'd have the results of their investigations in a couple of days, when he expected his reports to be brought in by friends who were attending the wedding.

"It's interesting you have so many questions about my family's past," Fitzgilbert said, drawing Gray's attention back to him. "After all, you have not exactly made it a secret that you don't approve of Celia and Stenfax's match."

Gray arched a brow. So now they were to the heart of it. "Celia told you this?"

"She was blubbering about it to her sister and I overheard. Though it wasn't so hard to believe. Anyone with eyes in their heads can see how you glare at her."

"And you think I've judged her too harshly?" Gray asked, preparing for a defense of Celia from this man, just as he'd received defenses of her character from Rosalinde.

Instead Fitzgilbert stared at him blankly. "I don't give a damn how you judge her. She's hardly worth considering, in truth. But what *is* worth considering is that your brother has already agreed to this union, sir. We have signed papers and arranged for monies to be exchanged. Monies that your family so desperately needs."

Gray drew back. "This is beginning to sound like a threat, Mr. Fitzgilbert."

"You may take it however you would like to take it." Fitzgilbert said with a dismissive wave of his hand. "It matters little to me. What may matter on a larger scale is how your family will survive if this money was taken away."

Gray pushed to his feet. "I think I've heard enough."

"How did your family lose their money in the first place?" Fitzgilbert asked, ignoring the warning in Gray's tone and posture. He even smiled up at him in the face of it.

"You had best watch yourself, sir," Gray growled.

"No." Fitzgilbert pointed a finger at him, jabbing it like it was a knife. "You best watch *yourself*, Mr. Danford. After all, your brother has as much to lose as I do if this marriage doesn't go through."

"My brother would find another match, I assure you."

"With two broken engagements in just two years? Society could be made to see that in a very unkind light." Fitzgilbert leaned back, a smug smile across his round face. "I say this only to make you remember your place as quickly as I recall my own."

"I know exactly what my place is," Gray said as he turned and walked away.

He stormed out of the room with Fitzgilbert's chuckle ringing in his ears. Rage bubbled up in him. Rage that this man would threaten his family, but also rage that he could treat his own granddaughters with such distain and disregard. It made everything Rosalinde did make so much more sense.

And it made him wish he could help her, even as he fought to destroy the one thing she wanted most. He only knew he couldn't have both the things he wanted. At some point he'd have to choose. And someone he cared for would lose.

Gray strode down the hall from the backstairs. He hadn't wanted to see anyone in his current mindset and so had gone the back route to the main floor. His mind still roiled with thoughts of his encounter with Fitzgilbert. The man's cruelty and his threats were hardly to be born.

And yet they would have to be, for at least a little longer. Fitzgilbert would be at the supper table in an hour, smugly overseeing this engagement that suited his own purposes.

Which drove Gray even harder to explore the past of Rosalinde and Celia's mother and see if he could find—

The thought in his head was cut off as he passed by the closed door to the music room. Inside, he could hear someone playing the pianoforte. It was a mournful song, but played impeccably. He was drawn to the sound and leaned toward the door to listen to it longer. But just as the notes wrapped around him, sank into him, there was a crashing, discordant sound of fingers mashing on keys.

He shoved the door open and found that the mysterious player of the music was none other than Rosalinde. And now she sat, head hung over the keys, her shoulders shaking. She obviously had not noticed his entry, his intrusion on her private heartbreak.

He had two options on how to proceed. He could quietly shut the door and never tell her that he'd seen her in such a state—or he could go inside and comfort her.

He was already moving into the room. It was too late to do anything else but whisper, "Rosalinde?"

She jumped at the sound of his voice and staggered to her feet to face him. She swiped at the tears which clung to her cheeks, and refused to meet his eyes.

"G-Gray," she stammered, her voice thick with tears. "I didn't hear you there."

He reached into his pocket and withdrew a handkerchief. He held it out wordlessly. She hesitated, but then took it, her fingers brushing over the monogram his sister had stitched on the cloth some Christmas years ago.

"Thank you," Rosalinde whispered before she turned away to gather her composure and blow her nose. "I'll have it washed and return it," she said as she tucked the handkerchief into her pocket.

"Come for a walk with me," Gray said, uncertain why those words had burst from his lips. "In the garden."

Rosalinde wrinkled her brow in confusion. "At dusk, in the cold?"

He nodded. "The night air will do us both some good. As long as you won't be bothered by the scenery."

She let out a laugh that was pained. "The garden is brown and dead now. That rather fits my soul at present."

He moved on her, unable to stop himself. "You are the

most alive thing I've ever known, Rosalinde."

She blinked at this compliment and he could see her hesitation. He supposed he'd earned that. After all, he hadn't been trustworthy, at least not in her eyes. She had to doubt his motives now. Motives he could hardly define they were so twisted in his own mind.

"Please," he said.

She nodded slowly. "All right."

He took her arm, guiding her to the foyer where he called for their coats to be brought. He watched as Stenfax's butler, Taylor, assisted her with the same hooded red cloak she'd been wearing the night she entered the inn. Once he had left them, Gray turned toward her to button her jacket slowly. In silence, she watched every movement of his hands.

Finally, he took her hand and they went down to a parlor with an exit to the terrace and the garden down the stairs below. She was silent the entire time, just watching until they stepped into the cold maze of the dead garden.

"Why are you being so kind to me, Gray?" she whispered at last. "Is this an angle to take me to your bed again?"

He flinched at her cold assessment of his intentions. "When it comes to you, I am always thinking about having you in my bed," he admitted. "But taking you for a walk tonight has nothing to do with that." She gave him a look, and he smiled despite himself. "Very well, it has *little* to do with that."

"Then why?" she pressed.

"I heard you playing the pianoforte and it drew me in," he admitted. "I saw you weep and it brought out a desire to comfort you."

She pursed her lips. "And if there is no comfort to be offered?"

He frowned at the idea that she could not be helped. It made him want to rip the world apart to find a way. Instead, he said, "Then perhaps a few moments to forget."

"And how do you suggest that I forget?"

"We'll talk about something else," he said, guiding them

forward once more. "You can tell me which of these dead flowers is your favorite."

She laughed, and the sound warmed him to his center. He could spend a lifetime making this woman laugh. Feeling the beauty of it wrap around him tighter and tighter until there was room for nothing else but the pleasure she brought.

He shook those feelings away. They served no purpose in heaven or on earth.

"I would rather talk about you," she said.

He looked at her from the corner of his eye. "Me?"

"Yes. You and I have gone about our entire acquaintance backward. We made love before we knew each other's name, we hated each other before we knew the other. It seems time now that we truly meet."

He shifted with discomfort at the idea that she wished to know him better. Just standing next to her made him feel vulnerable. Giving her more was…it was like arming an enemy with information on how best to destroy.

"And what about what I want to know about you?" he asked.

She shrugged. "You know I was married before, you know my grandfather raised me and my sister after our mother's death—you know a great deal. And all I know is that you're Stenfax's younger brother and you have some kind of business to the north."

"When you put it that way, it does sound unfair," he conceded slowly.

"You and your brother seem as close as Celia and I…" She trailed off, and there was a twisting sense of pain to her tone. She swallowed and said, "You are lucky to have such a tight-knit family."

He let his gaze slide away as he considered her statement. The truth about his family wasn't something he shared. Hell, he hardly spoke of it with Felicity and Lucien. And yet he found himself longing to tell Rosalinde more. He tried to tell himself it was only to lower her guard. But it was more than that.

"We look close," he admitted. "Felicity and Lucien and I are close, indeed. But our family isn't as intact and wonderful as perhaps you picture it."

She stopped in the path and turned toward him slightly. "No?"

"My father was a hard man. With vices and arrogance that did nothing to help refill our coffers. Oh, there were times he could be kind, at least to others, but with his family he was more often distant. He saw little value in his children except for the one who would take his place: Lucien."

He heard the pain in his voice, the pain he so rarely allowed and never addressed. Rosalinde took his hand and squeezed, and it was like it opened the gate to feel everything he normally repressed. The agony spread open his chest and exposed his heart to the cold air.

He clung to her hand, holding it too tightly until the emotion faded.

"You had no relationship with him?" she asked.

He shrugged, able to pretend that truth had no meaning again. "Not unless I could stand behind Lucien and wait for whatever scraps the old man had left to give. Which was little."

"But you don't resent Stenfax for that," Rosalinde said softly.

Gray wrinkled his brow. "How could I? Lucien didn't want it that way. I even sometimes overheard him trying to encourage our father to pay me some heed, for all the good it did. My brother is my best friend, Rosalinde."

He said it, knowing what it meant to her. Knowing she understood how far he would go, but also why he would do so.

Immediately he saw her appreciation for what his words meant. "You are lucky to have such close bonds with your siblings. Not everyone feels this way about their blood."

"No, I know many who war with their brothers for position and power." Gray shook his head.

Rosalinde nodded. "With women it is the same, although it is a different kind of power."

"And yet you would do anything for Celia," he said, watching her face. He asked because he wanted to know. He asked because her answer might help him in his quest. He hated himself for the second reason.

Rosalinde caught her breath. "Right now Celia may not believe that."

Gray drew her closer in the cold and stepped out to make them move again. He wanted to know what Rosalinde would confess, and he thought she would be more likely to say difficult words when he wasn't staring at her, making her question what he would do with the information she shared.

"Is that why you were crying?" he pressed gently. "Did you two have a row?"

She was silent for what felt like a very long time, as if she were considering what to do and say. "The truth affects you, I suppose."

He arched a brow as he looked at her. "Does it?"

She stopped and fully faced him again. The cold had made her cheeks pink, and in the faint light from the house behind him she was pretty as she'd ever been.

"Celia knows about...about what has happened between *us*," she whispered.

Gray's entire body tensed and he released her, his hands fisting at his sides. "About you and me?" he clarified.

She nodded.

"About us sharing a bed at the inn the night we met, about us being together since your arrival," he continued.

She nodded again, this time more slowly. "And she is upset with me," she whispered.

Gray frowned. This put a new wrinkle on an already complicated situation. After all, Celia was aware of Gray's disapproval of her. She might be able to use this affair against him as much as he was trying to use the truth against her.

"I'm shocked you would tell her about us," he said, keeping his tone neutral.

Rosalinde dipped her chin. "You say Stenfax is your best

friend. Well, Celia is mine, although I have let her down so many times."

Gray thought of her grandfather's words just a few hours before. Fitzgilbert judged Rosalinde harshly for some unnamed crimes, as well as for marrying beneath her station. If Celia felt the same, that only solidified Gray's poor opinion of the young woman.

"How have you let her down?" he asked, his voice barely carrying in the cold.

She met his gaze, and he saw her hesitation. He hated it, even though he deserved it. "My marriage," she said softly.

His eyes narrowed. It seemed it was just as he'd thought. "She didn't like you marrying a man with no standing?"

"No!" Rosalinde shook her head swiftly. "You misunderstand. My grandfather is such a...he's horrible, Gray. He may pretend to care when it suits him, but he doesn't."

Gray's thoughts turned again to the dismissive words Fitzgilbert had had for the remarkable woman standing before him. He'd wanted to smash a fist through the old man's nose at the time. Now he wished he had when it was clear how much Rosalinde was grieved by Fitzgilbert's lack of care.

"What does your grandfather's treatment have to do with your marriage?" he pressed, turning them back toward the house.

She sighed. "I was angry, hurt by him and his slurs against me, against my mother. I met Martin Wilde, who was a shopkeep, and I knew he was beneath what my grandfather would want for me. I admit that was part of the appeal, to defy him."

She lifted her chin as she said it and her face lit up with the defiance once again. It made her look like a warrior in the moonlight, and Gray had to fist his hand at his side not to touch her right there and then.

"So you married him, despite his standing," he urged.

She nodded. "I did. I left my sister behind in a fit of pique. And that left my grandfather able to..."

She trailed off and turned her face, as if she had thought better then to tell Gray the truth. As if she'd remember they were enemies, not friends, even if they were lovers.

"So your sister was angry because you left?" Gray pushed. "That seems unfair. You couldn't have been expected to stay with her forever."

"But I shouldn't have left for *him*!" she snapped, anger and pain changing her tone as well as her expression.

He leaned in, capturing her stare even as she tried to dodge him. "Why?" he asked.

She stared at him, her lips slightly parted, her body stiff in reaction. She stared at him, and he realized that her answer was suddenly desperately important to him. Not because of Celia. Not because of Lucien. But because he wanted to know her. He wanted to understand.

He wanted to connect, despite how foolish an inclination that was. And yet he needed it, needed her, like he needed air or blood or food. He could only pray she might let her guard down and give this gift to him. This gift he hadn't earned, but wanted more than anything.

CHAPTER THIRTEEN

Rosalinde stared at Gray. In the dim light from the house, she could see the oddest expression on his face. Where he was normally hard, unreadable, now there was a hint of desperation. Like he truly wanted to understand her. Like he truly *needed* to know what had driven her into her marriage and what forces she had found there.

There was tenderness in his expression as he tilted his head to be nearer to her. It was like he cared. *Could* he care? Was that possible that he cared even a little, despite his singular drive to draw her family far from his?

"I want to know, Rosalinde," he said softly, as if he'd read her mind and was answering her question. "To understand."

She shook her head. "Why?" she asked, her voice cracking.

"Because it's you," he responded, finally unfisting his hand and lifting his fingers to trace the line of her cheek.

She closed her eyes, reveling in the gentle caress of his warm fingers on her cold face. It was hypnotic, mesmerizing and she let out her breath in a shuddering sigh before she confessed, "I thought he cared for me, but in truth Martin only wanted me for my money, for my connections. When my grandfather cut me off after we wed and it became clear he would not change his mind, my husband grew..."

Gray's hand stopped moving, his fingers became stiff. When she opened her eyes, every fiber of his body was tense. "What? What did he do, Rosalinde?"

She lifted her chin. "He was not kind."

"Did he hurt you?" he asked, his voice cracking with an anguish she'd never heard from him before. There was a wildness in his eyes now, a caged animal that would be dangerous if freed.

"Not physically," she assured him. "But he was cruel beyond measure in the way he spoke to me. Some days I wished he'd just strike me rather than say those horrible things."

She hadn't realized she was crying until Gray's thumb wiped away a droplet from her cheek. He leaned in, his warmth cocooning her. "I'm sorry."

She shook her head. "I deserved it for being so foolhardy."

He clenched his jaw. "No, you didn't. You never deserved that, sweetheart."

His arms came around her, drawing her against his chest, and she didn't fight him. She rested her cheek on his shoulder and let his strength and his warmth bleed into her skin, filling her up in spaces where she'd been empty for so long. He cradled her, his hands smoothing over her back, not speaking, not judging, not excusing or telling her to forget. He just held her, and in that moment she felt like everything would somehow be all right.

She sighed, breathing in his cinnamon scent, and then she pulled away. Not because she wanted to, but because if she stood there in his arms too long, she might forget herself. Forget Celia. Forget everything but him.

"I-I should go inside. We're to gather for supper soon and..." She lifted her hands, unable to finish that sentence.

"Very well," he said, though there was disappointment in his tone. "Would you like me to take you?"

"No. I'll go up myself," she said. "A moment alone in the cold may clear my mind. But, Gray?"

He took a step closer. "Yes?"

"I—whatever happens in the next few days, whatever the outcome, I don't regret this." She motioned between them with one shaking hand. "Our stolen night or scandalous affair, whatever you want to call it, I'm glad our stars aligned."

He nodded. "I am too, Rosalinde," he whispered.

She turned then and left him. But she also left a part of herself with him. The part that had recognized a powerful truth.

She was in love with Gray. And it was impossible. Not only because they were on opposite sides of a battle that would tear them apart forever, but because he could never love her back. He wouldn't let himself.

And so instead of being joyful, she caught her breath and ran.

Gray shed his coat as he entered the house, handing it over to Taylor as he let the foyer's warmth seep into him. It wasn't enough. He still felt empty without Rosalinde.

"Did Mrs. Wilde make it back inside?" he asked.

The butler inclined his head slightly. "Yes, sir. She retired to her chamber briefly. She did say she would come down for supper in a few moments."

"And my brother, where is he?" Gray asked.

"Lord Stenfax is in the billiard room, I believe," Taylor intoned.

"Thank you," Gray said, heading in that direction when what he really wanted to do was climb the stairs two by two and burst into Rosalinde's chamber.

Quite a spectacle that would make.

So he didn't do something so foolhardy. Instead, he made his way up the hall. The main rooms of the house had been well kept, but back here, in the places where normally only family went, the truth of their financial situation was clear. The wallpaper peeled slightly, the furniture was rickety.

Gray pursed his lips. *This* was why Stenfax was so desperate to match "well" in Celia's inheritance. And perhaps his brother wasn't wrong in it. After all, everyone kept reminding Gray that people arranged these kinds of unions every Season.

But Gray couldn't get the image out of his mind of Lucien perched on the edge of a terrace wall, so close to oblivion, his face twisted in pain. The helplessness of that ugly night, the reason behind it…

Gray still feared the mindset his brother could be put in with this grasping, loveless match.

He neared the billiard room and stopped. He had assumed he would find his brother there alone, but there were voices coming from the chamber. Lucien's was one of them. The other was Celia Fitzgilbert's.

"I understand," she was saying in that soft tone Gray could hardly trust. "But you must understand, he only wants access. Could it hurt to introduce him to a few of your friends, see if he might be occasionally included in their circles in London?"

Gray clenched his fists at his sides. Rosalinde might wax poetic about what Celia's true motives were, but here she was, pressuring Lucien to grant her grandfather access where he very much did not belong. Furthering him and herself, just as Gray had always believed she would.

Lucien let out a long sigh, one filled with exhaustion. How long had she been haranguing him this way? "I will do so if it will make it easier for you," he said, his tone stiff and formal, despite the fact that he was alone in a chamber with his fiancée.

Gray heard Celia's skirts rustle, but was uncertain if she moved closer to or farther from Lucien. "I think it might," she said. "It would help me concentrate on matters at hand a little more."

"I think you're doing fine."

"But to be a good countess, I will need more focus." She cleared her throat. "At any rate, I appreciate your attention to the matter. I will see you at supper shortly."

Gray backed up, finding the shadow of another door nearby to stand in. He watched as Celia exited the chamber, but instead of going up the hallway, she stopped and looked back over her shoulder into the billiard room. Her expression caught the light, and Gray shook his head. She looked...*upset*. Frustrated. Like she wanted more.

But of course she did. Nothing would ever be enough for a woman like that. He waited until she moved up the hall at last, then slipped into the billiard room and shut the door behind him.

His brother was leaning over the table, cue in hand, and he looked up. "Gray."

Gray waited for him to take the shot. It didn't arc as his brother had intended, though, and Lucien let out a sharp curse. Gray's eyebrows lifted. Stenfax was one of the best players in their circle. He never missed a shot. That and his angry outburst proved his brother was not content. Clearly his conversation with Celia was troubling him.

"I'd offer you a game, but everyone will be gathering for supper in a few moments," Lucien said as he leaned on the table with both arms, staring at the scattered balls.

"You always beat me anyway," Gray said carefully.

Lucien jerked his gaze up. "You might be luckier tonight."

"Perhaps after supper," Gray suggested. "Though your fiancée's grandfather would likely insist on joining us."

Stenfax flinched almost imperceptivity. "I suppose he would," he conceded.

"And that would make things 'so much easier' for Celia," Gray said.

Lucien's gaze held his. "Lurking in halls like a villain, are we? Spying on private conversations."

"Overhearing isn't the same as spying," Gray said, but he knew they were hitting upon an issue of semantics.

Lucien shook his head. "No. I suppose on a point of technicality, it is not. I can only assume you have come here to lecture me about Celia once more."

"Do you two feel *any* connection toward each other?" Gray asked. His brother seemed surprised at that question and drew back a fraction. When he didn't answer immediately, Gray moved closer. "I only ask because despite my feelings regarding Miss Fitzgilbert, one cannot deny she has a certain beauty. Though I think her sister is far prettier."

Lucien's gaze narrowed. "Celia is lovely. No one could state otherwise."

Gray watched his brother's face. There was no passion there, hardly even the barest interest, despite his claim of his fiancée's loveliness.

"I hear told from both Mrs. Wilde and Felicity that Miss Fitzgilbert is also clever."

"Indeed, she is that." Lucien's lips pursed and he folded his arms. "What the hell are you about, Gray? Are you trying to convince me of Celia's better attributes now? What happened to warning me off?"

Gray put his hands behind his back and widened his stance. "I only want you to see that when you speak of her, when you speak *to* her, there seems to be no connection. You could be talking about a stranger with as much passion as is in your voice when you mention Celia."

"And your point in all this?"

"Don't you *want* her?" Gray asked. "Isn't there some part of you that craves touching her? And if the answer to that is no, doesn't that make you question the success of this union?"

Lucien shook his head. "I'm not about to walk around here with a cockstand for my future wife. This is a ludicrous conversation and I refuse to have it. Celia and I will wed, this is the end of it."

He was going to walk out, Gray could see that. The topic of desire had done nothing except make him think of Rosalinde and the heated longing she inspired in him. But it also made him think about her confessions to him in the garden. And her grandfather's unintentional words earlier.

"Look into their father," Gray said.

Lucien had already passed him, but now he stopped in the doorway, posture stiff. He didn't turn. "I beg your pardon?"

"Celia and Rosalinde's father. He's a mystery. And I have heard implications that he may not have been entirely proper. Look into it."

Lucien faced him now. His older brother's mouth was drawn down into a deep frown. Unmasked disappointment was slashed over his face and Gray flinched at the sight of it. It cut like a knife and filled his every pore with deep regret. He'd rarely ever seen such judgment in Lucien's eyes. Such censure.

"You would truly sink so low?" Lucien asked, his voice barely carrying in the quiet room.

"To protect you?" Gray jerked out a nod. "I feel I must do so if you are unwilling to protect yourself. I've already set the wheels in motion to do so. When Folly arrives tomorrow, he will likely bring a packet from my investigator on that very subject."

"You involved Folworth in this?" Lucien's expression darkened further. "When?"

"I don't know. A month or more ago. And before I left London, I asked him to collect the investigator's information before he and Marina came."

"You are a bastard, to put him in the middle of your inquiries. To make the inquiries at all is bad enough," Lucian spat.

Gray flinched. It wasn't as if he liked doing this. "Folly is not in the middle. I mentioned my concerns and asked him to do me this favor. He doesn't know what the packet contains, but even if he opened it, which he won't, I doubt there is anyone either of us trusts more. He's an old friend and one who understands the stakes."

Lucien's cheeks reddened slightly, and Gray knew he was thinking of that terrible night on the terrace too. "And what good do you think it will do?" his brother croaked.

"You are protecting our name, not just rebuilding it," Gray said. "If there is something in those notes that will threaten that name, I would assume you will at least have to *consider* changing your plans."

Stenfax shifted and a great exhaustion crossed his face. Gray frowned at the sight of it. His brother looked not just annoyed, but truly troubled.

"Lucien—" he began.

His brother lifted a hand to stop him. "Enough. You want me to look at evidence you collect, I will. But I make you no promises. You need to stop this foolishness, Grayson. Before you do something that cannot be undone."

He said nothing else, but strode from the room. Gray watched him go and sighed. "Lucien, that's exactly the mistake I'm trying to keep you from making."

Rosalinde took a long breath and forced her gaze away from Gray's. He sat at the opposite end of the table from her, next to his mother and sister. Of course, he had been stealing glances her way all through supper, but that was no reason to ogle him.

Especially since each time she did so, she saw Celia stiffen slightly up the table. Her sister had hardly spoken to her since her revelation of their affair earlier in the day, but Rosalinde could tell she was deeply troubled.

She forced her attention to the man at her side. Lord Stenfax had been an extremely quiet companion for nearly an hour. Even now he had a faraway expression, like he was lost in thought.

Rosalinde observed him while he was distracted. He was a well-favored man. Not as hard as Gray, nor as intense, but with handsome features. There was a slight sadness around his eyes and in the downward turn on his lips. She could well see why he had been considered such a catch, despite his family's financial issues.

And yet he and Celia seemed to have no connection whatsoever. Her beauty moved him not, nor his her. That seemed wrong, even though it was exactly as they had planned.

"My lord?" she said.

He jerked his head, almost as if he were coming awake from a daydream. "I'm sorry, Mrs. Wilde. How uncommonly rude of me."

She smiled in reassurance. "No need to be sorry. The entire table seems a bit out of sorts. I suppose one can expect it with all the excitement about to come."

"Yes. Tomorrow the guests who will be staying at my home will arrive. Friends and family, all." He hesitated. "I'm sorry no one from Celia's family will be part of our day."

Rosalinde shifted slightly. "Well, with our mother gone, I suppose our family is small in comparison."

His lips thinned a little. "And what of your father's side of the aisle? You have no one remaining from his family?"

She shot a quick glance at Gray. There was something in Stenfax's tone that made her wonder if Gray had spoken to him about her father. She swallowed and carefully considered her words before she spoke again.

"We know little of his family, I fear. As you know, we were raised as Fitzgilberts after the death of my parents. So it is a cozy group of two who will stand for my sister. That and the friends who come, though I believe all of Celia's friends will be staying at the inn in the village."

He nodded, but she watched as his gaze slid to Celia slowly. He seemed to be seeing her for the first time, yet she couldn't read his expression. He was good at hiding. It worried her.

Oh, he was a gentleman. Of course he was. But what was this man like in private? What were his passions? What were his feelings at all about Celia? Was he truly only mercenary? Would he have a gaggle of mistresses the moment the I dos were spoken?

Rosalinde hated having these questions. Worse, she hated having no answers. Damn Gray.

"Have I offended you?" Stenfax asked. "You are frowning

rather intently."

She forced a light laugh. "Oh, gracious, no. Just thinking that soon my sister will be a married lady. I hope I will be able to see her often."

Stenfax's expression softened slightly. "I would never keep my wife from her family. You will always be welcome in our home here or London, as I know how close you are. You are like me with my own siblings."

Rosalinde caught her breath. She'd always viewed Stenfax as a rather cold and distant man. Always polite, but never emotional. And yet here was a softness to his expression she'd never seen before. A warmth that was never spared for Celia, but could be conjured for his brother and sister. That meant he *could* feel.

He just didn't feel for Celia. And not she for him, when Rosalinde *knew* she was capable of so much more. Anxiety hit her stomach, forcing her to set her fork aside as the wave of it made her sick.

"I appreciate those kind words," she managed when it became clear he was awaiting her response. She took a deep breath and let her gaze slide to Celia again. Her sister was talking to their grandfather and did not look happy.

And behind her was Gray, always in Rosalinde's sightline. Always confusing already complicated issues.

"You and your brother do seem especially close, despite his living so far away. That must be difficult."

"I do miss seeing him more regularly." Stenfax shrugged. "But I am proud of what Gray has accomplished. He's an entirely self-made man."

"I've heard as much," Rosalinde said. "How exactly has he made himself?"

"A variety of industries. He's been investing in the canals since our father died. But his true love is mechanization of all kinds. You should hear him ramble on about increased productivity and safety when it comes to machines in various workplaces."

Rosalinde nodded. It was easy to see how a mind like Gray's would be fascinated by the intricacies of a machine. "I've heard told steam is the future, though," she said.

Stenfax laughed, and it felt like every eye at the table shifted to them. The rest swiftly returned to whatever had their attention initially, but Rosalinde felt Gray's gaze linger.

"You and my brother are of a mind," Stenfax said. "He claims the steam engine which pulled that train to Wales six years ago will one day take over travel all over the world. It will either bankrupt him or make him unfathomably rich. It's his own form of gambling, I believe."

"But more informed gambling," Rosalinde suggested, feeling an odd desire to stand up for Gray.

Stenfax nodded. "Exactly. Now I know some people turn their noses up at such things, but I admire how hard he's worked."

Rosalinde shifted. She had spent her life with a man who tried to claw his way up via pretended connection. A man who would trade relationships to get what he wanted.

Gray was the polar opposite. And in that moment she wanted more than anything to reach out and touch him. To burrow into his fascinating world and find out more about steam engines and canals and how he planned to build a road all the way to a sparkling future.

Before Rosalinde could respond, Mr. Fitzgilbert asked Stenfax a question and the earl's attention was drawn away from her. She supposed it was for the best. If she'd been allowed to praise Gray, she feared her growing feelings for the man would have been evident to all at the table.

And those were feelings she could not share. Not with him. Not with anyone. They were bound to be enemies. And even when their war was over, that didn't mean they had leave to even be friends. She would be pulled from the warmth of his life, back to the chilly existence her grandfather allowed.

It was better not to grow accustomed to Gray's fire. Or to even so much as imagine she could find a permanent place in his arms, in his world, or in his life.

CHAPTER FOURTEEN

Gray stepped into the parlor, his brow wrinkled as he scanned the room. The previous night he'd been roaming the halls, unable to sleep when he was plagued by thoughts of Rosalinde. He had secretly hoped to find her and perhaps purge his building desire once more. Instead, in his distraction he'd lost track of the book he'd carried with him through the dark.

"Are you looking for this?"

He turned to find Celia seated in a chair beside the fire. She was holding up a slim volume, the very one he sought.

"Indeed, I am," he said, hearing the harshness that always seemed to accompany a conversation with this woman. He'd found the best way around his contempt for her was to avoid her. "Thank you."

He slipped the book free from her fingers and bowed slightly.

"You needn't go," she said, stopping him before he could exit with any semblance of grace or politeness. "Won't you join me?"

He barely held back a curse. Well, there was no avoiding this now. He would have to sit with her. *Talk* to her.

"Of course," he managed through clenched teeth, and took the place across from her.

"Tea?" she asked, motioning to the pot on the table beside her.

He shook his head. "No, thank you."

A slight smile turned up her lips, a secret one like she'd

thought of something amusing that she did not share. "All right, then it is straight to business, yes?"

Gray blinked in confusion. "Business? Do we have business, Miss Fitzgilbert?"

She tilted her head slightly. "Come now, of course we do. I have long been wanting to speak to you alone, Mr. Danford."

He leaned back in his chair and folded his hands in his lap, trying not to react to this unexpected development. "So you are to be direct."

"You may not believe this—in fact, I suspect you will not—but I try as often as I can to be honest and direct in all things." She lifted her brows, as if waiting for him to deny what she said could be true.

"I don't think I know you well enough to call you a liar," he said, refusing to allow her the satisfaction she sought.

If he had expected her to scowl or whine at his attitude, she didn't. Instead, she laughed. He'd never heard her laugh before. Celia was almost always somber around his brother or the family. Now he found the sound was actually pretty, though certainly not as moving as when her sister did the same.

"We both know that you *believe* me to be a liar," Celia finally said. "There is no use pretending something else."

He pursed his lips. "And did you want to talk to me in order to convince me otherwise?"

She shook her head at once. "Heavens, no. That would very likely be an exercise in futility, for once you believed me a liar, my denying the same would be fruitless. I can only hope that my actions will eventually speak for themselves and that at some point you will come to at least accept me."

"And at most?"

"It might be too much to hope that one day you would like me." The laughter left her voice, and she sighed. "But that is truly *not* what I wish to discuss with you."

"No, so you said," he drawled, watching her face carefully. "Which leaves me to wonder what other topic you and I could possibly discuss, given all you've said."

"I want to talk to you about Rosalinde," she said, this time her voice soft yet firm.

Tension coursed through his body. He knew Celia was aware of what had gone on between Rosalinde and him. He supposed he should have been ready for such a confrontation. Of course, he had no idea of Celia's motives when it came to this. She could be hoping to use the indiscretion to keep him from pursuing his campaign to prevent her marriage from taking place.

And if she was, well, that would certainly reveal a great deal about the character she claimed to possess.

So as uncomfortable as the prospect was, Gray nodded slowly. "I suppose it is not out of the ordinary that you would wish to speak to me about your sister. After all, I believe she spoke to you about how...*close* we have become."

"She told you that, did she?" she asked, her tone carefully neutral.

He pursed his lips at the memory. "She was very upset."

"She would be," Celia whispered, and her voice broke slightly. "I was harsh when I heard the truth. Did you comfort her, then?"

He wrinkled his brow. "Are you asking if I...if we..."

"No!" Celia's pale cheeks suddenly flooded with dark pink color. "Good Lord, no! I have no interest in the details of your...your...whatever you would like to call this affair between you. I am only trying to determine what exactly your intentions are. You say you came upon my sister upset and I am asking if you reached out to her."

"Yes," he said, thinking of Rosalinde's confessions in the dark garden the night before. Thinking of the sparkle of tears on her cheeks in the moonlight. Thinking of how she had stepped into his arms and it felt like she belonged there.

"Yes," he repeated. "I spoke to her and tried to ease her as best I could. To reassure her that she was not nearly so vile as she believed herself to be. Or perhaps what you wanted her to think she was."

Celia's lips parted. "Mr. Danford, you may accuse me of a great many things, you may decide that I am mercenary and cold. But please do not make the mistake of believing that I do not love and respect my sister. I have *never* wanted to hurt her, nor do I think she has ever purposefully hurt me."

"Then why be angry when you found out she and I had been together?" he asked.

"Beyond the obvious scandal that could be created by your indiscretion? Beyond the fact that you have made it clear that you will go to *any* and *every* length to destroy my engagement to Stenfax?" she asked. "My truest concern was for Rosalinde's well-being."

"How noble of you," Gray murmured.

Celia's eyes flashed, and for a moment he was put to mind of Rosalinde. To his surprise, that made him actually *like* Celia more.

"You have known my sister for less than a fortnight. I have watched her all my life. I know what a risk she is at when it comes to such things."

"A risk from me?" he asked, laughing, though he knew her words were true. "How so?"

"Not just from you," she said. "My sister leads with her heart. She is entirely open, no matter how many times the world punishes her for it. She somehow still believes in the best in others, in a possibility for some kind of bright, happy future. And that makes her remarkable. It also leaves her vulnerable to the pain that will inevitably come when her hopes are dashed."

Gray hesitated, for Celia had just struck upon exactly what he'd thought of Rosalinde from nearly the moment he'd met her. What he'd thought, but never been able to fully label in his mind. Celia had now summed Rosalinde up five sentences and he would never be able to forget each one.

"Why do you think her hopes will be inevitably dashed?" he asked.

Celia shrugged and looked away from him. "Bitter

experience tells me they will. My mother died when I was young, taking my sister and me away from whatever life she had hoped for us and to my grandfather, who is…"

"A bastard," Gray supplied.

She let her eyes slide to him. "Yes. That is as good a term as any. Any time we wanted anything, it was denied us. Oh, we were given food and shelter, education and opportunity, but never love or affection. We sought that from each other and were denied it any other place we looked. I learned to stop looking. Rosalinde decided to look all the harder."

"Why is that a negative thing?" Gray asked.

"Because sometimes she found it where it didn't truly exist," Celia all but hissed.

Gray stiffened. "You are referring to her marriage."

Celia's eyes narrowed, and she couldn't hide her surprise that he had brought up that delicate subject. "She told you about her marriage?"

"A little," he admitted through clenched teeth. "Enough."

She stared at him, silent for what felt like an eternity. Finally, she whispered, "She is more trusting of you than I thought if she would tell you about Martin Wilde."

"I'm glad she did," he admitted for the first time out loud. "And I wish I could take away that terrible time in her life."

Celia's expression softened slightly. "As do I, more than anything. But it is proof of what I said earlier. Rosalinde was easily swayed by what that man pretended to be, pretended to offer. She grabbed on to the possibility of love so tightly that she refused to see anything else. She suffered greatly for it. And though I think she is wiser for the experience, I also know she remains vulnerable to lies."

Gray arched a brow. "And you think I am lying to her?"

"I don't know what you are doing," Celia admitted. "I don't know what bond you've formed with her, if any at all. I hope you wouldn't be so cruel as to use her, to hurt her, in order to lash out at me somehow. But I cannot rule that out."

"And that is what you wished to speak to me about here

today," he said.

She shrugged. "I am not certain that my speaking to you will change anything you plan to do. As I said, I am unaware of a great many things when it comes to you and Rosalinde and how true you are. But I do know one thing: my sister *is* true. And if you cut her, she will bleed. I love her, Mr. Danford. I love her with all my heart. And I ask that if what you share with her is only about this war you wish to wage with me, that you not allow her to be a casualty. It would be too cruel."

She got to her feet, and Gray was forced to do the same out of propriety.

"You have said quite a lot," Gray said, surprised that his voice shook slightly. He cleared his throat and settled himself before he continued, "And I will think about all of it, I assure you."

"Good," she said. "And now I must excuse myself to ready for the arrival of the other guests."

She inclined her head and moved to the door, but there she stopped and faced him once more. "I do understand your position, you know. I too am the younger sibling, yet driven to protect the elder after seeing them go through pain. The impulse is one I respect. I hope you will *always* protect Stenfax, as I will always protect Rosalinde. And I also hope that perhaps one day you will understand that I am no threat to him. Or to you. Good day."

She departed before he could respond, and Gray found himself staring at the door for a long time after he had been left alone. He'd spent so much time building Celia up to a monster in his head, he hadn't allowed any other possibility to shine through. Now her passionate defense of her sister changed his thoughts on her. Whatever else she might be, he believed she truly loved Rosalinde.

And her parting words about younger siblings protecting the elder gave them a connection he hadn't expected. Celia knew what he felt, perhaps more than anyone else he'd ever met.

So either she was very good at manipulation, or she wasn't exactly the ogre he had made her out to be in his mind. Either way, he was left uneasy.

He turned and poured himself a cup of the tea she had left behind. He sipped the warm brew as he stared out the window at the rolling hills of his family estate. Even dead as they were, even with the trees empty of their leaves, the sight was still beautiful. Stenfax wanted to protect all this.

And Rosalinde wanted to protect Celia. He shut his eyes and could see her before him, bright eyes flashing, slender body trembling, chin lifted in defiance. She was passionate. She was lovely.

And goddamn, but he wanted her to be his. He had never imagined that would be true when he realized who she was that terrible morning he'd found her in the breakfast room with his family. He'd not allowed himself to want more of her than whatever passion declared he must take.

But when he thought of Celia's words…

She leads with her heart.

Rosalinde did do that. He'd seen it. He'd felt it. He'd benefitted from it. She was unlike anyone he'd ever known. And he…

No, he wouldn't finish that thought. The fact was there were so many complications that would keep them apart. His own schemes alone were enough to break her heart the way Celia had warned him not to. And he didn't want to hurt her any more than he had to.

"You have to let her go," he whispered to himself.

The cup in his hand began to shake, and he set it aside so he wouldn't slosh liquid all over himself. He stared at the desolate landscape once more and realized it was the same as his heart. Empty.

"You *have* to let her go," he repeated, stronger now, knowing it was true. Hating it was true.

But how could he do it without breaking her heart? How could he do it without destroying himself in the process?

He didn't know. But he'd have to do it soon. Because plans would be in motion in the next few days that would not be able to be undone. Plans that would change everything.

CHAPTER FIFTEEN

Gray stepped from the house onto the stone steps and watched as the next carriage in a seemingly endless line of them pulled up. But as he caught the symbol on the door, his boredom with performing host duties faded and his pleasure increased.

He leaned over to Lucien and elbowed him. "Folly," he said.

Stenfax responded with a wide grin and they headed down the steps together to greet their newest visitors. The footman held open the door and a tall, wiry man stepped out. He turned back to help a beautiful redheaded lady down before the two stepped forward. Both were smiling as they caught a glimpse of the two brothers.

"Stenfax, Gray!" the Marquess of Folworth said, releasing his wife, Marina, and coming up to exchange a slap on the back with each. "Great God, it's good to see you."

"Folly, you old—" Stenfax began, then cut off whatever salty name he was going to call his friend. He glanced behind them where the rest of the family, Celia, Rosalinde and their grandfather stood, and shrugged. "Well, you know what you are."

"He does," Marina said, slipping up to press a kiss first to Gray's cheek, then Lucien's. As she stepped back, Gray saw her watching Stenfax carefully. He just barely held back a flinch at her obvious concern.

"Come on, then, meet my future bride and say hello to the

rest," Stenfax said, guiding them up.

The couple said their hellos to Felicity and Lady Stenfax and went through the introductions with the others. Once again, Gray felt them both watching Celia carefully, judging her, he supposed. He wondered what they thought, with all they knew and had witnessed. After all, it had been their terrace Stenfax had nearly thrown himself from after Elise's ultimate betrayal.

They were all four of them bound together by the horror and terror of that awful night. It had solidified a friendship that had already been strong.

"Oh, here comes the next carriage already," Stenfax said, casting his head toward the drive as they stood chatting about unimportant things. "I hate to be rude."

Gray shot a glance to their friends and said, "Why don't you let me see to them getting settled, Stenfax? You don't need me for a few moments."

"As long as no one minds us stealing you," Marina said, "I'd love to catch up."

The rest nodded, though Gray caught Rosalinde watching him carefully. She had sent several curious glances to Marina since her arrival. And of course she was always finding him, analyzing him. Making it hard to think or breathe.

"Come then," Gray said, both relieved and sorry to walk away from Rosalinde. "We'll get you tea while Taylor makes sure your chambers are ready."

The three entered the house together and Gray guided them down the winding halls to the parlor. Once they were settled, he wrapped an arm around Folly's shoulders once more.

"Damn, I am pleased to see you both! Alone as I am in the wilds of the North Country, I miss our gatherings."

"We miss you, as well," Marina said, pouring tea like she was the hostess. "The next few days promise to be rich with opportunities to spend time together, though I assume Stenfax will be busy with the wedding plans."

Folly nodded, his gaze even on Gray. "Unless you still

intend to break the match."

Gray shifted. Folly had not approved of his desire when he'd first shared his plans over a month ago. His disapproving tone said he still didn't.

"I simply don't want to watch Lucien endure any more unnecessary pain thanks to someone bent on only taking a title," he said.

Marina bent her head. "I don't think any of us want to see him in pain given all he's been through. But Miss Fitzgilbert seemed nice enough when we just met her."

"So did Elise," Gray said, his tone hard as stone. He might soften to Celia, yes, but no one would ever convince him to do anything but despite Elise to her core.

Now Folly shifted in the discomfort. "Well, if you are determined, I *did* pick up the information you asked me to retrieve from your investigator before we left London." His friend reached into his jacked and pulled out a thick packet of papers, bound together by a heavy ribbon.

Gray took them slowly. "Did you read them?"

"You are the one out to destroy this engagement, not me," Folly said, raising his hands. "I'm merely the messenger. I have no interest in knowing the details."

"Although we do have other news to share with you," Marina said, sliding up to her husband and taking his hand. "That has a great deal to do with Stenfax."

Gray pushed the papers into his inside pocket to review later and looked at them both. "News? What kind of news?"

"I don't know how to make this easy, so I will simply state it," Folly said. He drew a deep breath. "The Duke of Kirkford is dead."

Gray's ears began to ring and he blinked at his friends as he tried to keep his vision clear. "Elise's husband. *That* Duke of Kirkford?"

Marina's smile was soft, filled with understanding. "Yes, Gray. The only one."

"How?" he croaked out. "When?"

"The when was a week ago. The how is still being determined, but it has been whispered that it was a duel. Over another man's wife, though I would wager that will be covered up by the family," Marina said. "You know I am related to that bastard—third cousins, I think."

Gray staggered back and sank into the closest chair. The room was still spinning as he digested this news and all its ramifications.

Elise, the woman who had once ripped his brother to utter shreds with her lies, with her breaking of their engagement, with her marriage to a man with higher title and more money...she was once again free. And while Stenfax might pretend that wouldn't bother him, if he knew...

Lucien had loved her. Completely. Desperately. Was it possible his brother would see this death as a way to be with her again? Would he be driven not by reason, but by emotion, the same way he had the night he nearly killed himself?

The very idea made Gray's blood run cold.

"Who knows?" he whispered.

Marina and Folly exchanged a look. Folly shrugged. "Because of the scandal, not many. Kirkford was buried very quickly and quietly, in a funeral attended only by family. The only reason we know is because of Marina's connection."

"There's also some dispute over inheritance of the title," Marina explained. "Since he and Elise had no children, there are two cousins vying for it. Until that issue is resolved, there will be no announcement."

Gray nodded. "So likely no one who comes here will share the rumor with Lucien?"

Marina's lips parted. "I...I suppose it's possible. Though we intended to share it, or thought you would, Gray."

"No!" Gray leapt to his feet. "That would be a terrible mistake. You know what happened when she left. I have no intention of sharing this with my brother while he might still be vulnerable to *that* woman's wicked wiles."

Marina stepped closer to him. "Gray, what are you saying?

141

You cannot keep this from Stenfax forever. It will come out, probably in a matter of days, weeks at most."

"By then he could be married," Gray said. "And it will be too late for him to do something foolish or for her to call him to her."

"I thought you didn't want your brother to marry Celia Fitzgilbert," Folly interjected. "Wasn't that the point of the investigators? The scheming? Are you now saying Miss Fitzgilbert is a better option?"

"Than the she-devil I know?" Gray spat. "I'm not certain at present. Neither option makes me happy, I will tell you that. Look, you've told me the truth now and brought me this evidence, whatever it is. Let me handle it. Let me look at the information you've brought on Celia and determine what is the best course of action. You can pretend you knew nothing if it comes up, put the blame on me."

Marina sighed as she and Folly exchanged a long look. "I would not cause your brother pain. We can allow you to decide what is best. Though I would suggest that best might be simply letting Stenfax take his own path, Gray. Whether that path takes him to Miss Fitzgilbert, to Elise or to no one at all, let it be *his* decision."

Taylor stepped in at the door and cleared his throat, drawing attention away from the matter at hand. "Lord and Lady Folworth, your room is ready."

Gray forced a smile for his friends. "Go up, rest yourselves after your long journey, will you? There is a ball tonight to celebrate the impending nuptials and to welcome our friends. I promise you, I will speak more to you about this at length. If you can promise to stay silent until then."

Folworth nodded. "We will, though I do question the prudence. Come, my dear."

He took Marina's arm and they left, worried expressions on both their faces. As they departed, Gray sank into the chair he had vacated and covered his head with his hands. Here he had been fighting so hard to protect his brother from the clutches of a title-grabber, he'd never thought he'd have to protect Lucien from the talons of someone far worse.

And now he was stuck. The only way to be entirely certain that Lucien would not be seduced in by the idea of being with the one great love of his life was to ensure he was married before he knew Elise was free. But to do that meant turning his back on the plans Gray had been pursuing for months. It meant taking the opposite side, supporting the marriage to Celia, with all its unknowns. All its potential dangers.

And he had no idea what to do now. No idea how to best handle his brother, his future and Gray's own confused needs. But he had to decide and decide quickly. There would be, after all, a wedding in just three days.

Felicity tilted her head and laughed at something Celia had said, and Rosalinde couldn't help but smile. Despite Gray's best efforts, it seemed he had not swayed his younger sister against her own. And Stenfax had made no movement to end the engagement either. With just a few days until the wedding, with the other guests arriving and public parties being held, the danger to Celia was beginning to fade.

And yet Rosalinde felt little joy at the idea of her sister being bound to Stenfax. She'd been trying to tell herself it was just not yet safe for her to relax, not until the two had said their vows.

But it was more than that which trouble her. She felt a niggling worry that she had not yet named, but created tension every time she pictured Celia pledging her life to the handsome earl.

Felicity touched her hand, and Rosalinde came back to the present. "Oh, here is Marina, er, Lady Folworth. You two met her earlier today."

Rosalinde stiffened despite herself as she watched the

marchioness approach. Although she had met more than a dozen people during the arrivals and countless others since the party began tonight, Rosalinde remembered Lady Folworth above the rest. The marchioness was beautiful, with a coil of thick , ruddy hair wound on the top of her head, her dress impeccable and her smile wide.

The lady had also greeted Gray with such familiarity earlier in the day that Rosalinde's fists had tightened at her sides.

"She is as close to your brothers as her husband is, it seems," Rosalinde managed to croak out.

Felicity's smile wavered a fraction. "They shared a very…they shared a traumatic experience not so very long ago. So yes, I think it bound them. She is a lovely person, Rosalinde. I'm sure you and Celia will like her so much."

"Felicity," Lady Folworth said as she arrived to their group, putting out both her hands to catch Felicity's with a laugh. She pressed a warm kiss to her cheek. "And Miss Fitzgilbert, Mrs. Wilde. I'm so happy to see you both again, and to have more time for us to get to know each other."

"I'm very pleased to see you again," Celia said, her tone slightly stiff and awkward. But her smile was genuine enough. "Especially since Felicity was just telling us what good friends you and your husband are to Stenfax."

Lady Folworth nodded. "Oh yes, indeed, we are very close. Gray and Lucien and Baldwin have been great friends since school, but they were kind enough to welcome me when Baldwin became the first to fall victim to the marriage mart."

"Posh," Felicity said with a giggle. "Folly jumped, he never fell."

"Folly," Celia mused. "I heard Stenfax call him that earlier, as well. I realize it is a play on his title, but a rather odd nickname."

"Fitting, though," Lady Folworth said. "My husband was not always the proper marquess who stands across the room speaking very seriously about politics with his friends." She motioned her head toward him and Rosalinde found herself looking at Gray once again. He was leaned in, listening to whatever Lord Folworth was discussing. He looked very serious in that moment. And oh-so-very far away.

She dropped her gaze with a small sigh and continued to listen to Lady Folworth. "No, my Baldwin was once known for getting into terrible scrapes. Hence, Folly. For his life was full of it."

"He is lucky you married him and set him to rights," Felicity said, pretending seriousness.

"*I* am the lucky one," Lady Folworth said with a rather romantic sigh of her own.

Rosalinde noticed how some of the color drained from Celia's cheeks at the display of affection. "It was a love match, then?" she whispered.

"Indeed, it was. It *is*." She shook her head. "We have gone off course considerably, though, talking about my husband and me. I meant only to say that certainly we shall become great friends, Miss Fitzgilbert, as the men spend a good amount of time together in London. And Gray joins us often when he is in Town."

Celia was nodding, but Rosalinde froze at the panic that lit up her sister's blue eyes. "I-I look forward to spending time with you, Lady Folworth," she choked out. "I'm certain we will get along splendidly."

Lady Folworth tilted her head. "Are you all right, my dear?"

Felicity leaned closer. "Your face is a bit flushed."

"Yes, I'm warm. I think I will step out on the terrace for just a moment of air," Celia said.

Rosalinde moved for her, hand outstretched. "Why don't I take—"

Before she could finish, her sister backed away. "No, stay. I'll only be a moment. Excuse me."

She gathered up her skirt and all but ran for the terrace, leaving the women behind to watch her go. Lady Folworth turned back with a thin smile.

"I'm certain she must be nervous about the upcoming wedding. Such a to-do."

Rosalinde forced herself to stop staring in the direction her sister had gone and nodded. "Oh yes. So many people to meet and preparations to make."

"Brides are always nervous," Felicity said, but there was a stiff quality to her words. Rosalinde wasn't certain if that came from Celia's odd behavior, or her memories of her own wedding and the apparently very unhappy marriage that followed.

"But I know she will be fine," Rosalinde lied. Lied because she *didn't* know. Celia had always been the steadier of the two of them, despite being the younger. She'd never seen such abject terror on her sister's face before.

"Of course she will," Lady Folworth insisted. "Now, why don't you tell me a bit about yourself, Mrs. Wilde?"

Rosalinde drew back a fraction. "Me?"

"Yes," Lady Folworth pressed. "Not only did I have an immediate sense that you and I should be friends, but that was bolstered by Gray's high opinion when he spoke of you tonight."

Rosalinde let her gaze slide to the man in question yet again. He was still standing with his friends, but he was now outside of the conversation, watching her. Just watching, those dark eyes boring into her, filled with intensity and all the desire she knew hung between them. She shivered.

"He spoke of me? I'm surprised to hear Mr. Danford is so complimentary," she whispered.

Felicity frowned. "He is a little hard on Celia," she explained to Lady Folworth. "You know how protective he is."

Lady Folworth paled, but she didn't look surprised at Felicity's assertion. Rosalinde clenched her fists. It seemed Gray's disparagement of Celia had gone beyond just his family. And yet Lady Folworth was kind to Celia, at least.

"Indeed, I do know of Gray's proclivity to ride to the

rescue when it comes to Stenfax or you, Felicity," the lady said. Her tone was tight, but when she spoke again, it was softer. "And yet whatever he thinks, he clearly does like you, Mrs. Wilde. Just before they started talking about Whigs and what's going on in America, Gray was just telling us what a fascinating woman you are."

Rosalinde felt heat flooding her cheeks. Heat that multiplied when Felicity turned her attention toward her. The viscountess had a certain expression on her face, but Rosalinde couldn't tell if it was supportive or in upset.

"*Fascinating*?" Felicity repeated, still staring at Rosalinde as if she were seeing her for the first time. "That is interesting."

"I—I'm sure, Mr. Danford is only referring to the fact that we have similar taste in literature," she whispered. "We discussed it when—"

She broke off. Great God, they had discussed books the night they spent together at the inn. Now her cheeks felt like they were on fire.

"—we discussed it over supper one night," she said, formulating words that somehow resembled the truth. She glanced toward the doors where her sister had departed. "You know, I ought to go after Celia. Make sure she's all right."

Felicity was still staring, but she nodded. "Of course."

"It was lovely speaking to you both," Rosalinde managed through tightly clenched teeth. "I-I will see you later, I'm certain."

The two said their farewells, and Rosalinde began to make her way through the crowd. She felt their stares on her back, felt Gray's stare on her back, as she did so and a thin layer of sweat made itself known on her brow. Gray's offhanded comment had certainly raised the interest of the women, which was bad. And yet the fact that he was telling people who were important to him that she was fascinating still warmed her to her toes.

She exited to the terrace, shutting the door behind her. The night air was chill, which meant no one else was outside, and she breathed a sigh of relief. At least she could have a moment without eyes watching her.

She looked around, expecting to find Celia standing at the wall or pacing the length of the terrace. But her sister was nowhere to be found.

Rosalinde walked out farther, seeking Celia in the shadows. "Celia?" she called out, but to no response. A breeze blew across the walkway, and she shivered. Celia had been out here for a while, she had to be freezing.

"Celia!" Rosalinde repeated, this time louder. She moved along the length of the terrace, worry building in her. Could her sister have gone to the garden? In this chill? She would catch her death.

But just as Rosalinde moved toward the steps to go down and search, she caught a glimpse of movement in a window nearby. Relief flooded her. Celia sat in one of the other parlors which was also attached to the terrace. But through the window, Rosalinde saw her sister's head in her hands. She was weeping.

Rosalinde caught her breath and rushed to the terrace door, pressing it open and entering the chamber to join her sister. Celia looked up, her red face pained and tear-streaked.

Rosalinde shut the door and rushed to her, putting her arms around her. "Oh, Celia!" she murmured, drawing her closer.

Celia let out a gasping breath and then continued to cry, this time into Rosalinde's shoulder.

"This is a mistake," she sobbed, her words garbled by her tears. "Oh, Rosalinde, whatever am I to do?"

CHAPTER SIXTEEN

Rosalinde caught her breath as she smoothed Celia's hair gently. "A mistake?" she asked, even though she knew exactly what her sister was referring to.

"This marriage," Celia wailed.

Rosalinde squeezed her eyes shut. It was as she feared. And despite what had been said earlier, she knew full well this was more than mere bridal nerves.

"Why?" she said softly. "Tell me what you're feeling. Tell me what he's done."

Celia drew away from her shoulder. "It isn't anything he has done. I don't hate him, I don't fear him. But I do not love him, Rosalinde. I will *never* love him. I know that as I know my own face, my own hands, my own heart."

Rosalinde nodded slowly. "I see."

"And he feels nothing for me either. I see it and I feel it every time he looks at me."

Rosalinde steeled herself, for she would have to tread carefully in order to understand. She kept her tone calm and gentle as she said, "But you knew this from the start, Celia. We've even spoken before about the nature of your relationship with Stenfax. What has changed that makes you so unhappy with the decision now?"

Celia rubbed her neck. "I was never fully comfortable. I felt what was lacking between us from the first moment we met, but I somehow convinced myself it might change. I tried so hard to make it change, because who wouldn't want such a man? When it didn't, I kept telling myself that I would live with it. That I could live without love or affection or passion of any kind. That it would be worth it. But then…then…"

"Then?" Rosalinde squeezed her hand. "You needn't hold back. I want to hear it all—it's the only way I can help you."

Celia nodded. "It will help to say it, I suppose. But then you told me about you and Gray."

"Me and Gray?" Rosalinde gasped. "*That* changed your mind?"

"You were describing a passion I will never feel." Celia sighed. "And when I spoke to Gray, there was this…this expression in his eyes that said more than any words. What he feels for you after just a short acquaintance is more than Stenfax has ever felt for me in almost a year of courtship. It is more than the earl will *ever* feel for me."

Rosalinde could not find her breath as she stared at her sister. "You spoke to Gray about me?"

"Of course," Celia said with a shake of her head. "If you are involved with the man, I must know he is worthy, mustn't I? That is my duty as the person who loves you most. And while I do not like him, I cannot deny that there *does* seem to be a connection between you. From his side as well as yours."

Rosalinde fought the impulse to leap to her feet and run away. Celia was saying words she longed to hear, making her want things she had convinced herself were not possible, despite how much she had come to love Gray.

"Dearest, I don't know what you saw," she said. "But he has made no promises or offers to me. So you cannot compare this to your situation."

Celia shrugged. "Perhaps not. And perhaps I could have continued on as I was even with that niggling doubt, but then I saw Lord and Lady Folworth."

Rosalinde's lips pressed together. "Their love match."

Celia nodded. "I had convinced myself love matches didn't truly exist in the *ton*, I suppose. That they were a fairytale. But they love each other, Rosalinde." Her sister's tears began to flow anew. "They love each other so deeply and I...I..."

"You want that," Rosalinde whispered. "Despite any threats leveled at you by Grandfather, you want it. You *deserve* it."

Celia had gone still and she wiped her eyes slowly. "Yes, Grandfather. If I break this engagement, his punishments to both of us will be swift and vicious."

Rosalinde shook her head, even though she knew her sister's words were true.

"He will cut me off," Celia said. "And likely you, too. And there will be nowhere to go for us. We'll have no money, no references."

Rosalinde swallowed past the fears those words left in her stomach. "We would work out a way," she said, though she could think of nothing. "Because like you, my job as the one who loves you most is to protect you. If you will be so unhappy with Stenfax—"

"We'll never learn the truth about our father," Celia continued, and now her voice was flat and emotionless.

"It doesn't matter," Rosalinde reassured her. "We'll—"

Celia pushed from the settee and walked to the fire. She stared at the dancing flames a moment, then turned back to face Rosalinde. "I am being foolish," she said, her tone suddenly very calm. But her eyes were so empty, so lost that Rosalinde nearly burst into tears herself. "I am reaching for things that most never find, and throwing away opportunities we will never have again."

Rosalinde stood and moved toward her sister. "Celia, you were just describing a highly unhappy and empty marriage. You cannot pretend—"

"There is no choice!" Celia interrupted, her voice elevating to near hysteria. Then she took a long breath and grew calm again. "The deal is done, the contracts signed, the license obtained. There is no choice in the matter. And the alternative if I made another choice is bleaker than anything I shall endure if I marry as planned."

"Celia," Rosalinde whispered, moving toward her.

Celia caught her hand and squeezed. "I was only feeling bridal nerves," she said. "That is all. Please forget all I said here tonight. It matters not, and we will continue on just as before."

She released Rosalinde and moved to a mirror on the opposite wall where she smoothed her gown and pinched her cheeks to put color back in them. Rosalinde watched her perform the motions and her heart broke.

Celia faced her again. "I should return. It is rude of me to be gone so long from a party in my honor, after all. Please promise me you won't say anything to anyone about my foolishness tonight."

Rosalinde caught her breath. She had so much to say to Celia. So much she wanted to do. But she could see her sister would not allow it. She was determined.

"I won't say a word," Rosalinde whispered.

Celia nodded and then moved to the parlor door where she stepped out and left Rosalinde alone.

She stood at the fire a few moments, shocked and numb from what had just happened. She had promised not to say anything about her sister's hesitations, and she would do her level best not to. But she could not make the promise to forget. She would never forget Celia's panic, her uncertainty, her regrets.

But Rosalinde had no idea what to do about any of it. She had no idea how to save the person she loved most from a future that might crush her beneath its weight.

Hours after the ball had ended, hours after everyone else had retired to their beds, Gray sat in his chamber at a table near the fire. He was wide awake. The papers delivered by Folly were spread out before him. He had read them over and over again until he could almost repeat them verbatim without looking at the pages.

Agatha Fitzgilbert had not married, as had always been reported. She had certainly not married anyone who was deemed appropriate by Society. No, Celia and Rosalinde's mother had run off with a former servant of her father's. No one knew his name, no one had a record of him, it seemed Fitzgilbert had very carefully taken care of that information.

But the bare bones were enough to ruin the young women. They were not only bastards by law, but bastards created by a scandalous relationship with a man far below their mother's status. Even Stenfax would have to think twice about a marriage now. After all, he was trying to not only return the coffers of their family to their former glory, but make people forget the shameful decisions that had emptied those coffers in the first place.

Marrying a bastard daughter of a servant would do little to elevate him.

Gray knew that he held a bullet in his hands that would jeopardize the engagement he had worked so hard to end. And yet he had no idea what to do with what he knew.

A day ago, he would have been perfectly clear. He would have taken this information straight to his brother and revealed all. He wouldn't have felt good about it, he wasn't a total cad. But he would have done it to protect Lucien. He would have calmly reminded his brother about all the issues the information could create.

He might not have had his way, but it would have been his best play in this game of chess.

Now, though, there were new revelations, new problems that kept Gray up, staring at the papers before him and completely unsure what to do.

The Duchess of Kirkford was widowed. And if Stenfax found out and was unattached, there was no telling what he would do. Love was a powerful thing. Even hate couldn't fully destroy it.

But love and hate mixed so potently could destroy Stenfax. They had already nearly done so.

So Gray was left with a choice: leave his brother to marry Celia and risk the harm she might do, or free his brother from this trap only to leave him open to a far more damaging one.

"Bollocks," he grunted, slamming a fist down on the tabletop.

At almost the same moment, there was a light knock on his door. He glanced at the clock on the mantel in surprise. It was after two in the morning. Far too late for anyone to trouble him unless…

Unless it was an emergency.

He pushed to his feet and hurried to the door, throwing it open with the expectation that he would see a concerned servant or ragged family member on the other side.

Instead, he found Rosalinde standing in the hallway. She wore a robe tied tightly around her waist, the same robe she'd been wearing that night in the library when the desire between them had overflowed and he'd surrendered to the need he had to touch her.

"Rosalinde," he whispered, her name a benediction and curse all at once. Saying it warmed him to his core, but it also reminded him of the decisions he'd made earlier in the day.

He had to let her go. But staring at her in the hall, seeing her looking up at him, lips slightly parted, hair down around her shoulders, he couldn't do that. Not yet. Not yet.

She was silent as she slipped past the space next to him at the doorway. She said nothing as she took his hand and led him back inside.

He shut the door. He knew what it meant to do so and he still did it. She wound her fingers through his, leaning in until her body brushed his. She lifted to her tiptoes and kissed him. He shut his eyes with a shuddering breath and just sank into the feeling of her soft lips brushing his. He wanted so much to have this. To have her.

Even if he knew it was yet again, a stolen moment. And that was all they'd ever have in the end. Moments that hadn't belonged to them. If this was to be the last, then he was going to take it.

He caught her upper arms, not tightly, gently, letting his thumbs brush over the soft cotton of her robe, feeling her arms tense beneath. He deepened the kiss, opening to her tongue, meeting her with his, tasting the sweetness of her and memorizing it as best he could.

They backed together toward his bed, and he shivered. It had been a long time since he'd been able to take his time with her. Tonight he intended to do just that.

He broke the kiss and backed up, looking at her in the dim light of his dying fire. She smiled, just the slightest expression, and he was lost. He was hers.

He never wanted to be anyone else's. But he squashed that thought and instead reached out to untie her robe. When he parted the fabric, he gasped. She was naked beneath. Utterly, beautifully and completely naked.

"Rosalinde?" he groaned.

She smiled again. "If I found the courage to knock on your door, I couldn't leave without having you. I knew I couldn't. If you refused, this was to be my ammunition."

"I can't refuse you," he whispered as he leaned in to brush his lips along the column of her throat. "You should know that by now. Even when I should, I can't."

She shuddered when he pushed her robe away, but as soon as her arms were free, she lifted them around his neck, leaning into him with a shuddering sigh. Surrender was in her body, on her lips, in her taste, and he took it gladly.

"Won't Celia notice you're gone?" he asked.

She shook her head. "She's asleep. I can't talk about her now. Later, later we must. But right now I want you. You and only you. I want you to make the rest go away."

His brow wrinkled, for there was a soft desperation to her words, her tone, her expression. And it mimicked his own. Like

155

her, he wanted to forget everything else, all the decisions he had to make. She was the only one capable of such a thing.

So he shut down his mind, shut down his arguments and kissed her once more. Everything else was silent. Silent as he tasted her, molding her to him by gliding both his hands to the curve of her naked backside. Silent when he somehow forced a space between them to unbutton his shirt.

Silent when she shed that same shirt and stared at his bare chest.

"The first time I saw you like this," she whispered, staring at the plane of muscles, "I wondered if you were real. I wondered what I had done to deserve you wanting me."

He laughed softly. "You deserved it by being extraordinary and undeniable. By being Rosalinde Wilde."

She lifted her gaze to his face. "I want to give you pleasure, Gray. I want that so much."

"You already have," he assured her, reaching up to touch her face with the back of his hand. "Every time I look at you or touch you or taste you, it is pleasure beyond imagining."

"Not like that," she said, her cheeks flaming. "A different kind of pleasure."

His eyes widened. "Rosalinde, are you saying you want to—"

She nodded even as she made a strangled sound. "I want to taste you."

He swallowed. Most ladies did not wish such a thing. But this was no average lady. This was sweet and passionate Rosalinde, who, as Celia had said, led with her heart in all things. Gave of herself completely.

And he selfishly wanted to take. To let everything good about her bleed into his empty spaces until he was somehow whole again.

He let his trembling hands drop to his trouser waist and unfastened the rough fabric. She slid her hands beneath, her hands warm on his flesh. He hissed out pleasure as she shoved the trousers away and left him as naked as she was.

"Sit?" she asked, motioning him to the soft chair near the fire.

He moved toward it, taking his seat without looking away from her. She drew in a long breath, like she was readying herself, and then slowly moved to her knees before him. She scooted forward, forcing him to open his legs, to create a space for her to rest.

And then they froze. Her gaze was locked on his, her cheeks were flushed, her hands shaking as her fingers moved on him. He waited, not breathing, not thinking, not focused on anything but how she closed her fist around his already hard and ready length.

They both eased out a long breath at the touch, and Gray couldn't help when his eyes fluttered shut. She began to gently pump her hand over him, her grip just right, her movements perfect. Already he felt close to spending and she had just begun. He tried to think of other things, to wait, but he felt her hot breath on the sensitive head of his erect cock and he couldn't help but moan.

"Rosalinde," he began, uncertain what to say, whether to warm her off or order her to take him.

She took the decision from his hands swiftly enough when her lips closed over him and her tongue swept the thick length of him gently.

He made a low sound deep in his chest that was hardly human, hardly recognizable, and he felt her smile against him as he opened his eyes. She was looking up at his face even as she lowered her mouth over him, sucking until his vision blurred.

She was not practiced in this, he could tell. But it was incredible despite her innocence. Or perhaps because of it. She was driven to pleasure him, to do this even though it was foreign. That was how much she wanted him, how much she cared.

He deserved far less, but he greedily took more, tangling his fingers into her dark hair as she moved her mouth more quickly over him, around him. His balls were beginning to tighten, his seed flashing hot through him. He was going to come and he didn't want it to be this way. Not this time. He wanted to be inside of her, to claim her even though she wasn't his.

He caught her arms and dragged her away from his cock, pulling her up his body. She made a sound of disapproval, but didn't fight him as he lifted her into his lap. She straddled him, her eyelashes fluttering as he eased her down over him, feeling her body accept him inch by inch.

"I wanted to finish," she all but pouted even as her breath came short.

"Next time," he said, even though he was certain there wouldn't be a next time. He couldn't allow it.

But the lie seemed to appease her, for her arms dropped around his neck and she let out a low cry as he seated himself fully inside of her. He clutched her backside, tugging her even closer until there wasn't an inch separating them.

Then he stood. She yelped in surprise, even though her long legs came around him as if she had been trained to do so. He held tight as he carried her to his bed and settled her upon the pillows, her dark hair spanning the white fabric.

She stared up at him, her blue eyes bright and her slight smile welcoming. He was drawn in, lost in her. He lowered his mouth to hers and kissed her as he thrust gently into her welcoming body. She lifted to meet him, but he forced himself to keep his tempo slow, easy. He wanted this to last. He never wanted to let it end.

Her fingernails dug into his arms and her moans dissolved against his lips as he built her pleasure bit by bit, slow swivel by slow swivel. Finally she let out a soft cry, turning her head as her body pulsed around him in orgasm. He watched her through the crisis, memorizing how her face twisted and her flesh grew pink with pleasure.

She went limp against his pillows and he chuckled. He felt so damn close to coming, but that would end this encounter. He didn't want that. So he withdrew, though it was almost physically painful to do so.

"What are you doing?" she gasped, gripping at his arms.

He shook his head. "I'm not finished," he promised. "Far from it."

CHAPTER SEVENTEEN

Gray said nothing more, even when Rosalinde repeated his name. At least, she did until her breath was stolen by pleasure. Gray dragged his mouth down her throat, her chest. He paused at her right breast, laving her nipple until her back arched and she gripped the coverlet beneath her with both hands. This man was magic, pure magic, and he had woven a spell over her that she feared could never be broken. She would be his forever, a part of her never able to let go of these stolen moments, stolen kisses, stolen nights.

Gray smiled against her skin, his dark gaze coming up to hold hers, taunting and teasing. She reached down and touched his rough cheek.

"Please," she murmured, not knowing exactly what she was pleading for.

"Please you?" he suggested. "Oh, I shall. Don't you worry."

"I was never worried," she croaked.

His face grew more serious, more determined. He ceased the torture of her nipple and continued his way down her body, rubbing his stubbly cheek against her belly, tasting her hip, her thigh, and finally he settled between her legs.

Her sex was slick and exquisitely sensitive from her recent release. He stared for what felt like an eternity at the flexing entrance to her body. She held her breath as she waited, waited.

Finally, he dropped his head there, just as he had the first night he made love to her. He swiped his tongue over her quim and she jerked, letting out a low gasp of pleasure and relief. Oh, how many times had she dreamed of this exact act since he first performed it? How many times had she pictured his hard mouth against her soft and yielding flesh?

Now it was not fantasy, but reality. And a better reality than she had even remembered. His tongue traced her entrance with delicate licks. She lifted, but he laughed and pressed a hand to her hip, holding her steady so he could guide the torture to come.

He used his other hand to gently spread her open, revealing her further. Yet she felt no embarrassment at being so exposed. On the contrary, she felt proud. Proud that he wanted her. Proud to give herself fully to this man, this amazing, complicated, generous man who made her want things she had never known existed.

He glided his tongue in a slow, firm circle around her clitoris, and Rosalinde's head lolled back. Thoughts exited her mind, her body began to shake out of control.

"So close already," he whispered, his breath stimulating her further. "How many times could I make you come, Rosalinde?"

She gasped as he licked her clitoris again. She was on the edge already. "I-I don't know," she moaned. "Please."

He looked up the length of her body and their eyes met. He held the stare as he licked again, again, and then he was sucking, and she shattered as she fell over the edge of pleasure for a second time. She reached for him, grabbing for his hair, his shoulders, anything to center herself as swirling, pounding pleasure roared through every fiber of her being.

But he offered her no relief. He kept sucking, kept forcing her over-stimulated flesh to give more and more, until she was weak with release, until she thought she might just combust in his unrelenting fire.

At last, the tremors began to fade, the world slowed from its ceaseless spinning and he lifted his head from her sex. He crawled up the length of her body, positioning himself back at her entrance. She was so slick now that when he pressed his cock against her, he slid forward, fully seating without resistance.

They sighed together as he thrust again, short, hard thrusts, punctuated by pivots of his muscular hips. She drowned in sensation, her body still clenching from the previous two orgasms. His mouth found hers, filling her with the flavor of her pleasure and the heat of his need.

She held him close, whispering mindless, headless words of need and desire and care. And just when she thought she could not feel more, her body rocked again. He began to pound harder as she cried out beneath him and then he was gone, his slick seed pumping between them before he collapsed over her.

His arms came around her, tucking her into his side. His fingers tangled in her hair as he drew one of her legs over him and kissed her deeply, tenderly.

"I needed that," he mused at last, when moments had ticked by, when their breath and heart rates had slowed and matched like they were made to do so.

She cuddled deeper into his embrace. "After today, so did I."

He pulled back a fraction and looked down at her. "After today? What happened today?"

She sighed as he stroked back a few locks of hair from her face. "I-I am beginning to see your side of the argument."

He blinked, and she could see he didn't understand. "What do you mean?"

She traced one bicep with the edge of her fingernail. "You have been strenuously arguing that our siblings should not wed. I am beginning to wonder if you are correct in that assessment."

He released her and straightened up. His dark stare held hers as he gaped at her. "You think I'm *correct*?" he repeated. "You're saying you don't want Celia and Lucien to wed now?"

She let out a long breath. Now that it had been said out loud, the truth of it felt so clear. "My sister is not wicked, as you want to believe. I'm not agreeing to your reasons."

"I understand that part, Rosalinde. What I don't understand is why you would change your mind about this marriage."

"Gray, you and I both see the same thing when we look at them. Your brother does not care for Celia. And she doesn't care for him. Tonight I realized just how much they would be giving up if they marry."

"Love, you mean." His voice was raw and his expression taut.

She nodded. "Love, but also desire." She reached out and touched his chest, feeling the muscles there ripple when her fingers brushed them. "Passion. Perhaps it is naïve, but I don't want my sister to be in a loveless union where she someday wonders what she missed. Regret is a cold bedfellow."

He pinched his lips. She had expected him to be pleased that she had come around to his side of this situation. And yet he didn't look happy.

"So you are saying you want to stop their marriage?" he said.

"I want to make sure they will be able to live with their decision to wed, at the very least. I want to encourage them to reconsider if this empty union will be fulfilling enough," she clarified. "And if that means they part, I'll support that. Though I know not what Celia and I would do. My grandfather will be livid."

"Christ," he muttered, and got to his feet.

He paced the room, naked and seemingly unaffected by that fact, even though she was. She was even more affected by his demeanor, though.

"Why are you angry? Don't you *want* an ally in your quest to end this union, even if we come at it from different motivations?"

He barked out a laugh as he faced her. "Oh, my dear, if this wasn't so entirely depressing, it would be funny."

She pulled the coverlet around herself, suddenly feeling

vulnerable. "What are you talking about?"

"Tonight you decided that Celia must not marry Stenfax. Well, tonight *I* decided the absolute opposite. My brother *must* marry your sister."

Rosalinde's mouth dropped open at that declaration and she stared at him. At last she found her breath. "I-I am dreaming. This cannot be real."

"I'm afraid it is," he said, running a hand through his thick, short hair. "God's teeth, what a bloody mess."

"You can't just make a statement about how you've changed your mind and not explain yourself," Rosalinde said. "Especially about something so important. Why do you want Stenfax to marry Celia all of a sudden?"

He let out a sigh, and in that sound Rosalinde heard how broken he was. How upset. She wanted to comfort him, but by the way he went back to pacing, tense and unhappy, she recognized that she couldn't. He might share pleasure with her, but if she touched him now he might recoil.

She couldn't bear the rejection.

"Gray," she said softly, forcing her tone to be even and unemotional. "*Please* explain."

"I met with your sister before the others arrived," he admitted. "And I couldn't help but be impressed by her. Perhaps I have simply come to see she is what you say."

Rosalinde arched a brow. "And so you claim you have changed your mind on such a flimsy reason? After months of being determined to end this union, you wish me to believe that a single conversation with my sister has changed your heart?"

"I suppose that would be sporting with your intelligence." He let out a long groan.

She shot him a look. "Just a bit, yes. I'm willing to believe that Celia might have softened you to her, but not that it has made you turn around and change your mind. Don't you have any trust for me, Gray? Won't you tell me even a fraction of the truth after all we've been through and shared?"

He moved toward her, and her heart stuttered as he sat

down on the bed next to her. He observed her for a moment before he said, "Being honest, being open, it doesn't come easy to me. It is not my nature."

She wrinkled her brow. "Sharing ourselves with others is *entirely* our nature. But it leaves us vulnerable and that makes some recoil. I promise you, Gray—whatever you tell me, it will stay between us."

Gray reached out to take her hand. He held it, staring at it, and then he shook his head almost in surrender. "Did anyone ever tell you about Elise?"

Rosalinde hesitated. "I admit I know of her. Everyone knows Stenfax was engaged before and that the engagement was broken."

Gray flinched. "Yes. But do you know anything more about her?"

"Not much. Just the basics that gossip retells. She left Stenfax and married—the Duke of Kirkford, I think I remember. I've never met her, if that's what you're asking," Rosalinde said. "And as far as I know, Stenfax hasn't told Celia anything about her. Why?"

"Of course Stenfax wouldn't speak of her. He refuses to do so. And most of the whispers have died down now that so long has passed." Gray rubbed his eyes. "Where do I begin?"

She squeezed his hand gently. "At the beginning seems as good a place as any."

He exhaled a long breath before he said, "Very well. Elise's mother and our mother were good friends, and she used to come here in the summers and spend a few weeks every year. She was younger than us, seven years younger than Lucien, four younger than me. She and Felicity were thick as thieves, of course, but they always insisted upon tagging along with us. And she was…well, she was fun. Both she and Felicity could hold their own when it came to boyish pursuits, so though we groused, I don't think either of us cared all that much when they made themselves part of our expeditions."

"She was a childhood friend," Rosalinde said slowly.

Gray's face was hard to read as he spoke, like he'd put a flat mask over his features.

"I suppose I would have called her that once. Felicity certainly would have. But the year Elise came out, it became clear that something had shifted. Lucien couldn't stop *looking* at her. They weren't officially courting, but anyone could see they were bonded, closer than friends."

"Ultimately he courted her, though," Rosalinde interjected.

Gray rubbed a hand over his face. "Stenfax was young, not sure he wanted to settle down. I…encouraged him, God forgive me. After dancing around it for almost three years, he finally began to court her. I was happy for him at the time, it seemed they would be a good match."

"But the engagement was broken," Rosalinde said softly.

Gray bent his head. "Oh yes. Elise showed her true colors eventually. Just a few weeks after their engagement, she broke with him. She married a duke instead, Kirkford, who had more money and whose title had more weight than ours. She wrote Lucien a letter to end it. A goddamned letter. When he came to confront her, to force her to look him in the eye when she said she didn't love him, she refused to see him."

Rosalinde drew back, her hand coming to her lips. So much made sense now. "*That* is why you were so loath to let him marry someone you believed only wanted a title."

"Elise all over again," Gray said. "Though at least Celia was honest about her desires."

"Stenfax must have been devastated," Rosalinde said.

Gray swallowed hard. "He was torn to shreds. The man you see now? The one who does not show emotion? He didn't exist before that summer when Elise threw him over. He loved her with all he was, and she destroyed him." He shifted, and for a moment pure pain was reflected in his face, his eyes, his entire being. "It got so bad that one night after too many drinks at Folworth's, he climbed up on Folly's terrace edge and declared he would throw himself to his death."

Rosalinde let out a pained sound. "Oh, Gray!"

"It took Folly, Marina and me two hours to talk him down." Gray clenched his fist. "Do you know what it's like to have someone you love try to end himself in front of you?"

"No," Rosalinde said, swiping at a tear that slipped from the corner of her eye. "I can hardly imagine how shattering that must have been for you."

"Shattering," he repeated, meeting her stare. "That was the word for it. I had long watched Felicity suffer cruelly at the hands of her husband without any way to help her, and now I nearly lost my brother. Both because of their choices in love. I vowed I would never allow them to make those kinds of mistakes again. That I would protect them."

Rosalinde nodded. "I can understand why you would make that vow, Gray. But what I don't understand is how this has *anything* to do with your changing your mind about Celia and Stenfax marrying."

Gray was silent for a long moment. "Elise's husband is dead," he all but whispered, as if he said it too loudly it would be heard by more than just her.

Rosalinde's eyes went wide. "The Duke of Kirkford?"

He jerked his head once. "Very few know because according to Folly and Marina, there is some scandal the family is keeping quiet. It will come out soon enough, though. And if my brother is unmarried when he hears the news, he might—"

He cut himself off, and the way he flexed his fist spoke of his fears more than any words. Rosalinde covered his tight fingers gently. "You think he might go to Elise."

"He might," Gray admitted in a broken tone. "And if he does, this time I fear there is nothing I could do to protect him from the damage she would cause."

"But if he is married to Celia…" Rosalinde said.

"He would be true. I *know* him. He might pine for Elise, he might regret that he wasn't free, but Lucien would never break his vows to his wife. He would be safe."

"Just loveless," Rosalinde reminded him.

"Love has not treated him kindly in the past," Gray said. "Perhaps it is better to leave it be."

"And you get to decide that?" Rosalinde asked.

He pushed to his feet and walked away. "You think I haven't punished myself for wanting to control his future? I have. But I have looked at all alternatives. I could tell him what I know about your family and possibly end this wedding—"

Rosalinde got to her feet now, his words ringing in her ears. "What?"

He stopped and looked at her. His cheeks were pale, as if he hadn't meant to say those words. But he'd been so wrapped up in his emotional response he hadn't been more prudent.

"What do you know?" Rosalinde burst out, moving on him.

His gaze shifted to the table across the room, and she followed it. There was a stack of papers there. She faced him again.

"You investigated us?" she asked, hardly able to raise her voice high enough to carry with all the pain blooming in her chest like a poisonous flower.

He nodded. "I'm sorry, Rosalinde. I felt I had no choice. I had to pursue every avenue to protect my brother."

"It sounds as if you found something out. What did you learn?" she asked, breathless.

There was only one secret she knew for certain her family carried. If Gray had uncovered the truth about her father's identity, then she and Celia didn't have to live under their grandfather's thumb as prisoners of his whims.

"You might not want to know."

"Did you find out about my father?" she asked, forcing herself to keep her gaze even when she wanted to grab Gray, when she wanted to scream and plead, when she wanted to make him understand just how important the truth was.

His brow wrinkled and he took a step back. "You know?"

The world began to spin and she grasped the edge of the

bed to stay upright. "Do you know who he is?"

"I—"

"His name!" she cried out. "Please?"

"I'm sorry," he said, moving toward her, holding her up by the hands he cupped at her elbows. "I'm sorry, *that* I don't know."

She tipped her head back in pain, in disappointment. He drew her closer, holding her. Not speaking, not demanding, just holding her.

"We were always told the same thing the world believed," Rosalinde said against his chest. "That my mother had married someone of appropriate rank and that they had tragically died together, leaving my grandfather to care for us. But after I married Martin, my grandfather revealed the truth to Celia in a rage. He told her that our father is alive."

"Alive?" Gray repeated, and there was shock to his tone.

"Yes," she said, drawing back to look up at him. "Isn't that what you determined in your research?"

He shook his head. "No, not that. Are you telling me your father lives and that Fitzgilbert…"

"Took us away from him after my mother's death," she said. "And he won't tell us the truth about his identity, perhaps even his location, unless…"

"Unless?" Gray encouraged her softly.

She forced herself to look at him at last, knowing her cheeks were tear-streaked, knowing she was handing him the keys to her pain and trusting he wouldn't use them.

"Unless Celia marries a man with a title. To make up for the shame brought upon his name by my mother when she married a man who was obviously beneath her. To make up for the shame brought by me when I married the same. He *forced* Celia into a corner. Lose any chance of finding the man who fathered us, or marry a man she does not love."

Gray shook his head. "And now your motives are as clear as mine. You and your sister needed Celia to marry a title for more than mere mercenary reasons. In fact, it sounds to be as noble a cause as my own desire to protect Lucien."

She blinked at tears. At last they understood each other. And yet they were still on opposite sides. "Here we are, brought together by the strangest of circumstances, the deepest of betrayals and lies."

Gray drew back. "But wait, then why do you suddenly want Celia to break her engagement? You will not only be punished by your grandfather, but he may never tell you the truth about your father."

"Because my sister's happiness today is worth more than the vague promise of a man who does not give a damn about us," Rosalinde said, lifting her chin in defiance. "Celia could wed and our grandfather could just as easily decide to hold the information hostage for some other reason. Until I marry or until there is an heir or until Stenfax allows my grandfather entry into some club. It might never end, and then Celia would have sacrificed herself for nothing. I would never forgive myself if she did that."

"You are a good sister," Gray whispered, and dropped a gentle kiss to her lips.

She let out a sigh and smiled up at him sadly. "And you are a good brother. Which means we are at cross purposes yet again."

"We are," he said. "But by God, I will tell you all I discovered in my investigation. You deserve that truth, Rosalinde. You deserve so much more. Come, get dressed. I'll show you everything I have."

CHAPTER EIGHTEEN

Rosalinde tied her robe shut and looked at the hand Gray now held out to her. She took it, leaning into his bare forearm. He had put on his trousers but nothing else, and she squeezed his hand tightly, craving the warmth of his skin as he guided her to the table across the room.

She found herself leaning back slightly as she approached, as if that could help her avoid what was about to happen. Ever since she and Celia had learned the truth that their father lived, she had longed to know more. Now she feared it. What if what she saw proved he was just as wicked as her grandfather?

Gray brushed her fingers to his lips, almost as if he'd read her mind, understood that she needed his support and comfort. Having it gave her the bravery to take the last step and sit down at the table. He swiftly reorganized the papers and then stepped away, silent as she read through the tangle of information. It took her half an hour to do so, but when she was finished, she sat back with a sigh.

"There's not much there, is there?" she asked, hearing her voice shake.

He stroked his fingers over her shoulder gently. "Your grandfather covered up as much information as he could."

"There was never a record of her marrying," Rosalinde whispered. "That is the part that stuns me, not that my father seems to have been a servant in their house. I knew he was likely below her because of my grandfather's cruel remarks, his fury when I followed in her footsteps. But I always believed they were married. What kind of man could he have been to father two children with her but never marry her?"

Gray sank into the chair next to hers. He smoothed a few locks of hair away from her cheeks and said, "Rosalinde, your grandfather seems to me to be the vindictive kind."

She shivered. "Indeed, he is. Cruel and punishing as the harshest winter."

"Your mother was his only child, yes?"

She nodded. "Yes. He often laments that, blames my grandmother for it, though she's been dead in the ground longer than my mother."

"Then he saw her as his only bargaining chip, just like he sees Celia as such. If she ran away, it is possible he might have wanted to find her, yes? After all, he was telling everyone in Society a fabricated story about how she was visiting an aunt during the time she was missing. He was trying to keep her from scandal, I assume so that when she returned, he would still be able to marry her off to a man of rank and title."

Rosalinde wrinkled her brow. "Certainly, I would wager that is true. And?"

"Your mother must have known his character just as well as you do. That he was looking for her in order to force her hand. If he was tracking them, they might have feared that having the banns read for three weeks, both in the parish where they planned to wed *and* in London where your father was watching…it might have exposed them. He could have come and forced her home."

Rosalinde drew a breath. "I suppose that might be."

"So do not judge your father too harshly. I doubt he could have afforded a special license to subvert the issue, or even a trip to Gretna Green. Remaining unmarried, at least in the eyes of the church, could have been their best recourse."

"You don't want me to hate him," she whispered. "Why?"

"Because finding him is important to you," he said. "And I don't want you to break your own heart before you even have a chance to know his name."

She leaned up and kissed him, finding solace in the soft brush of his lips. He leaned away at last and smiled at her. "Now, let us address the finding of him. This is the best information my man could find in his investigation. Your grandfather did a great deal of covering the truth over the years. But certainly if this man was a servant in Fitzgilbert's house, he would be remembered. Is it possible you could obtain more information from those who serve him now?"

Rosalinde ducked her head. "Grandfather is mercurial. He fires servants for the smallest of infractions. No one on his staff now has served for more than five years. I doubt anyone knows, and if they did, they wouldn't tell in fear they'd be sacked without reference."

"But it *is* something. We could use this information in the future to perhaps track down some of the old servants and question them." Gray rubbed his chin. "It will take some doing, but—"

Rosalinde stared at him. "The future, Gray?"

He stopped talking and stared back, but his face had lost some of its life, its connection to her. He said nothing.

"Do we have a future?" she whispered.

She hadn't intended to ask the question, but tonight had opened her eyes to so much. As much as she didn't want Celia to face an empty future, she didn't want that fate for herself either. She loved the man sitting across from her. She knew it as clearly as she had ever known anything.

And he cared for her. She could feel it in the way he treated her. With his passion, yes, but also this moment. Sitting here with her, sharing with her the information that could change the course of her life, trying to reassure her when she needed it.

He cared for her.

But that didn't mean he loved her. That didn't mean he wanted any more with her than the few hours they'd already had. Or more than just her willing body beneath his.

She'd been with one man who didn't love her. She wasn't

about to be with another. Even if she adored him beyond reason.

He was still silent, still watching her. But then he turned his face slightly. "Rosalinde," he said.

He said nothing more than her name, and yet he answered every question she would ever have about what they could and could not have together.

She nodded, trying not to show her pain, trying not to force his hand through misplaced guilt. "We both know this was all a stolen moment. The moment just lasted longer than either of us ever could have imagined." She pushed to her feet. "Thank you, Gray."

"Thank me?" he repeated, also getting up. His hand fisted at his side, like he wanted to touch her but couldn't allow himself to do so. "Why are you thanking me?"

She almost laughed. He truly had no idea of her heart. Probably because he felt nothing like she did.

"For being so kind as to share your information. I don't know what to do with it, but at least it gives me a start. Now I should go."

He moved on her then, crowding into her space, and yet still he didn't allow himself to touch her. "Rosalinde," he said, pleading in his tone. She waited for more, but he gave nothing else.

She smiled through the swell of her pain. "Good night, Grayson," she whispered, touching his cheek for what she knew would be the last time. "Thank you again for your honesty. It was a precious gift."

He opened his mouth, as if he wanted to speak, and she waited, hoping that he would. But finally he bent his head, and she sighed. Without another word, she slipped from the room. She shut the door behind her and leaned against it for a few breaths.

Tonight had started just as a need for his touch, for his comfort. And it had ended with what felt like a goodbye to everything they'd shared. Not an ugly goodbye, not a cruel one. But one that had to happen. He couldn't give her what she desired.

She straightened up and walked down the hall toward the opposite wing of the house and her own room. There Celia slept. Celia, who had shown the truth about her heart tonight, even if she later tried to deny it.

Rosalinde had spent her life living by her own heart. Celia had suffered for it. She was still suffering for it. So the best thing she could do now was set her love for Gray aside and focus on what her sister needed.

Even if it meant betraying just a little of what Gray had told her tonight.

Gray stared at the door where Rosalinde had exited and his entire body felt numb. She was gone. He could tell himself she had only left his room, that he would see her tomorrow, and that was true.

But her leaving meant more than that and they both knew it. She had asked him a question about the future and he had remained silent. He saw how that hurt her. Still, she had steadied herself in the pain and found the strength to accept his unspoken rejection. She hadn't raged at him, as some women in her position would. She hadn't threatened him, even though their affair could have easily been used to twist him to her will.

No, she had done none of those things. Because she was Rosalinde. Living life with her open heart, but never taking more than what was freely given.

What was strange was that when she'd asked the question about the future, his silence hadn't actually *been* a rejection. It had truly been born from confusion.

He'd spent the eight years since his father died building himself up—and watching his siblings be torn apart. Those two facts had merged together and made him into what he was. He shunned connection and had done his level best to block out passion and even emotion because he'd seen how weak those things could make a person. Because he thought he'd be in control if he never let anything or anyone past the walls he'd built.

And yet Rosalinde Wilde had breached those walls with just the tilt of a smile, the touch of a hand, a sigh of pleasure. She was inside now. And it terrified him.

So when she had asked about the future, he'd had no answer because he didn't know what to do or say. He could offer her safety and security, certainly. His fortune was growing nearly every day. But she wasn't asking about safety and security. She was asking for feelings he had long packed away. Ones he didn't know if he could find or share.

Earlier that very day, he had told himself he had to let her go, to keep her from feeling the very pain that had flickered across her face when he was silent in the face of her question. He had failed in doing that.

And yet her reaction had been to let *him* go. She had released him with her goodbye, released him from the connection she thought he didn't want. He should have been happy for that.

And instead, he stared at the door, completely unable to find the strength to go after her. To change his answer. To be the kind of man who was worthy of her heart. Worthy of her future. Worthy of more than the stolen moments they had taken since they first met.

Knowing he had lost something precious.

CHAPTER NINETEEN

Gray took a long breath as he entered the breakfast room the next morning. For over a week, the house had only contained the two families, so Gray had been able to brood if he wished, without too many eyes on him.

But this morning, just two days before his brother would wed, the house was now stuffed full of guests. When he entered, his name was called out by more than one person as hands were lifted in greeting.

"Good morning," he said to the group, hearing the rasp to his voice, the strain he was trying to hide.

Stenfax was already at the head of the table with their mother on one side and Celia on the other. The intendeds were not speaking to each other as they sat, and Gray frowned. There was proof once again of what Rosalinde had said the night before. Proof that the two cared little for each other. God, if it were him marrying Rosalinde in two days, he wouldn't be able to stop looking at her. Touching her, even in passing.

He jolted. Where had that damned thought come from? He'd spent a night tossing and turning as he relived her question about the future over and over. Now he was imagining one that didn't exist.

"You look tired," Felicity said, suddenly at his elbow.

He turned to face her. "I—yes, I didn't sleep well."

She tilted her head and examined him more closely. "I am worried about you, Gray. You haven't been yourself lately. Are you still determined that Lucien is making a mistake?"

Gray stared again at his brother. "I don't know," he admitted. "My mind is a jumble on the topic."

Felicity pursed her lips. "He's grown, Gray. You must allow him to make his own decisions."

Gray squeezed his eyes shut. Felicity didn't understand. Lucien *couldn't* make decisions because he was being denied information, both about Elise and about Celia. Gray's head spun with all the possibilities. Should he break up the wedding or make damned sure it happened? Should he tell his brother the truth about Elise? Or was it Celia? Or was it himself?

"Gray?" Felicity said, and her voice sounded very far away. The world was beginning to spin and Gray felt like he was drowning, drowning.

"Good morning."

Air filled his lungs again as a voice cut into his spinning mind. Rosalinde's voice. He turned toward it, toward her, like she was a lighthouse beacon guiding him to safety through the fog. She stood in the doorway to the breakfast room in a dark blue gown that made her eyes look like sapphires. She was smiling, but he knew her now. He knew that smile was empty.

It was also never turned on him. She didn't even look at him as she entered, greeting guests before she went to her sister and kissed her cheek, acknowledged Gray's mother and brother, then took a seat beside her grandfather. She was stiff in her posture as she said hello to him. Gray could see the contempt dripping from her.

And yet she still didn't look at *him*. She never looked at him.

"Gray?" Felicity said.

He blinked and looked at his sister. "I'm sorry. I must be more tired than I thought," he choked out. "My mind was entirely gone."

Felicity stared at him and then looked at the table. He couldn't tell if she was staring at his brother or at Rosalinde. Both were in her sightline. But she didn't reveal herself. She merely squeezed his hand.

"Eat," she suggested. "I'm sure you'll feel better once you do so."

Gray nodded as Felicity returned to her seat, but he had no certainty about that statement. *Better*. What was better when he held the keys to his brother's demise? Or was it his salvation?

He walked to the table and took a place next to Marina and Folly. Servants came with dishes and the breakfast meal was lively and bright with conversation. Gray took part in none of it, eating slowly as he kept stealing glances down the table at Rosalinde.

Rosalinde, who still didn't look at him. Never looked at him. She just ate, as quiet as he was, equally as watchful, only her attention was turned on Celia and Stenfax. He could almost read her mind as she sat there. She was trying to decide if she would indeed do as she had said she would last night.

She was trying to decide if she would make known her case for dissolving the engagement. As the meal ended and everyone began to rise and talk about a croquet tournament arranged as entertainment for the rest of what remained of the morning, Rosalinde took a deep breath and got to her feet.

For one fleeting moment, her gaze slid to Gray at last. He saw her hesitation in that look, but also her strength and her determination.

Gray found himself rising, found himself saying her name, *sotto voce*. She looked away.

"Lord Stenfax," she said, her voice cracking slightly before she regained her composure. "I wondered if I might have a private word with you and Celia before we join the others for croquet?"

Stenfax was already standing and gave her a look of surprise. But before he could answer her request, Fitzgilbert jolted to his feet. His glare at Rosalinde could have frozen the lake at the bottom of the hill, it was so cold. Cold and cruel, like the man who wore it. Gray saw hate in that stare. Somehow Fitzgilbert could only see the disappointment Rosalinde had brought to him. He was incapable of more.

"What are you about, girl? You've nothing to say to anyone," he growled.

The response to her was so violent, so cruel, that the room grew silent in response. It felt like every eye in the room slowly turned to Rosalinde. She must have felt it, too, for her cheeks filled with high color. But she kept her back straight and her gaze even on Stenfax. She did not yield.

Of course she didn't.

Stenfax shot Fitzgilbert a harsh look at his nasty response and then smiled at Rosalinde. "Certainly, Mrs. Wilde. Why don't we go to my private office? The rest of you begin without us. Mama, you and Felicity can host, yes?"

Lady Stenfax nodded, though her expression was worried. "Of course. Come, everyone. And don't forget to bundle up. It's chilly out, but that will only add to the stakes of game."

"Whoever wins gets to go inside by the fire first," Marina said with a laugh that lightened the mood considerably. Gray could have kissed her for that, and smiled at Folly before the couple started out the door as if nothing in the breakfast room was amiss.

There were some who hesitated before they followed, as if they were more interested in the strange interaction between the bridal families, but eventually Lady Stenfax got them moving. "Come, my dear," she said to Felicity.

Felicity moved to follow her, but grasped Gray's arm before she did. "Go with them," she whispered.

Gray, of course, had every intention of doing just that, but he was surprised his sister would believe as much. "You think I have a place there?"

Her gaze narrowed. "Please, I am not blind. I see *exactly* where your place is. And I fear what Rosalinde's grandfather may do. Now go."

Gray caught his breath. Felicity's implication was clear. Had he been so obvious in his attentions to Rosalinde or did his sister simply know him so well?

Felicity squeezed his arm, then followed their mother out

into the hall. All this time, the others had been unmoving, almost in a standoff. Fitzgilbert glared at Rosalinde, and finally she turned her attention on him.

"You needn't join us," she said softly.

Fitzgilbert's face was turning redder with each passing second. "You don't tell me a damned thing, girl. I'll come right along."

Rosalinde let out a long sigh, and it was Stenfax who broke the tension. "Come, let me escort you, Mrs. Wilde."

"A good idea," Celia responded as she gave a nervous glance at her grandfather.

Celia took his arm—reluctantly, it seemed—and followed Stenfax as he escorted Rosalinde out of the room and down the hall. Gray followed quietly, watching as Celia whispered into her grandfather's ear. Clearly she was trying to mitigate the anger Rosalinde's request had inspired. And it didn't seem to be working.

Gray shook his head. He could only imagine the response that would be evoked once Rosalinde said her piece about why she wished to talk to the couple.

They entered Stenfax's office and Gray shut the door behind them. As Lucien released Rosalinde, he caught Gray's eye, but he did not ask him to go. Instead, his brother's gaze slipped to Fitzgilbert and then back, and a world of meaning passed between them.

Gray nodded to indicate he would monitor the situation just as his brother did. Then Stenfax moved to his desk. He didn't go around, but perched himself on the edge. He smiled at Rosalinde and said, "What did you wish to discuss with Celia and me?"

Rosalinde was worrying a handkerchief in her hands and Gray watched as she did so, turning and twisting the fabric until she almost rent it in two. He drew back. That was *his* handkerchief. The one he'd given to her earlier. Now she held it, taking out her nervous energy on the neatly stitched lines of his initials.

He found he wished he could slip his hand into hers instead. Smooth a thumb over her skin and whisper soothing words into her ear.

But he couldn't. He had no right.

She cleared her throat. "I suppose there is no easy way to say this, so I will come right out and do it. I-I don't think the two of you should wed."

There was a moment when her words hung in the air, echoing like a gunshot in the small room. And then all hell broke loose.

Rosalinde had never heard such a cacophonous and terrifying sound as the screeching voices that bombarded her from all sides. Her pronouncement had gone over just as she had expected, but she didn't regret making it. She had to be strong now. To face the consequences.

Her first instinct was to carefully watch her grandfather. Fitzgilbert was shouting at her, his voice breaking with the force of his anger, spittle flying from his lips as he fumed at her. She blocked out the specific words. She knew them all by heart. The slurs against her character, the ownership he claimed over her and her sister and their futures. None of it was a surprise. And though his reaction spurred the most physical fear in her, she found her gaze slipping away to Gray.

He had followed them, unbidden, to the office. At first she had hated him being there, for she feared that he would try to silence her. But he hadn't. He'd allowed her to say what she'd said, even though it went against whatever new plan he had concocted to save Stenfax. Gray watched her carefully now, his arms folded. Not angry, not controlling, not denying. Just there, as if he were ready to offer a lifeline if she needed it.

And she might. For she forced herself to look in the direction that was her chief concern. She looked at Celia.

Celia, who she loved. Celia, who was pale and pasty, her eyes wide. "Please don't do this, Rosalinde," she pleaded, her voice hardly carrying. "Please don't ruin everything."

But though her lips spoke those words of denial, of rejection of Rosalinde's statement, her eyes said something different. Rosalinde looked into her sister's eyes, so dark and so blue, and she saw a flicker of…hope. This statement that the marriage should not go forward gave Celia *hope*.

"Please be quiet!"

Rosalinde jolted as Stenfax slapped a palm hard on the desk beside him. His tone was so sharp it silenced even Fitzgilbert and reminded Rosalinde just how much power the earl wielded. But his face was unreadable, neither angry at her declaration nor surprised, nor sad.

He held her stare with evenness, fairness. "I want to hear what Rosalinde has to say," he continued. "You have always supported this union and now you say this, just two days before the deed is to be done. Tell me, were you influenced somehow?"

Stenfax glared at Gray, and Celia followed his stare. She caught her breath. "Did Mr. Danford *make* you say this, Rosalinde?"

"No!" she burst out, raising her heads in pleading. "God, no. Gray has had nothing to do with this at all. In fact, I would wager he would stand up against what I am saying if he could speak freely."

Celia folded her arms. "He has made clear his intentions to break this union by any means. Of *course* he would not argue that we should wed, not when he now has an ally in my closest family member."

Gray stepped forward and cleared his throat. "You needn't talk about me like I am not here. Rosalinde is correct."

"What?" Celia choked out, her eyes widening. "You cannot be serious."

Gray inclined his head. "I can see why you would doubt me, but I must admit to a recent change of heart on this subject.

I now think you *should* marry Celia, Stenfax. I think that would be best for you."

Stenfax jerked his gaze toward Gray and his eyes narrowed. "*Best* for me," he repeated.

Fitzgilbert leapt in. "You're damn right it's best for you, Stenfax. Our arrangements have been made, our contracts signed. You have a special license burning a hole in your desk drawer. You wouldn't dare back out now or you would face such a scandal."

Stenfax's lips thinned, and he slowly turned away from Gray and back toward Fitzgilbert. "I have asked you once to shut up, sir. I don't want to ask you again. Everyone in the room has given me their reasons for what they think should happen except for the one person who has declared we should not wed. Rosalinde, I ask you again, why do you now oppose this union?"

Rosalinde took a deep breath. "You are clearly a good man," she began. "I like you a great deal."

"That is a relief," Stenfax said, his tone dripping with sarcasm, though it wasn't cruel. Rosalinde smiled at him.

"I hope it is, for this is not about you. I hesitate about this marriage because…because I see no connection between you and my sister. This is not a slur against you. But I know my sister is capable of great love. I have a feeling you are, as well. So when I see you two together, looking as though you were mere acquaintances rather than two people who will in forty-eight hours be bound together for life, well, I fear that your happiness is at risk."

"You have created this entire situation because you want some fairytale version of love for Celia?" Fitzgilbert bellowed. He was moving toward Rosalinde now, and she fought the urge to back away. "You need to shut your mouth before you ruin everything we have worked for."

"I don't want either of you to regret your decision, for it cannot be undone," Rosalinde continued, ignoring her grandfather's looming presence.

Celia looked at Stenfax, and he looked back. Rosalinde realized it might have been the first time she'd ever seen them look each other in the eye. A moment of silent communication went between them, a moment where the hesitation her simple truth created was obvious.

"Do you forget what I can take away?" Fitzgilbert said, directing the comment to the room at large. Rosalinde supposed he meant his money when it came to Stenfax.

And his secrets when it came to her. Secrets he had lorded over them for years now. Secrets that she knew could easily put the final nail into the coffin of his ambition.

"Are you referring to the way you blackmailed Celia into accepting Stenfax's proposal?" Rosalinde asked softly.

Stenfax pushed off the desk. "What?"

Celia covered her mouth with one hand. Her voice was muffled as she said, "Oh, Rosalinde. Don't, don't…"

She faced her sister, tears stinging her eyes. "We will live under his thumb forever, Celia. We will be his puppets *forever* if I don't. And he'll never tell us the truth. *Never.*"

"What are you holding over Celia's head?" Stenfax asked, and suddenly he seemed to have gotten even taller. There were storms on his face, passions that he had never revealed because he never felt them for Celia.

But there they were, and Rosalinde caught her breath at the power Stenfax exuded now. Money or not, he was most definitely the man with the most power in the room.

Fitzgilbert shook his head. "It's none of your concern!"

"I think it is," Stenfax growled. "You have made it my concern."

"You can tell him or I will," Rosalinde said softly. "You can tell him about our father. About who he was. About how you stole us away from him. About how you held his true identity over our heads like cheese to a rat, forcing us to run your maze and do your bidding."

"Shut up," Fitzgilbert said.

"He was a servant," Rosalinde said, turning her attention

back to Stenfax.

Celia caught her breath. "What?"

Rosalinde nodded at her, seeing her reel with the information as much as Rosalinde had herself the night before. "We may not know his name, but now we know he was nothing but a servant to our grandfather. That's how much our poor mother wanted to escape him. She would run away with a servant and bear that man two daughters out of wedlock rather than be held hostage one more moment. Gray has the proof."

Stenfax pivoted on Gray and stared. "You have *proof* of this?"

Gray opened his mouth, and Rosalinde forced herself to look at him. He might see this as a betrayal. Only he didn't look betrayed. He met her eyes, nodded slightly and opened his mouth to answer his brother.

But he didn't get a chance. Before he could speak, Fitzgilbert suddenly rushed across the room toward her. She let out a truncated scream and tried to back away, but it was no use. Her grandfather had the element of surprise in his attack. He caught her throat in one big hand, even as they fell backward together.

She hit the floor, what little air he wasn't choking from her lungs exiting with the blow. She stared up into his face, this man who was meant to raise her, protect her, love her, and all she saw was his insanity. His hatred as he closed both hands around her neck and began to squeeze. Squeeze even as she clawed at him, even as the air disappeared from her lungs and the world grew blacker and silent.

CHAPTER TWENTY

Gray was moving and he hadn't even given his legs the order to do so. He was just flying across the room at Fitzgilbert as he leaned over Rosalinde, choking her as Celia screamed and clawed at his shoulders in a vain effort to make him stop.

Stenfax was moving too, but Gray reached Fitzgilbert first. He pushed Celia aside, knocking her on her ass before he ripped Fitzgilbert off of Rosalinde. As she was freed, she gasped for air and shoved herself backward, out of the range of her grandfather's swinging grip.

Gray threw him across the room, into a chair that shattered into splinters, and then he jumped on top of him. Rosalinde was free, safe, and it didn't matter—because Gray was going to destroy this man. For threatening her, for hurting her, for trying to kill her.

Gray was going to annihilate him.

He threw the first punch with all his might and felt the older man's nose break beneath the weight of Gray's fist. Blood splattered both across his face and Gray's knuckles. Gray threw more and more punches, raining them down without stopping, without speaking, without thinking about anything but Rosalinde's face when Fitzgilbert had grabbed her throat.

He felt arms and hands on him, but didn't stop his assault until he was yanked away. Only then did his mind clear, and he became aware that he was being held by both Stenfax and Folly. Except Folly wasn't supposed to be here. But then it also became clear that the door to the office was now open and half a dozen curious, whispering faces were peering in at the carnage in the room.

Celia moved toward her grandfather cautiously, digging in her pocket for a handkerchief.

The man needed more than that. His nose was shattered and his face was bruised. Gray didn't feel the least bit sorry, either.

"Get away!" Fitzgilbert cried as Celia reached for him.

She skittered back and returned to at once to Rosalinde's side. Celia helped her to her feet and immediately the sisters fell into each other's arms.

Gray looked at Rosalinde. There were finger-shaped bruises on her throat. His vision went red again at the sight and he lunged toward Fitzgilbert, but Folly and Lucien kept him steady.

"Enough," Lucien said in his ear. "Enough."

"Keep him away from me," Fitzgilbert said, covering his bleeding nose and pushing through the crowd to exit the room. Gray could hear him calling for his horse as he left.

"All right," Gray said, shrugging from the hold of his brother and friend. "All right."

They released him at last, and he straightened his coat as he made his way directly to Rosalinde. He took her hands and guided her to a chair. She sat and he knelt down before her, tracing her face with his fingers as if to tell himself that she was whole.

She was pale and shaking, her eyes filled with tears as she stared at him.

"Are you all right?" he whispered.

She held his stare. "Yes," she whispered, but her voice was rough from being choked.

He squeezed his eyes shut. "I should have killed him."

She covered his fingers with her hands and squeezed. "You did enough, Gray. Thank you for coming to my aid."

"Everyone out," Stenfax said, looking toward the crowd.

It was only then that Gray really realized what was happening. A good portion of the party had seen at least some part of his pummeling of Fitzgilbert and all of his comforting of Rosalinde. They were staring, whispering. The story was too good not to spread like wildfire.

"I'm sorry," he whispered before he stood. She clung to his hand a moment, then released him.

As Lady Stenfax hustled the crowd from the room, exhaustion on her face, Felicity entered and crossed to Gray. She looked up into his face and sighed. "You don't know how to do anything by half."

He shook his head. "Fitzgilbert tried to kill her."

Felicity jolted back. "Oh, Rosalinde," she said, looking toward her. All the blood had gone out of her face and she swayed ever so slightly as she saw Rosalinde's bruises. Gray frowned as his sister lifted her hands to her own throat in response, as if remembering. "I'm sorry," she said at last.

Rosalinde blushed and dipped her head. "I'm fine. I'm fine."

Felicity hugged Gray and he felt her tremble for a moment before she whispered, "I'm sorry. I tried to keep them out. The noise was so loud, I couldn't distract them all."

"It's not your fault," Gray reassured her.

Stenfax sidled up and Felicity stepped back. "I'll try to help Mama mitigate the damage," she said, squeezing first one brother's hand then the other.

She departed the room, leaving only Folly behind. He shook his head slowly at the brothers and bowed to Celia and Rosalinde. "I'm glad you were not injured, Mrs. Wilde."

"Thank you for your help," Celia said when Rosalinde didn't look up.

Her gaze seemed locked on the floor now, and Gray wasn't certain if she was reliving the moment when her grandfather had actually tried to kill her or if she were swamped by the humiliation of what had followed.

Perhaps both.

It stung Gray to see her so still. So somber.

Folly closed the door behind him, leaving Gray, Lucien, Rosalinde and Celia alone at last. Celia took a place beside her sister and took her hand as she stared up at the two men.

Stenfax took a long breath and moved to the women. "Rosalinde, are you certain you aren't injured?"

She looked up at him. "I'm certain, my lord," she said, though the scratchiness of her voice persisted. "Gray's quick action kept me from any permanent harm. I was shocked more than anything."

"As were we all," Stenfax said with a shake of his head. He paced away across the room. "That was a damned spectacle," he murmured.

Gray watched his brother. Waves of tension coursed from him, as well as anger and outrage. He was surprised to find he was *happy* to see Stenfax so emotional. This wasn't dangerous like the night on the terrace wall. But it was real. And he hadn't seen his real brother for nearly two years.

Rosalinde was watching him, too. "My lord—" she began.

Stenfax turned, his hand up. "Forgive me, Rosalinde, but I believe you have said enough. About what you think should happen, about truths that have shocked us all. You and my brother have said a mouthful lately. Now it is between Celia and me." He motioned to Celia. "Will you come here, please?"

Celia rose slowly and walked toward Stenfax, her shoulders back and her chin raised. She looked like she was marching to her execution. Gray could hardly blame her. After everything they had been through in the past half an hour, she had to believe his brother might be cruel.

Which proved she didn't know Lucien at all. And proved Rosalinde's earlier point about the poor quality of their match.

"Are *you* all right?" Stenfax asked, his tone softer, warmer.

Celia blinked as if surprised by his inquiry. "I-I can't believe he would do that. I always knew his capacity for vindictiveness, but if Gray hadn't stopped him—"

Stenfax took her hand. Gray realized it was the first time he'd ever seen him do so, unless it was required. He held it gently. "But Gray *did* stop him," Stenfax said softly. "I'm so sorry, Celia."

She nodded. "Thank you. But you must think so little of me now. Seeing what my grandfather did. Hearing the truth about my parentage. I know it shocked me, I cannot imagine your reaction."

"Celia, I think no less of you than I did the day I asked for your hand," Stenfax said with a shake of his head. "You are no more in control of your grandfather's actions than you are of the wind or the rain. As for your parentage, yes, I suppose that secret coming out could cause a scandal, but that wouldn't stop me from wedding you."

"You still wish to wed me?" Celia asked, her tone filled with disbelief, and Gray thought some disappointment.

"Your sister's points before the chaos were very good ones," Stenfax said. "And I think we both know that to be true. So before I answer your question about whether we should wed, I think you need to answer this one: do you care for me, Celia?"

She hesitated for a moment, and Gray could see her fighting with herself. Then she smiled. Perhaps it was the first real smile he had ever seen from her. He had to admit, it was an appealing expression.

"No," Celia said with a small laugh. "I do not love you even in the slightest. Do you care for me?"

"Looking at you, so beautiful, knowing your intelligence and your kindness, I'm sure this answer speaks of my poor character, but no, Celia. I don't. Not the way a husband should. Do you want *more* than what a marriage between us would entail?"

Celia nodded without hesitation. "I thought I didn't, but I find that I do, Stenfax. I do. And I think *you* deserve more."

Gray shut his eyes. They would not wed. This had been his desire for months, only Elise's situation had changed his mind. But now he found he was not upset by it. He was not pleased by it, either. In the end, it had been his brother's decision. And Gray couldn't fault him for making it. Even if he was terrified about what Lucien would do once he found out Elise was free.

But that was a matter to be dealt with another day.

"Are you saying you two are breaking the engagement?" Rosalinde said softly as she slowly rose from the settee.

Celia smiled once again at Lucien and then slipped off the ring she had been given just that summer. She handed it to him, then leaned up to kiss his cheek.

"Yes," she said before she turned to go back to her sister.

"Yes," Stenfax agreed as he placed the ring in his front pocket and patted it to ensure its safety.

Stenfax smiled, and Gray stared in wonder. His brother looked…*happy*. He couldn't recall the last time he'd seem him thus.

Celia returned to Rosalinde and slid an arm around her. They rested their heads against each other a moment before Rosalinde's smile fell.

"I'm happy you are doing what is in your heart," she said. "Though I do worry about Grandfather." Her delicate hands came up to touch her throat, and Gray flinched.

"I do, too," Celia said with a shudder. "How could we go home with him after what he tried to do to Rosalinde?"

Gray stepped forward. "We'll work it out." Rosalinde looked at him, a question on her face. Doubt. And in that moment, he knew exactly what he would do to save her. "We'll work it out," he repeated, firm and certain.

Celia cocked her head. "You sound like you have an idea of what happens next. Would you care to share it?"

Stenfax leaned against the edge of his desk again. "So much has happened. Why don't we start with simply discussing how we will announce the breaking of the engagement? And the arrangements for the next few days? We will work out the rest as we go."

Celia and Rosalinde exchanged a glance, then nodded together. "Very well," Celia said. "Let's talk about the end of the engagement."

Gray stretched his back as he stood. It had been an hour since the four of them had started this conversation about their next step. There seemed to be few good answers for what they would tell the others about the broken engagement, but at least he knew Rosalinde and Celia would be safe for the time being. Stenfax had agreed to let them stay a week and to keep Fitzgilbert away from them if he returned.

Everything else was still to be worked out, but he wasn't about to reveal his plan in front of everyone. He wanted to talk to Rosalinde alone.

"I'll have supper sent up to you," Stenfax said with a smile for the women. "And I'm sure no one will be surprised by your absence after all that has happened today."

"They'll whisper more," Celia said with a shake of her head. "But if it buys us more time to come up with a story, then I suppose I have to accept that."

Rosalinde squeezed her hand. "We'll find something to say. *I'll* take the blame."

Celia didn't seem convinced, but she smiled at the two men as she left the room. Rosalinde followed, but stopped before she exited.

"Gray," she said softly, meeting his gaze from across the room. It was like she had tied a string between them. He couldn't help but take a step toward her, pulled toward her by their powerful connection.

"Yes?"

"Thank you again," she whispered. "You saved my life."

He could think of nothing to say in the face of her bald emotion. So he merely nodded and watched as she left.

When he could find the strength to move, he turned back to his brother and found Lucien staring at him, arms folded. "Close the door," Lucien said.

Gray wrinkled his brow. "Very well." He did as he had been asked and then returned to Lucien. "You have more to discuss with me?"

Lucien laughed, but the sound held no humor. "I have so many questions that I hardly know where to start. I suppose first must be, how long have you known that Elise was a widow?"

Gray froze. Lucien's mouth was a hard line and his hands were fisted at his sides as he waited for the answer to his very direct question.

"Elise is a widow?" Gray repeated, more to buy time than because he intended to lie.

"I didn't think you knew—I thought it was a secret until you said that marrying Celia was *best* for me. That word, your sudden about-face on the topic of my fiancée revealed you, Gray. So don't sport with my intelligence. How long?"

"Only since yesterday," Gray admitted. "Who told you, Folly and Marina?"

Lucien let out his breath in a burst. "No. But of course they would know. And they hid it, too. With friends like these…"

Gray shook his head. "You want to pretend you don't know exactly why we didn't tell you? Why the three of us might want to keep such information from you?"

A cloud crossed Lucien's expression and he nodded. "Very well, I understand your reasons, I suppose. I have reacted imprudently in the past when it came to Elise."

"Imprudently?" Gray repeated. "You call nearly killing yourself imprudent? It was one of the most horrifying experiences of my life."

Lucien swallowed. "The point is, you kept it from me. In fact, you decided I *must* marry because of it."

"I know you and I knew you wouldn't go to Elise if you

were wed. You wouldn't break vows like that, it isn't in your nature."

Lucien shrugged. "But you think I'd go to her now that I'm free. Or soon to be."

"Will you?" Gray asked, leaning forward as he awaited the answer.

Lucien rubbed a hand over his face. "What would I have to say to that woman, Gray? Nothing. She is nothing to me and she never will be again. Her being a widow changes…it changes nothing."

Gray frowned. There was something in the way his brother's voice caught that made him doubt the veracity of his statement. But it was done now.

"If Folly and Marina didn't tell you, who did?" he asked.

"I overheard one of the women whispering about it. The family may be trying to keep whatever happened quiet, but it's about to explode."

"Well, perhaps that scandal will trump yours," Gray offered.

"No, it will be bound to mine," Lucien said, his voice faraway. "Even though I want nothing to do with her, people will whisper about *us* and *our* scandals, as if we were still linked." He shook his head. "But that leads me to my next question. How long have you and Rosalinde Wilde been…*attached*?"

Gray flinched at his term. "Attached?"

"You want me to be more direct?" Lucien asked, his voice elevating. "How long have you been bedding her? I assume from your behavior today that is what you've done."

Gray lifted his chin as anger pulsed through him. "Careful now. That is a lady."

"Have you treated her as such?" his brother countered.

"She is a magnet to me," Gray explained softly. "I am drawn to her without trying to be, sometimes without wanting to be. And I have failed in my behavior, I realize. But I intend to fix that now."

Lucien's anger faded from his face. "Fix it? How?"

"She and Celia need a savior. They obviously can never return to Fitzgilbert—he is too volatile. I'm going to ask Rosalinde to marry me. Celia can stay with us. My money and influence should ensure Fitzgilbert won't be able to say much about it."

"You're going to ask her to marry you?" Lucien was staring at Gray as if he had suggested he was going to breed poodles and start traveling in the circus with them.

"People marry, Lucien. You needn't look so surprised."

"You have always behaved as if you never would," his brother retorted. "So you must forgive my surprise."

"It is the right thing to do," he said.

"*Right*. Is that the only reason?"

Gray let his thoughts turn to Rosalinde. To all she had become to him, to all he wanted her to be. But to say those things out loud felt very dangerous, even to a person he trusted with his life.

"It will help you out of a mess," he suggested, changing the subject. "We can tell the world that Rosalinde and I fell in love, but that her grandfather refused to allow the marriage because he wanted his two granddaughters to give him connection to more than one family. That will explain my untoward behavior this afternoon."

"You snapped when he refused to let you have your bride," Lucien said. "So driven by your passions were you."

Gray nodded. "And you and Celia, with your arranged marriage, could see that your siblings would not be happy without each other. So you nobly stepped aside to allow us to wed in your place, freeing Celia to marry into another important family to appease her grandfather."

Lucien considered the story. "If told correctly, it might just make the *ton* support what was done, rather than shun Celia and despise me." Lucien sighed. "Of course, this assumes Rosalinde will accept your proposal."

Gray took a deep breath. "Yes, there is that. But I am off

to have that discussion with her right now. I didn't want to bring it up in front of everyone because the pressure might have been too much after what she went through today."

Lucien observed him for what felt like a very long time. Long enough that Gray shifted beneath his focused regard. Then his brother waved his hand.

"Off with you then. And I hope she says yes to your offer."

Gray smiled. "As do I."

"I also hope at some point you tear down that wall around yourself and actually let the girl love you as she obviously does," Lucien added as he turned his back and began to stack the papers on his desk.

Gray stared at Stenfax's back, but he had nothing to say to that statement.

"Yes, well, I'll let you know her answer once I have it," he said, and left the room. But as he strode up the stairs to the woman he hoped would be his bride, Lucien's words rang in his head.

And made him think of things he didn't want to think of. And want things he wasn't sure he was ready to accept.

CHAPTER TWENTY-ONE

Rosalinde sat at the small table in the chamber she shared with Celia, staring at the plates before them. Neither of them had eaten since the food was delivered. They had hardly spoken either, as the gravity of all that had happened that day sank in bit by bit.

"Do you think he'll come back?" Celia asked.

Rosalinde closed her eyes, but her mind conjured images of her grandfather's rage as he lunged for her. She could still feel his fingers close around her throat, closing off her air.

"I don't know," she whispered. "He lost control in front of a great many people. That might make him stay away. Either way, I think we both know what will happen next."

"He's going to cut us off," Celia said. "We'll be on the street."

"Perhaps not on the street," Rosalinde replied, trying to sound positive. "Stenfax and his family have been kind, and they say they won't let us fall to complete ruin."

"Yes, it was generous of Felicity and Lady Stenfax to come up when the food was delivered to reassure us we were still welcome," Celia said, her cheeks filling with color. "But their charity cannot be expected to last. This will ruin us, ruin *me*."

Celia put her head in her hands and began to cry. Rosalinde slid closer to her, wrapping her arms around her in what she knew was cold comfort. There was little to be done to mitigate the damage. Once the engagement was broken, Celia might be right that they would be shunned.

"Was I too hasty to walk away from a marriage to a man who could protect us?" Celia whispered. "To do so for a chance at love that may never happen?"

"No," Rosalinde said, and grasped Celia's cheeks to make her look up. "No, not too hasty. You didn't love Stenfax. Perhaps that notion of a love match is a silly or naïve hope to have, but I'd rather have it than always wonder if you'd thrown it away. Darling, this will die down and you may yet meet the man of your dreams. The man who will sweep you off your feet and make you happier than you've ever been. When he arrives, we'll be glad you didn't settle for a title just to please grandfather."

Celia sucked in a breath. "When did you find out about father being a servant in Grandfather's house?"

Rosalinde let out a sigh. "Only last night, I promise you. Gray had us investigated in his quest to end the engagement. But the information didn't arrive until yesterday, and I discovered it then."

"Is there more than what you shared today?"

"Father's identity is still unknown." She frowned as her sister's face fell. "But we now have a big piece of the puzzle. More than we ever knew before!"

"Do you think...do you think Mother loved him?" Celia asked.

Rosalinde smiled. "I like to believe she did. After all, she took a huge risk running away with him, bearing him children without the protection of a marriage. I like to think she loved him desperately. I also like to think his lowered position was the only reason he didn't keep us with him."

"Grandfather would have swept in once she was dead and taken us," Celia whispered. "We were property to him. Chattel."

Rosalinde nodded. "And with no position and likely little money, our father would have had little recourse."

"If he's still alive, perhaps he thinks of us," Celia

suggested, her eyes brimming with tears.

"I hope so." Rosalinde took her hand and they sat together, lost in fantasy about a man neither remembered, a life they might have had. Of course, she knew the reality might be very different, but after today, they both deserved to dream.

There was a knock on the door, and both of them froze.

"Do you think it's him?" Rosalinde whispered, thinking once again of her grandfather's face before the attack.

Celia shook her head. "Stenfax and Mr. Danford would never allow *him* up here. *Especially* Gray. He'd kill him first." Her sister got up. "But *I* will answer, just in case."

Rosalinde stayed where she was, heart throbbing as she watched Celia open the door. It didn't stop throbbing when the person who had knocked was revealed, though the reason for her physical reaction changed.

It was Gray who stood there, peering past Celia and right at her. Gray who smiled, *smiled* as if there was something to be pleased about. And though she didn't agree, she found herself smiling back, for the expression on his face was so rare that she couldn't help but respond to it.

"Good evening, ladies," he said.

"Hello," Celia said before she shot a look at Rosalinde. "I'm surprised to see you at our door."

"I came for two purposes," he said, making no move to enter. "First was to apologize to you, Miss Fitzgilbert."

Rosalinde pushed to her feet as Celia blinked at him in shock and stammered, "A-apologize?"

"I realize that may not seem sincere given the way today went," he said, locking his gaze on Celia and holding it evenly. "And I do not expect forgiveness, at least not at this point. But it must be said that I was in the wrong to judge you so harshly, and I apologize."

Celia opened and shut her mouth before she looked again toward Rosalinde, almost for help. But Rosalinde was just as dumbfounded. She had never expected Gray to do something so...out of character.

"Th-thank you," Celia finally stammered. "And I *do* accept the apology, Mr. Danford. First because I *did* understand in some way where you were coming from. And secondly because you saved my sister's life today. So whatever bad blood was ever between us, I have already forgotten it."

Gray's smile softened. "Thank you, Celia. Your response shows you to have more character than I ever gave you credit for."

Celia blushed and dipped her head. "You said you have two purposes for coming to call. What is the second?"

Gray looked passed her again and speared Rosalinde with a look. She knew the look. She had been seeing it on his face since the first moment she met him at the inn weeks before. The look that spoke of desire she had never expected. The look that spoke of a connection they had both claimed was stolen, and yet felt so much like home to her.

A look that stirred the love she felt for him.

"I came to talk to Rosalinde," he said softly. "Will you come with me?"

Rosalinde swallowed hard. She knew what a precarious position she was currently in. She loved him, but he did not feel the same. With all the high emotion of the day, she would likely give him anything he asked for. She would want to give it. But later, she might regret it.

Later, there would be consequences.

"I should stay with Celia," she whispered.

Celia shot her an incredulous look. "Rosalinde, don't use me as a shield, for heaven's sake. After today, I might just want a lovely bath and a bit of time alone to ponder my next step. So please, go with Gray. I'm fine."

Rosalinde sighed. Gray had a half-smile on his face, almost amused when confronted by her reticence. But Celia had taken away her only excuse, so she nodded.

"Of course, Gray. I'd be happy to speak to you."

She passed by her sister, shooting her a glare, and stepped into the hallway with him. As the door closed behind them, he reached for her hand, interlacing his fingers with hers. Electric awareness shot up her hand at the act, which was so intimate and so meaningful. Far more than if he had merely taken her arm.

He guided her up the hallway toward the family wing of the house, and when he stopped at his door, she hesitated. "Your room?"

He nodded while he opened it and waved her in. "I wasn't lying when I said I need to speak to you. What I have to say requires privacy. Downstairs everyone is gathered for supper now, but soon enough they'll be roaming the halls again, some of them looking for more gossip about today than they already have. My rooms are the safest place if we don't want to be interrupted."

She shook her head. If this was a game, he was the expert at it. She had no words, no recourse, no retort. Partly because she was exhausted and arguing would take too much energy. Partly because she wanted so much to be alone with him, to be comforted by him and his searing touch.

She entered the chamber without further argument and caught her breath. He had prepared for her. There were candles lit across the room and a plate with fruit and cheese next to an opened bottle of wine on a table before the settee.

"Gray?" she murmured.

"I thought you might not eat whatever was sent to your rooms," he explained. "And so I first want to tempt you to have a bit of sustenance. Unless your throat hurts too much?"

He asked the last in a strained tone. She lifted her hand to her neck, feeling the bruises there. He frowned at the act.

"It only hurts a little," she reassured him.

"I should have positioned myself to better protect you," he said as he led her to the settee. They took their place together. "I could have kept that bastard from getting his hands on you at all."

She bent her head. "No one could have guessed he would become so violent," she whispered. "You are not to blame."

He pressed a finger beneath her chin and tilted her face up. "And neither are you."

When he said the words like that, she almost believed him. With a sigh, she leaned into him to rest her head on his chest, shivering as his arms came around her. He held her like that for a long time, wordlessly smoothing his hand over her hair. She was glad he didn't speak. An endless string of platitudes would do nothing to change what had already happened. His comfort was enough.

"I thought you would hate me when I began my speech," she murmured against his coat when she felt strong enough. "I ruined your plans, after all."

He made a low rumbling sound in his chest and his arms held tighter. "They weren't very good plans, Rosalinde. My only good plan, in fact, was you."

"Me?" she repeated, drawing back to look at him. His dark gaze was intent on her face, and when he was so close it felt like he could see all the way through her. She'd never known a man who could do that. She'd never known a man who wanted to. Even her husband hadn't tried.

Gray traced her cheek with a fingertip. "Approaching you at the inn that night. Making love to you, there and here. Those were my best plans ever."

His face was moving closer, and it felt like the air had been sucked from her room—hell, sucked from her very lungs. Something was happening here. Something she didn't understand, couldn't believe, wasn't ready for.

"Gray?" she murmured, holding tighter to his arm for purchase, even though it was him who was spinning her out of control.

"Rosalinde," he said, and took a long breath.

She waited as he struggled for words. It was like she was an arrow drawn back on a bow and all that existed was exquisite tension as she waited for him to speak. Waited for him to tell her that he loved her. Those had to be the words that were so difficult for his lips to form. And once she heard them, everything would be right again.

Only he pressed his lips together at last, and then he said, "You'll marry me."

She blinked. The sentence, stated as fact, not as a question, both moved her and cut her to the core. There was no declaration of love to go along with his statement. No romantic swell of passion to sweep her away.

Even Martin had *asked* for her hand, not told her it belonged to him.

"Is that a proposal?" she said, unable to keep the hint of disappointment from her voice.

He must have heard it, for he frowned. "Perhaps not artfully done, but yes. Let me try again. Please, marry me."

She drew her hands from his and got up. She had to put space between them in order to think clearly. Once she had, the true weight of what was happening settled on her shoulders. Marriage to this man who wanted her, yes. Cared for her, she believed. But loved her?

That still seemed in bitter question.

"Gray," she whispered.

He got to his feet and took a step toward her. "You don't know your future, Rosalinde. Stenfax can provide protection to a point, but if your grandfather wants you back in his house, we may not be able to stop him if you are two unmarried misses. But if you are my wife, you'll be safe. And I will leverage every bit of influence I have to make sure Celia is safe, too."

"Safe," she said. The word was what she needed right now, but oh, how bitter it tasted.

"In fact, Celia might be more than safe thanks to this. Stenfax and I believe if we tell tale of how you and I fell unexpectedly in love—"

She jolted. There was the word she had been looking for, but he said it in the context of a tale to tell to others. Not the truth, but a story meant to save them all from ruin.

He was still talking. "—your grandfather refused the marriage because he wanted you to marry into a different influential family…"

"It would explain away your actions today in the parlor," she said, "I understand you perfectly."

And she did. It was a good plan. The *ton* liked a good love story as much as it did a scandal. An engaged couple who stepped aside in their arranged marriage in order to clear the way for true love was something that would resonate even with the most jaded of lords. They might turn their noses up and laugh, but they would not tar Celia and Stenfax with a dirty brush.

"Rosalinde, I have wanted you from the moment I laid eyes on you," Gray said. "And I would be a good husband and partner to you. If you allow me."

She shut her eyes. Looking at him was physically painful in that moment. He offered her everything and nothing she wanted, all at once.

"Once Celia told me that I only did what I desired," she said. "That I only followed my heart and left the consequences to others."

She looked at him. He was frowning, as if he disagreed. But she knew better than he did.

"But if I do this, I'll be helping her. It will be my turn to do what is right and clear the way for her happiness." Rosalinde nodded. "How could I refuse? Especially since I think you and I *do* suit in a great many ways."

His frown deepened at that statement, though she had no idea of why. She hadn't troubled him with her heart. She hadn't required more than he would give. She was stepping in line to what he claimed to want from her. He should smile.

So she did, even though there was a piece of her that wanted so much more. But she would have him, hers forever. And perhaps at some point, he might come to care more. Deeper. It happened.

"Are you saying yes?" he asked.

She moved toward him, her heart pounding as she reached for him. She leaned up and pressed her lips to his. Immediately he grabbed for her, cupping her closer to him, his tongue waging war with her as he woke her body just as he always did.

She drew away, though it was physically painful. "Yes," she whispered. "I'll marry you."

He let out a breath like he'd been holding it, and smiled. "Excellent. We'll tell your sister the news and the plan, and we'll announce it tonight. Then there is much to arrange. I'll get a special license and we'll take over Stenfax and Celia's date."

"Two days?" Rosalinde gasped in shock.

He nodded. "Then everyone will remember our whirlwind, not the other."

"Yes," she said. "I see what you mean. All right. Two days."

Gray grabbed for her hand and lifted it to his lips. "It's all going to work out, Rosalinde, trust me. Now come, we have much to do."

He guided her to the door and she let him, for she knew there was no fighting this now. But though she was about to get everything she'd ever wanted, she also knew that she had perhaps let something go that meant a great deal.

And the future, though settled, she wished was a bit brighter.

CHAPTER TWENTY-TWO

Rosalinde looked at herself in the mirror and hardly believed what she saw. A bride looked back at her, a bride with her own face. Celia's silver-gray wedding gown, stitched with lines of beautiful pearls, had been hastily altered to fit her.

"I think it looks better on you," Celia said.

Rosalinde forced a smile. "And Grandfather hasn't made himself known?" she asked, her stomach queasy. Even now there were faint marks remaining on her throat, reminders of what had brought them here.

Gertrude scowled as she finished tugging and smoothing Rosalinde's gown. "There's been no word since he sent his letter demanding his things be returned to London along with Thomas and the carriage yesterday."

Celia pulled a face. "I wonder if he included us in his 'things'."

"I don't know," Rosalinde said. "I don't care. But the sooner I get through this wedding, the sooner we won't have to worry."

Celia met her eyes in the mirror's reflection, and Rosalinde saw her sister's concern. Celia turned to Gertrude. "Might I have a moment with Rosalinde?"

Gertie nodded. "Of course. I'll just go and see if any of the other servants need help with the final preparations."

"Thank you," Celia said softly as the maid left the room and shut them in alone.

Rosalinde turned to face Celia at last and made herself

smile. "Well, here we are, at your wedding day. I hope you don't hate me for requisitioning it."

Celia laughed. "You sound as though it is a military operation."

"It feels like it has been." Rosalinde shook her head. "In such a short time, everything has been set on its head. But at least that is what the guests are talking about, not your broken engagement."

Celia frowned. "When the guests do speak to me about Stenfax, it is to tell me what a good sister I am to sacrifice becoming a countess so that you could have true love. Stenfax and Gray's plan has worked exactly as they hoped."

"So has ours. Only we caught the wrong brother," Rosalinde said.

Celia reached out to twist one of Rosalinde's curls around her finger. "I think he might just be the right brother for you, Rosalinde. Have you told him you're in love with him?"

Rosalinde drew back. She hadn't realized her heart was so clear. What a cake she must be making of herself. Only it was hard to pretend when one was being washed away by a tidal wave. Every time someone referred to Gray as her fiancé, her heart leapt. Whenever she had to tell someone the story of their grand and undeniable love, *she* was speaking every inch the truth, even if he wasn't.

"I have eyes and I can see," Celia whispered. "I know your heart like I know my own."

Rosalinde turned away. "I haven't told him," she admitted. "Because I fear his response."

"My brave sister Rosalinde, the same one who flies into the world with her arms wide open, is afraid to say three little words to a man who obviously worships her?"

"There is a difference between desire and love," Rosalinde said. "And saying those three little words is asking to be shot through the heart."

"Or to be given wings." Rosalinde faced Celia again. She'd never seen her sister so open or so calm when speaking about emotion. Celia smiled. "It seems you cannot have one without risking the other."

"You think I *should* tell him?" Rosalinde asked.

Celia nodded. "Yes. And I think you should tell him before you wed."

"Before?" Rosalinde repeated. "But we are just an hour away."

"Exactly. If you tell him now, you'll go into this ceremony with your eyes wide open and be best prepared for what happens next. The longer you wait, the harder it will become. For both of you."

Rosalinde's heart began to pound. "He's probably in his chamber," she whispered.

"Perfect. You'll have privacy." Celia took her hand and the two of them moved to the door. Her sister pushed her out into the hallway. "I'll keep everyone away from you and give you even more."

"Why are you so determined to have me do this?" Rosalinde asked.

"Because making the biggest decision of your life should not be a sacrifice. Because you deserve to be happy, and I think you can be." Celia shrugged. "Because Stenfax and I made a wager that you would figure out you're in love before you wed, and I want to win."

"Celia!" Rosalinde gasped at the last.

Her sister laughed and pushed her down the hall gently. "Go!"

Rosalinde gave her a glare, but she didn't argue. She walked down the hall shaking her head at her sister's unexpected encouragement. But the more steps she took toward Gray's door, the more nervous she became.

What if she spilled her heart and Gray told her he didn't feel the same? Oh, he would be gentle about it, she was certain of that. And his answer wouldn't, *couldn't* change the fact that they would wed. It was too late for that. But it would start their union on a note of pain she wasn't certain she could survive.

So she stood outside his door, staring at the barrier between them, contemplating whether she should run or stay.

In the end, she didn't have to make the decision. The door opened and Gray almost walked right into her. He was devilishly handsome, dressed in his wedding finery. His crisp, white cravat made his fine jawline even more defined.

"Rosalinde!" he said, staggering back so he wouldn't trample over her. "What are you doing—"

He cut himself off and stared at her. Just stared, his gaze easing down from the top of her head to her feet. He was shaking his head, mouth partly open, eyes wide with pupils dilated.

"Why—why do you look at me like that?" she whispered.

He drew in a long breath. "You are beautiful."

Rosalinde lifted her hand and touched the silken gown she had all but forgotten she was wearing. "Thank you."

He blinked, as if trying to gather himself. "But what are you doing here? Nothing is wrong, is it?"

"No, I just…I needed to speak to you. Well, I *wanted* to speak to you," she corrected herself as her nerves returned. Now that she was looking at him, so handsome as he smiled, she was even less certain she wished to ruin this day. "But— but it can wait. It will keep until—"

He motioned her into the room. "I was just going to look for Lucien, he was meant to come up and let me know that the vicar had arrived. But I'm sure he's handling it. Please, let's talk."

She entered the chamber she now knew so well. Here he had made love to her. Here he had proposed. And now here she would spill out her heart. *If* she could find the courage to do so.

He shut the door, and she shivered. "What if Stenfax arrives? Won't he be shocked to find us alone?"

Gray laughed, a low, rough sound that sent answering vibrations of pleasure through her body. "He might be. And there would be consequences."

Her eyes went wide. "What kind of consequences?"

He leaned in. "I suppose he might force us to wed. But I'll risk it."

She smiled at his quip even though her ears were filled with the sound of her own rushing blood and her hands shook.

"Rosalinde, you're trembling," Gray said, coming toward her as his smile fell. He filled up her vision as he took her hand, smoothing his thumb over her flesh. This did not make what she had to do any easier.

"I'm sorry. I just needed to speak to you," she said, and blushed at the clumsiness of those words. Ones she had already spoken.

"Yes, so you said," he replied, and guided her to the settee. "What is troubling you?"

Rosalinde stared at him. Right now things were perfect. He was tender with her, sweet. If she told him she loved him, there was a chance he might recoil. Even grow cold in an attempt not to mislead her further. Did she want that?

"Er, I was just thinking what an expensive bargain you've made," she lied. "After all, Celia had most of her things here already since she was to wed and move here, but I-I have lost more than half my wardrobe. I don't know if it is fair to ask you to replace so much."

Gray blinked at her, as if confused. "You came to my chamber an hour before our wedding to talk to me about how unfair it is that I must pay for new clothing for you?"

"And...and Gertrude and Lincoln will be an added household expense," she continued. "And we'll have to find a place for them in your home in the north. Plus, there's the issue of—"

Gray cupped her cheeks and dropped his mouth to hers, silencing her ramblings in the sweetest way possible. At first the kiss was gentle, just a brush of lips on lips, but that didn't last. It never did. The passion that always seemed to flare the moment they touched rose to the surface once more. He angled his head for better access, sweeping his tongue across the crease of her lips.

She opened. Of course she did, for denying him was an exercise in futility. He tasted of mint as he delved inside, stroking and tasting and teasing until she went boneless and needy from her head to her toes.

Only then did he release her. He smiled at her bleary-eyed stare and smoothed the pad of his thumb over her cheek. "I don't give a damn about money, Rosalinde. I have plenty. I'll buy you ten new wardrobes just because it pleases me to see you in pretty things. My home in the north is small, yes, but once we arrive we will buy a new one. Or build something on the land I own there. Or both. The arrangements are not a concern, though this conversation is."

"Is it?" she asked, still shaken by the power of his kiss.

"Yes. Because I don't believe you decided to come all the way to my room to talk to me about this." He tilted his head. "So what do you really want to discuss?"

She reached up and closed her hand around his. "How do you know me so well?"

The corner of his lip quirked up. "Come now, Rosalinde, confession time."

She let her breath exit her mouth slowly, trying to slow her racing heart. Of course it was to no avail. She was sitting next to Gray, her hand in his, her heart was going to race.

"The past day and a half has been such a whirlwind," she began. "Between the events in Stenfax's office, to our decision to wed, to Celia's broken engagement. I've hardly had time to breathe."

He nodded. "It has been quite an experience. I felt like I hardly saw you at all yesterday with all the insanity involving the special license and your fittings and the like."

"Yes. But though I've been caught up, I have still had time to think."

He had been smiling slightly, and now that expression fell. "Think? Please don't tell me you want to change your mind, Rosalinde, because I don't think we could mitigate the damage done if you did that on the day we are to marry."

"No, I have no desire to stop this wedding," she reassured him. "But I do think we must go into it honestly. With both of us knowing exactly where we stand."

His jaw was tightening with every word and he slowly withdrew his hand from hers, like he was expecting an attack. "What is it you're trying to say, Rosalinde? Just be honest and come out with it."

She shifted. His withdrawal didn't make this any easier, but now she had started and she couldn't go back.

"I love you," she said, her voice breaking. She cleared her throat and repeated it with more strength. "I love you, Gray. And I wanted to tell you that before we married, so that you know where I stand. Now, I don't expect you to return those sentiments. But I wanted you to understand my heart so that we start out correctly."

The words were out and there was a part of her that felt free in saying them. But the other part looked at Gray, who was just *staring* at her, his expression unreadable, and wished she had kept her feelings to herself.

"Please say something," she whispered when he was silent for what seemed like an eternity.

"You love me?" he said, and his voice was rough as sandpaper.

She nodded. "I-I do. I have for a little while now. Before everything happened with my grandfather and the broken engagement."

"You love me," he said again, this time slower, like he was rolling it around on his tongue to test the veracity of the words.

"Yes," she said. "But as I said, I have no expectation that you—"

"Oh, please don't launch into a longwinded speech that excuses me from making a decision regarding this matter," Gray said with a shake of his head. "Let me respond before you talk me out of what I do or do not feel."

Rosalinde forced her lips together to keep from rambling.

He cleared his throat. "Emotion has never been easy for me. I never made a connection with a woman, certainly. After watching my brother crushed beneath the weight of what he thought was love and my sister nearly killed by the same, I shunned the emotion. And not just shunned it, I did my level best to shut it off. I even denied myself physical pleasures in the belief they would make me weak."

Gray had touched on those subjects over the weeks, so they weren't a surprise to her. She wanted to say something but forced herself to remain quiet and let him continue.

He scrubbed a hand over his face. "And then came *you*."

There was something accusatory in his tone, and she flinched. "Me."

He sighed. "Yes. When you walked into that awful inn, snow blowing around you, cheeks pink, you woke me up. I didn't want to be awake, but I had no choice. I thought I could walk away and pretend that night hadn't happened. When you arrived here, I realized I had to face what I wanted. What I *need*."

She bit her lip. "Wh-what do you need?"

"It turns out what I need is you," he said. "As much as I fought that, as much as I tried to deny it, as much as I pretended it was for some ulterior motive, the fact is that I couldn't walk away. Even when I tried, you were always there, pushed into my heart and my space and my everything."

"You sound like that is a bad thing," Rosalinde whispered. "Something you regret."

"Am I not making myself clear?" He dropped to his knees before her and leaned up into her. His arms came around her, tugging her close until there was nothing but breath between them. "I love you, Rosalinde Wilde. I may have tried not to love you, but I do."

She smiled, joy swelling up in her. She cupped his cheek, stroking her fingers over the harsh lines of his cheeks, his jaw, her thumb across his lip as if to memorize the feel of him in this moment. "You aren't just saying it?"

He shook his head solemnly. "I may be many things, but I'm not a liar. *I love you.*"

"But you still frown," she whispered, leaning in to press her lips to that frown.

He returned the kiss briefly. "I do. Because I don't know how to do this. To love you so that I won't hurt you. So that I won't disappoint you. So that I won't make you regret giving me the precious gift of your heart."

Gray's whole body hurt from the weight of the words he had just spoken. He'd never allowed himself to voice that fear. To allow himself to imagine that he would hurt Rosalinde. But now that she had given her heart so freely, now that he had accepted it because it was so precious, terror gripped him.

Rosalinde tilted her head and speared him with a loving yet questioning glance. "*That's* what you fear? That you might hurt me?"

He nodded. "Yes," he said, his voice cracking with the weight of those words and the consequences they might hold.

She touched his face, her fingers so light against his skin, so warm. "Gray, you *will* hurt me."

He flinched and tried to pull away, but she held him steady with a deceptively strong grip.

"Don't run. Pain is inevitable in this life. But if you never risk the pain, you will also never find the joy or the pleasure or the true connection. You'll never hurt me with ill intentions, never with cruelty. And I may hurt you in return out of misunderstanding or by accident. But more often than not, you'll heal me. You'll complete me. And I hope to do the same for you. *That* is life, that is love."

He mused on that for a moment before he stroked his hands along her spine. He felt her shiver beneath him, felt his own body react to the press of her, the weight of what they had just said to each other.

"Celia once told me you live your life with your arms wide open," he said, his voice soft and rough. "It is one of the things I have loved about you. Will you teach me how to do that?"

She nodded. "It's easy enough, my love. Just trust that you'll survive the flight *or* the fall. And trust that I'll always be there to catch you."

He pushed her back against the settee, his mouth finding hers, his body nudging between her legs. He had wanted her too many times since he'd met her, but never more than now. Now he wanted to feel her wrapped around him when he knew he had her heart. When he knew she held his.

"We have less than an hour before we are declared man and wife," he whispered as his lips dragged against her throat. "Just enough time to show you how much I love you, just enough time for us to try out our wings together."

She hesitated. "I want more than an hour."

He laughed even though her words made his cock even harder. "Mmm, one more thing I love about you. This time will be fast, but I promise you that tonight, when you are my wife, you will know it in every way."

"I know it now," she said, drawing him closer. "I know it forever."

He pushed up her skirt with one hand, splaying his fingers across her satiny flesh, marking it as his as he inched higher and higher. He so wanted to strip her bare, to take his time worshipping her, but that was not to be this afternoon.

Still, he had the rest of his life.

He smiled as he pushed his fingers through the slit in her drawers and stroked them over her sex. She was wet, hot, ready.

"Thank God," he groaned, covering her mouth as he unbuttoned the flap of his trousers. Her fingers tangled with his, and together they worked to free him.

She made a soft sound against his lips as she stroked him

once, twice, then guided him to her entrance. He pulled away from the kiss as he slid forward, breaching her, feeling her slick folds tighten around him and welcome him home.

"I love you," he whispered.

She smiled up at him, her eyes filled with tears, but happy tears. Joyful tears. "I love you."

He drove forward on those words, taking her slowly, rotating his hips to give her the most pleasure. He watched her face as he moved, marking every hitch of her breath, every gasping moan, every contortion of her face as her pleasure built.

Finally she buried her face against his shoulder, her entire body shuddering as she lifted hard against him in release. That was the permission he needed. He increased his pace, surrendering to the pull and grip of her body, the spasms from her orgasm milking him until he grunted and spent inside of her.

She smiled as she drew him down, his body covering hers, her hands smoothing over his shoulders.

"Today we'll say vows," she whispered against his ear. "But *that* was my wedding. My stolen moment to become yours."

He pulled away, smiling down at her. "They were never stolen moments, Rosalinde," he murmured. "They were always ours to take. And they always will be."

Then he dropped his mouth to hers, claiming her once more.

EPILOGUE

Four months later

Rosalinde stood aside as yet another servant passed by with a trunk. From her place in the foyer, she watched out the window as Celia directed the young man, who would place it on the wagon leaving for London in less than an hour.

Suddenly warm arms slid around her from behind and she smiled, leaning back into the solid chest of her husband.

"Celia is running the show," Gray murmured against her ear.

Rosalinde shrugged. "I think she's nervous about returning to London for a Season. Everyone at Caraway Court was kind about the breaking of the engagement, but you never know what the Town biddies will say or do."

Gray let out a long sigh that made Rosalinde turn toward him. He was frowning, his gaze distant as he watched out the window with unseeing eyes.

"Lucien arrived in London a week ago," he said. "His latest letter said he's encountered no resistance due to the broken engagement. It bodes well for Celia."

Rosalinde searched his face. In the months since their hasty wedding, they had returned to his home in the north, Celia in tow. In that time, she had truly come to know her husband. Not only as the giving lover and the kind brother, but as the fair employer and brilliant mind. She had fallen further and further in love with him the more she became able to judge his moods.

Right now he was pensive.

"Did Stenfax's letter include reference to anything else?" she asked.

Gray's dark gaze focused on her and the corner of his lip quirked up. "What have we talked about, Rosalinde? You shouldn't read my mind where the servants could hear. They'll start calling you a witch."

She laughed but swatted his chest. "Don't tease."

"But I like the sounds you make when I tease," he whispered.

Her cheeks flamed and the hand swatting his chest curled instead to stroke there. "So do I, but you are changing the subject."

He grunted in displeasure. "I was trying to, but you are too smart. If you are asking if Stenfax has seen Elise, it seems he has not."

Rosalinde nodded. "It isn't surprising. Lady Kirkford will be in mourning until the fall probably. By then, Stenfax may retreat back to Caraway Court, or maybe he'll even be courting a new love."

Gray's lips remained thin, and she knew that he didn't believe her. She didn't really believe that either. But she couldn't change what Stenfax would do, nor could her husband.

So she slid into his arms, smiling up at him in comfort.

"Are you worried?" she whispered.

He stared at her a long moment and the tension bled away from his face. He smiled down at her, his eyes glowing with love and passion and all the things that made him the only home she'd ever need.

"Worried?" he asked. "I have you. I couldn't worry."

Then he bent his head and kissed her, and all was right with her world.

Coming next from USA Today Bestselling Author Jess Michaels:

A wedding that cannot happen…

A man who is not what he seems…

A woman who betrayed for love…

And a couple who can never be.

It will all happen during one year of passionate Seasons. Turn the page to read an exclusive excerpt of Seasons book two - A Spring Deception, coming September 6, 2016.

Excerpt of
A Spring Deception
SEASONS BOOK 2

Celia smiled as she looked out over the dance floor and watched Gray and Rosalinde swirl by in the crowd. Gray's hand was firmly pressed into Rosalinde's hip and their gazes were locked on each other, proof once again of their loving bond.

"She does look happy."

Celia started and looked at the two young women who had stepped up beside her. She'd known Miss Tabitha Thornton and Lady Honora for as long as she could remember. They were old friends and ones who had stood staunchly beside her before, during and after her ill-fated engagement. She appreciated that beyond measure.

"She does," Celia said, addressing Honora, for it was she who had made the statement. "She is. Lucky her."

"Indeed, for Mr. Danford cuts a fine figure," Tabitha sighed. "And I've heard he's worth a fortune, even if father does turn up his nose that he made it by work and not inheritance."

Celia shrugged. "I don't care what he does to earn his keep, as long as he takes care of my sister. Which he does in spades."

"So you don't regret breaking your engagement to Stenfax at all?" Tabitha asked, curling a loose blonde lock around her finger.

Celia pursed her lips. Her friends had kindly danced around that subject since her return to London a week before, but here it was. She found herself searching through the ballroom and found the tall, stern figure of the Earl of Stenfax. He was talking to a few other men in a corner. He was very handsome, of course, but he had never moved her, nor had she moved him.

"I do not regret it," she said and meant it. "Things have worked out exactly right." She cleared her throat and looked around. The women who were not dancing were all gathered in clumps it seemed, and there was a crackling electricity in the air that made no sense to Celia. "Why is everyone so odd tonight?" she asked, hoping for a change in subject.

Honora grasped her arm in both hands, her face lighting up in excited pleasure. "You mean you haven't heard?"

"Heard what?" Celia asked, shaking her head. "What is there to hear that would inspire *that* expression?"

Honora leaned in, as did Tabitha. "The Duke of Clairemont is making a return to Society tonight."

Celia wrinkled her brow. "The Duke of Clairemont. I vaguely recognize the title, but why does that matter? We've a room full of stuffy old men as it is. One more duke is hardly any matter."

"Oh my lord, she doesn't know!" Tabitha squealed and now Celia was being held by both her arms, one for each friend. She rather hoped they didn't try for a tug of war.

Honora all but bounced. "His Grace is *not* an old man," she said, trying for a whisper but not really accomplishing it in her excitement. "He is barely above thirty and rich as Midas, himself!"

Tabitha tugged on Celia's arm none too gently. "His father died a decade ago and he took the title, but since then he has been a recluse, hiding away in his country estate, Kinghill Castle. No one has seen him in years and years."

"There are so many rumors about why he hid so long, Celia," Honora continued, pulling her back to her side. "Some say he was scarred in an accident-"

"A fire!" Tabitha said. "I heard it was a fire."

"Whatever it was." Honora shrugged. "Or that he was driven mad over his father's death."

"Oh there are a dozen stories or more," Tabitha said. "Whatever the truth is, everyone is agog over his return. He is quite the catch."

"Despite being horribly disfigured or mad? Or both?" Celia asked mildly.

Honora let out a huff of breath. "He's *titled* and *rich*, did you not hear that part?"

Celia held back a sigh. She hated to be mercenary, especially after all she'd gone through breaking her engagement to Stenfax, but the idea of this duke's title did appeal to her. Since Gray had had little luck in finding out her father's identity, she couldn't help but wonder if her grandfather might consider honoring his original bargain with her.

Marry a title to satisfy him and receive the information that was so well-hidden. Oh, Rosalinde would hate that. She wouldn't want Celia anywhere near the old man.

But Rosalinde didn't need the truth as much as Celia felt she did. It didn't eat at her at night, it didn't haunt her every time she looked in the mirror and wondered if she had her father's nose or chin.

"Are you well, my dear?" Tabitha asked, tilting her head to get a closer look at Celia. "You have gotten very pale."

Celia shook her head. These were not thoughts she should entertain. Likely when this mysterious duke arrived he would not be interested in her at all. He would probably be a boring, fat aristocrat who already knew exactly what family he would merge with his own. There was no use getting one's hopes up over a mirage.

"I'm fine, I was wool gathering," she said with a smile to reassure her friends.

Tabitha didn't look certain, but before she could follow up with more questions or concerns, the crowd in the room began to titter and shift. It seemed everyone in the room turned toward the door at once as the servant there made some muffled announcement.

Celia turned with them, lifting on her tiptoes to see who had caused the commotion.

"It must be him," Honora breathed, her hand coming up to fluff her hair. "It *must* be!"

Celia supposed her friend must be correct, for this mysterious duke was the only new addition to Society that would cause such a stir. The crowd began to part, splitting apart like a torn seam and then the few people before her stepped aside and she caught her breath.

An impeccably dressed man now stood not three feet from her. And he was utterly beautiful with dark blond hair and steely gray eyes that swept over the room. He had an angled face with a strong jaw and a slightly imperfect nose, like he had broken it at some point during his life. But the imperfection only made the rest of his face that much more striking.

He shifted slightly, revealing some discomfort on his handsome face. And something else, too. Sadness. There was a sadness in his eyes that spoke to Celia in a visceral and immediate way.

"That's him?" she breathed, unable to take her eyes off of him. Tabitha and Honora nodded mutely. "He certainly isn't scarred."

"Or fat," Honora added. "Or hideous."

"No," Celia whispered as he turned away and smiled as their host and hostess, the Marquis and Marchioness Harrington rushed to greet their coup of a guest. He was led off into the crowd and suddenly it felt like the air had been let back into the room. Celia sucked in a gulp of it with a shiver.

She had never had such a strong reaction to a stranger before. A man. It was like her whole body was tingling and her heart pounded so loudly in her ears that the rest of the sounds in the room were muffled by the rush of blood.

"I think he'll be even more of a catch now that we've all

seen him," Tabitha said with a sigh. "Some lucky girl will land him before the summer, I can almost guarantee it!"

Celia blinked as those words sank in. Of course that was true. The mamas would swarm on their newcomer before he could settle in for five minutes and he would be the focus of their manipulations until someone had landed him.

Someone who would almost certainly *not* be Celia Fitzgilbert. She turned away from where the duke had stood and took a few more deep breaths. It was foolish to be swept away by the appearance of a handsome face. And if she were smart, she'd just forget about the man.

Only she didn't think that would be so easy to do.

Other Books by Jess Michaels

THE WICKED WOODLEYS

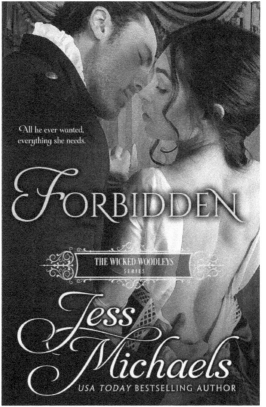

Forbidden (Book 1)

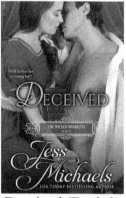

Deceived (Book 2)

Tempted (Book 3)

Ruined (Book 4)

Seduced (Book 5

THE NOTORIOUS FLYNNS
The Other Duke (Book 1)
The Scoundrel's Lover (Book 2)
The Widow Wager (Book 3)
No Gentleman for Georgina (Book 4)
A Marquis for Mary (Book 5)

THE LADIES BOOK OF PLEASURES
A Matter of Sin
A Moment of Passion
A Measure of Deceit

THE PLEASURE WARS SERIES
Taken By the Duke
Pleasuring the Lady
Beauty and the Earl
Beautiful Distraction

MISTRESS MATCHMAKER SERIES
An Introduction to Pleasure
For Desire Alone
Her Perfect Match

Jess Michaels raffles a FREE Kindle or Amazon gift certificate EVERY month to members of her newsletter, so sign up on her website:

http://www.authorjessmichaels.com/join-the-jess-michaels-newsletter/

About the Author

Jess Michaels writes erotic historical romance from her home in Tucson, AZ with her husband and one adorable kitty cat. She has written over 60 books, enjoys long walks in the desert and once wrestled a bear over a piece of pie. One of these things is a lie.

Jess loves to hear from fans! So please feel free to contact her in any of the following ways (or carrier pigeon):

www.AuthorJessMichaels.com
PO Box 814, Cortaro, AZ 85652-0814

Email: Jess@AuthorJessMichaels.com
Twitter www.twitter.com/JessMichaelsbks
Facebook: www.facebook.com/JessMichaelsBks

Jess Michaels raffles a FREE Kindle or Amazon gift certificate EVERY month to members of her newsletter, so sign up on her website: http://www.authorjessmichaels.com/

CPSIA information can be obtained
at www.ICGtesting.com
Printed in the USA
BVHW030954050120
568584BV00001B/102/P